Praise for *T*

'A twisty thriller . . . Possibly no cottage. I'll certainly be checkin holiday rental.'

The Age

'Chilling . . . Should keep readers up at night. Pomare knows how to keep the pages turning.'

Publishers Weekly

'An emerging master of the taut and fast-flowing psychological thriller.'

ArtsHub

'*The Last Guests* is a brilliantly executed siege set-piece that keeps readers guessing until the final few pages.'

Greg Flemming, Stuff.co.nz

'This is a rip-snorting read that burbles along on fine prose, from a novelist who while still early in his career has already stamped his mark as a masterful storyteller. An excellent read from a must-read author.'

Good Reading

'Pomare's strength is in the way he works the tension between his crisp writing and the often horrific instability of what it describes. Not just the violent events, but the sense of how fragile and easily manipulated our sense of self and relationship to the world around us can be . . . *The Last Guests* is the first novel I've read in years I wish was longer.'

Craig Ranapia, newsroom.

'Couldn't put it down, can't stop thinking about it. Bump it to the top of your must-read list immediately.'

Anna Downes, author of *The Safe Place*

Praise for *Tell Me Lies*

'Smart, deftly plotted and narratively sophisticated.'

Sunday Star Times

'A deliciously tight and twisty tale that is guaranteed to keep you turning the pages into the wee hours. If you enjoy your psychological thrillers at a breakneck pace . . . then add this to your wish list.'

Good Reading

'As taut a thriller as you could hope to find.'

New Zealand Woman's Weekly

'Some startling surprises towards the end and a dark, thoughtful conclusion will keep you frantically turning the pages.'

Canberra Weekly

'A thrilling story about a celebrated psychologist who gets too close to a patient.'

Who Magazine

'J.P. Pomare spins another intriguing tale in his latest thriller.'

Reader's Digest

'The acclaimed author of *Call Me Evie* and *In the Clearing* returns with this twisty psychological thriller.'

West Australian

'A twisty tale full of suspense and mystery.'

New Idea

'*Tell Me Lies* is a fast-paced mystery thriller.'

Sydney Morning Herald

'A whodunit with a limited number of possibilities that encourages the reader to guess between a handful of possibilities.'

Herald Sun

Praise for *In the Clearing*

'*In the Clearing* is written with a technical aplomb that proves [*Call Me Evie*] was no fluke.'

The Australian

'Pomare is able to pull off red herrings galore and crafty, satisfying twists. A heart-pounding novel made heart-rending by its reflection of real-life events.'

Kirkus Reviews

'*In the Clearing* will keep you on the edge of your seat and wide awake until you've raced to the end. A true psychological thriller that is totally believable and which will stay with you long after you've finished.'

Herald Sun

'Both [Pomare's] books are testament to the fact that he could be one of the most exciting literary thriller authors to come out of the country.'

The Saturday Paper

'There are lots of premium crime-fiction offerings this summer, but this bloodcurdling exploration of the asphyxiating grip of a cult on its followers deserves to be at the top of your pile.'

The New Daily

'A very fine thriller from a very fine author.'

New Zealand Listener

'If J.P. Pomare's *Call Me Evie* was a slow-burner of a psychological thriller, his follow-up, *In the Clearing*, is a pared-back firecracker.'

Books+Publishing

'I couldn't put it down. What a ride!'

Victoria Hannan, author of *Kokomo*

'Pomare's writing is clear and precise, with not a word wasted. The characters are especially well drawn, developed patiently and with empathy . . . It is the plot, however, of *In the Clearing* that is especially impressive – ambitious, audacious, and masterfully rendered.'

Australian Book Review

'*In the Clearing* is another breathtaking page-turner from the author of *Call Me Evie*. A dark, chilling, atmospheric thriller populated with mysterious and wonderfully flawed characters.'

Christian White, bestselling author of *The Nowhere Child*

'A chilling depiction of the ferocious hold exerted by a cult and its adherents. This is totally absorbing fiction, made all the more shocking by the realisation that these stories recur again and again in Australian society.'

Jock Serong, author of *The Rules of Backyard Cricket*
and *Preservation*

'J.P. Pomare captivates in this haunting novel, *In the Clearing*. I was utterly gripped with the stories of Amy and Freya from start to finish, and fascinated by the unexpected way the two came together . . . A sure-fire bestseller.'

Sally Hepworth, bestselling author of *The Mother-In-Law* and
The Good Sister

'*In the Clearing* is SO good. I love "The Family"-esque vibe, the characters are so well drawn. It's such a great follow up to *Call Me Evie*!'

Ruth McIver, author of *I Shot the Devil*

Praise for *Call Me Evie*

'A nerve-jangling debut infused with literary flair.'

New Zealand Listener

'Almost nothing will turn out as it initially appears in this devastating novel of psychological suspense.'

Publishers Weekly (starred review)

'Read this one with the lights on, and keep Pomare on your radar.'

Kirkus Reviews

'A whip smart debut from our newest thriller star.'

New Zealand Herald

'I felt pure dread reading this book. Enjoyable, exquisite dread.'

Sarah Bailey, author of *The Dark Lake*

'It's a tight, compulsive, beautifully written thriller with echoes of Gillian Flynn, with characters that keep you guessing and a plot that keeps you turning the page.'

Christian White, author of *The Nowhere Child*

'A striking and suspenseful read.'

Sydney Morning Herald

'Will have you guessing and second-guessing until the very end.'

Herald Sun

'A one-sitting kind of book, ideal for readers who enjoy fast-paced thrillers that keep them guessing.'

Books+Publishing

'Pick this one up when you have plenty of time as you're unlikely to put it down after a few pages.'

Daily Telegraph

For my daughter, Blake

THE
LAST
GUESTS

J. P. POMARE

hachette
AUSTRALIA & NEW ZEALAND

hachette
AUSTRALIA & NEW ZEALAND

First published in Australia and New Zealand in 2021
by Hachette Australia
(an imprint of Hachette Australia Pty Limited)
Gadigal Country, Level 17, 207 Kent Street, Sydney, NSW 2000
www.hachette.com.au

This edition published in 2022

Hachette Australia acknowledges and pays our respects to the past, present and
future Traditional Owners and Custodians of Country throughout Australia
and recognises the continuation of cultural, spiritual and educational practices
of Aboriginal and Torres Strait Islander peoples. Our head office is located on
the lands of the Gadigal people of the Eora Nation.

NATIONAL
LIBRARY
OF AUSTRALIA

A catalogue record for this
book is available from the
National Library of Australia

ISBN: 978 1 86971 821 3 (paperback)

Cover design by Christabella Designs
Cover photograph courtesy of Getty
Author photograph by Leah Jing McIntosh
Peephole image design by Dan Valenzuela
Typeset in Adobe Garamond Pro by Bookhouse, Sydney
Printed and bound in Australia by McPherson's Printing Group

MIX
Paper from
responsible sources
FSC
www.fsc.org   FSC® C001695

The paper this book is printed on is certified against the
Forest Stewardship Council® Standards. McPherson's Printing
Group holds FSC® chain of custody certification SA-COC-005379.
FSC® promotes environmentally responsible, socially beneficial
and economically viable management of the world's forests.

That's a secret, private world you're looking into out there. People do a lot of things in private they couldn't possibly explain in public.

– *REAR WINDOW*

PROLOGUE

HE IS ANYBODY, everybody, nobody. A black jacket, blue jeans, baseball cap and black sneakers. That's what the neighbours would see if they happened to glance out the window as he passed through the front gate and crossed the three metres of cobbled path to the front of the house. His heart is steady, his hand is still as he punches the code into the silver key safe bolted to the brick facade of 299 Hillview Terrace. Four-one-three-nine, then it falls open and he's staring at a simple silver key and a long brass mortise key attached to a key ring in the shape of New Zealand.

He pockets the keys, pulls his hat lower and walks back to the rental car parked on the street. He opens the boot, retrieves two large suitcases and wheels them to the house. He scans the entrance. *No cameras, no surveillance.*

He slides the keys into the locks, first the antiquated bottom lock with the long brass key then the modern lock. The door swings back, an arm opening to invite him inside. He drags the suitcases over the threshold and closes the door behind him. Open plan, as sterile and neat as a hotel room. Polished floorboards echo beneath his sneakers as he passes through the kitchen to the lounge room. Framed Ikea prints. A boxy couch that looks like it belongs in a furniture showroom. A beige rug. Outside, through the sliding door, a tiled courtyard and a potted lemon tree sit in the lukewarm sunlight.

He checks out the other rooms. There's a study just large enough for a pine desk, a chair and a bookshelf. The bedroom is generous: a king-sized bed, a flat screen TV bolted to the wall and a wardrobe. He knows the place is booked this weekend and most nights next week. It averages seven bookings a month, which isn't surprising. It's cheap and not too far from the CBD. Most importantly, it's available for single-night bookings. Ideal for a one-night stand. Perfect for his needs.

He sets both suitcases down in the living room and opens them to reveal a handheld vacuum cleaner, a number of white cardboard boxes, a cordless drill, screws, screwdrivers, chisels, a paint roller. He also has a plaster kit.

His eyes roam the walls and the ceiling, his gaze coming to rest on the black pendant light fitting hanging down. Lights are good; people tend not to stare directly at them. He takes one of the four chairs ringing the dining table and places it at the centre of the room before climbing up to examine the elaborate bowl-shaped design of the lampshade. He lowers himself back to the carpet again and pulls a bluetooth speaker from one of the suitcases. He puts on music, 'Paint It, Black' by the Rolling Stones. With the volume up high, he climbs onto the chair again and begins drilling a tiny aperture. It's an expensive drill, much quieter than the splash of the cymbals coming from the speakers, the rolling thud of the bass drum. He hums the tune.

Back down from the chair, he opens the white boxes, looking for the size he is after. *Bingo.* A three-millimetre fish-eye lens. He removes the camera, about the size of a pen nib. He climbs back up, presses it through the hole in the light fitting and fastens it in place. He returns to the floor and inspects his handiwork. Unless you knew exactly what you were looking for, you would never notice it.

Next he goes to the bedroom, eyes searching. There's a smoke alarm. He could punch out the tiny light that only flashes when the battery is low and put the camera eye in its place. He brings the chair in from the lounge room, climbs up. As he reaches for the alarm, he hears something over the music and freezes. It's a rattling sound coming from outside. Could it be someone dragging their bin out? He doesn't move until the sound is gone. Then, exhaling, he completes the installation. The alarm won't work anymore – he takes the battery out just to be sure.

Now the bathroom. He stops at the door and considers the layout, his gloved hands gently sliding across the wall tiles. He has to have a camera in here, but there is no obvious place to conceal it. If he puts one in the ceiling beside the fan, the steam will likely obscure the vision. And he needs to find somewhere that will capture both the shower and the rest of the room. Or use two cameras. He takes option B, better to be safe than sorry. He runs hot water in the shower with the fan turned on, watches where the steam comes to rest on the surfaces. The glass of the shower screen, the mirror, the steel handrail next to the toilet. Anywhere lower than waist height is good, any higher and you risk fogging the lens. The towel rail is attached to the wall with a small screw. That'll do. He carefully removes the screw from the rail and replaces it with an expensive camera mounted in a screw head. Then he places the second camera in the light fitting above the mirror, just below the fan where there's no steam on the tiles.

Back out in the hallway, the walls are thin plasterboard. Tapping with his knuckles he finds the stud near the meter box and cuts out a square beside it with a jab saw; the hole is just large enough for his remote-access 5G wi-fi router which is already configured with the cameras. He can't stream through the house's wi-fi in case the hosts change the password or have enough technical nous to check how many devices are currently connected to the network and realise there are four extras unaccounted for – the four cameras. Some savvy travellers also have apps and devices which check to see if any cameras are running through local wi-fi networks.

He installs a power point within the wall and plugs the router in. He finds the switchboard just inside the front door and opens it to reveal a panel of new circuit-breakers. He runs the cable from the router through the same switch as the hot water service. Kill the hot water and the cameras will drop out. It's not ideal, but it's least likely to be switched off and a new circuit-breaker might get noticed.

Then he takes a piece of plaster from his kit and cuts it to shape, fitting it into the square to hide the router. He's a perfectionist. It's a flaw as much as an asset; he can't leave a job until everything is polished, finished. What calms him most is sanding down a jag in a wooden bench or buffing out a scuff in floorboards. The sort of work that soothes him but doesn't pay well. This job has made him the most money; and while this work may not be calming, it is, oddly, the most satisfying. There is enough risk to keep it interesting, but when you're this careful and precise there's almost no chance of getting caught.

Now he mixes a little plaster and smears it over the seams. While it dries, he goes to the kitchen, fires up his tablet and logs on to the surveillance software.

The screen shows a man in a cap hunched over a faux stone benchtop, with boxes open on the carpet of the adjoining lounge room. He clicks through each camera: the bathroom, a view of the shower and then a view of the toilet, then the bedroom.

'Shit,' he says to himself. 'You idiot.'

The bedroom camera catches only two-thirds of the bed. He can see everything except the pillows. He grinds the heels of his palms into his temples. The bed yields the most sought-after footage – that's why he is here. He strides back into the bedroom, searching for a better spot. He could shift the smoke detector, sand and paint where it was, rewire it to the new spot. But a cleaner might notice if it has moved; a nosy cleaner might even take a closer look. That's the easiest way to lose his equipment and possibly get caught. *I could turn the fitting, so the camera is aimed closer to the bed*, he decides.

He climbs up to start turning the alarm fitting. As he examines it, though, he sees that the smoke alarm has a smear of paint on one side, from the last time the room was painted, he guesses. It's dusty, too, clearly a few years old, and his gloved fingers have left tiny smudges. He chews his lip, his frustration growing. Should he put a second camera in this room? But where? *How many viewers will I lose if I don't have the pillows in the frame?* He thinks for a moment. *Full HD streams with night vision*, he tells himself, *it doesn't matter if you miss the pillows, the viewers will still flood the streams.* He wipes the dust on his shirt away and climbs down.

Back in the lounge room, he takes a coin-sized chip of paint from the removed square of plaster and puts it in his pocket. Then he cranes his head out the door before striding to the car. A modern white Toyota, the most forgettable car on the roads. He removes his hat and gloves, starts the car and heads up the street. He goes the long way around the park at the top of the street, taking the same route he came earlier to avoid the CCTV at the corner store. He drives north, over the harbour bridge and west to a part of the city where no one would ever recognise him.

The sign above the door reads, 'Speedy Shoe Repairs and Key Cutting'. A man is grinding a key when he enters, so he waits with his head down, pretending to study a display of key rings near the counter. The grinder stops, the portly man blows away the steel files, rubs the key on his blue apron as he walks towards the counter. 'How can I help you?'

'I just need another copy of these.' He holds out the keys. 'These are the wife's.'

'Lost yours, eh?'

He answers quickly, the first thing that comes to mind. 'Mine are at the bottom of the Pacific.'

'Right,' the man says with a smile. 'Fisherman.'

'You bet.'

The man takes the long mortise key now, peers closely at it. 'Don't see these too much these days.'

'It's an old unit. Still got the original lock as well as a deadbolt.'

'You in a rush?'

'I am actually.'

'It'll probably be half an hour.'

'That's fine.'

'Five bucks for one copy of this one and twenty-nine for this one.'

He smiles. 'Sure.'

'I'll grab a number to call you when they're done.'

'I'll just come back in half an hour.'

The man's eyes linger on him for a moment. *Suspicion?* Maybe. He's sizing him up. 'Right.'

He returns to the car, sits in the driver's seat, brings up the camera streams on his phone. With the curtains closed, the bedroom is dark, so he turns on night mode. The screen goes from black to a shade of green, like the bottom of the sea. The shape of the bed is sharp, the pattern on the carpet is clear – it's good. Much better than he was expecting.

The keys are ready and waiting for him when he returns. There's a tiny orange buoy attached to the key ring.

'Now they'll float,' the man says with a wink.

'Thanks,' he says, annoyed that he is making himself more memorable. Easy to imagine this chipper bloke in a dim police interview room. *Yeah, the fisherman. I remember him clearly.* Maybe he should have done one key at one locksmith and the other at a different one. Maybe he should have kept his mouth shut. In the future, he'll be more careful.

He pays cash, pockets the keys and heads back to the car. He drives to another shopping strip, with a hardware store. He finds an uninterested teenager leaning on his elbow over the paint desk.

'Hi, just need something that matches this.' He lays the paint chip on the counter.

'Sure, how much?'

'Enough for ten metres.'

It takes five minutes to mix. When it's done, the youth paints a spot, blow dries it and compares the dry paint to the chip. It looks perfect.

'Great,' he says, taking the can.

The youth picks up the chip.

'I need that,' he says quickly.

'Sorry?' The teenager looks at him.

'The chip, give it to me.'

'Okay, sorry, I didn't . . .'

He takes the chip from the teenager's hand and turns, striding towards the checkout.

Back at the house, wearing his gloves and hat once more, he tests the new keys and finds they both slide in and turn smoothly. The door unlocks. He can return whenever he wants. Some months from now, when the place isn't booked, he can slip in and uninstall the cameras.

His repairs have dried while he has been out. In the kitchen, he lays out a sheet of newspaper before returning to the hallway to study the wall for a moment, noting the original paintwork, the telling strokes. It was clearly a roller job, using decent paint that has been there for a while. His tin is enough to do the entire wall if he needs to. He has drop sheets with him. The fine sandpaper rasps as he smooths the edges of the new plaster. Then he cleans it with an alcohol wipe, fills the paint tray and begins rolling it on, covering only the new square of wall and ten centimetres around it.

While it dries, he repacks all but a few of the white boxes into his suitcases. Again, he finds the street empty when he opens the door. He quickly drags the suitcases back out to the rental, stowing them in the boot.

He packs up the last of his things, pulls a chair out from the table, half-closes the curtains, tips a third of the complimentary carton of milk down the sink. He sprays air freshener, hoping to neutralise the paint smell. He walks to the bedroom, pulls a small ziplock bag from his pocket and opens it to pluck out one of the long blonde hairs inside. He lays it on a pillow. He'd collected them from the drain at a swimming pool across town.

He pulls the blankets back on the bed and rumples the sheets. He empties the remaining five hairs from the ziplock bag into the shower, then he runs the hot water for a moment. He mops up a little of the water with one of the towels then leaves it on the floor. He does one last walk-through, searching for any sign of his presence, but everything is in place.

Under the glow of a streetlight, he locks the keys away, as per the instructions on the listing, and gets into the rental car. Now he waits.

PART ONE
THE VOYEUR

ONE

'LINA,' CAIN SAYS.

A current shoots down my spine. I'm deleting the app before he has a chance to see what it is. When the blue square disappears from my screen, I turn my head.

'Yeah?'

'What are you doing?'

I turn and face him with the rest of my body now, phone still squeezed in my fist. 'Oh, nothing, I just downloaded the wrong app.'

'Right,' he says. He's in his towel, heading for a shower. He picks up his protein shaker and gives it a few pumps. 'I'll be quick. Are you ready?'

'Yeah,' I say, my voice a little tight. 'Almost.' He doesn't seem to notice the slight tremble in my hand holding the phone as he drains the liquid, the muscles in his throat working. He has clipped his hair again, a few millimetres of salted black. The towel is loose on his waist and beneath the kitchen downlights he looks as lean as he ever has. He's getting his SAS body back, but it's more than that, more mass, a bulging chest and shoulders.

'Love you,' he says, stepping closer now, placing a kiss on my forehead.

'Quick,' I say. 'We've got to go.'

Everyone has secrets, I tell myself. Or is that just one of those things people, bad people, tell themselves? Whispering little lies to get through the days. Just how my mother had done. A secret like mine is a snake in a box – so long as it's trapped inside, it can't hurt. He goes to the bathroom and a small surge of relief floods through me. But this night is far from over.

•

I watch him get dressed, his body mapped with pale scars up his left side, concentrated between his knee and hip, with slashes reaching up to his shoulder. Surgeons managed to cut out most of the shrapnel and his body has since squeezed out more, but there are still scraps encased in knots of scar tissue that'll be there until he dies.

He pulls his shirt on, climbs the buttons with his fingers. I adjust his collar, find it still warm from the iron. A smile now. Pale brown eyes that catch the light. And those dimples bracketing his mouth deepen, almost too charming for his weathered, rugged face. I think about the app again. *Stay the course*, I tell myself.

'You set for work later?' he asks.

'Yep, I've got my uniform in the car.' Nerves crest beneath my sternum; I push back against the feeling. He can't complain about me picking up shifts, his recklessness is partly to blame for putting us in a financial hole. Our monthly repayments on the credit card barely cover the interest, let alone pay off the debt.

We are heading about twenty-five minutes south-east of the CBD, an area full of big two-storey places whose residents all work in the city and whose yards are full of harmless dogs: labradors or collies.

Cain steers through the streets to the motorway heading south and soon we are rolling along the tree-lined streets. I'm grateful he's driving; I spend half my day behind the wheel – people think an ambulance officer's job is performing CPR and administering EpiPens when really we spend much more time navigating traffic and waiting in car parks for our next call.

I should have taken something, a Valium maybe. For the first time in months, I crave a drink. It's like I can taste an earthy red on my tongue.

'Knock, knock,' I call through the screen door when we arrive. 'Hello.'

'Come in,' Axel's deep voice calls. 'It's unlocked.' We walk through to the living room, white walls, pale timber floorboards. They bought this place a few years ago and it's much bigger than our rental. A show home; it barely looks lived in at all.

'Hello, lovelies,' Claire says, striding to Cain first for a hug. 'Jesus, you need to chill on the bench press.'

'Tell me about it,' I say.

Taj, their twelve-year-old beagle, is at her heels.

Claire hugs me, kisses the air beside my cheek. She calls herself the yogoth – she has bottle-black hair, shellacked nails and tattoos, and owns her own yoga studio in the city. I've gone along once or twice; I always feel good afterwards but horribly inflexible during.

'I love your hair,' she says. 'Very short, very chic.' She might as well be complimenting her own hair, which is shorter, darker and undeniably *more* chic. But I appreciate it. Claire is one of the good ones. We'd caught up for wine a few times when the boys were away. We'd joked about getting matching tattoos: *WW*, war wives. It was nice to have a confidante, someone I could talk to about what Cain did, other than the dismissive, 'He's in the army.'

Axel comes over in an apron with Michelangelo's *David* on the front. He's not quite as tall as Cain but otherwise they could be twins. Maori boys with perennial tans, and salt and pepper hair, although where Cain's is receding and clipped short, Axel's is long and slicked back. Both gym junkies and still built like rugby players. Their hands clap together, palms thump backs. *The alpha of alphas*, Cain had once said, *but I love him for it.*

Axel steps back now, gives me that grin that belongs on a salesman, or a politician. Dentist-white teeth. He's not vain but he looks after himself; looks good in designer jeans tight around his muscled thighs and a loose linen shirt. Hard to imagine him as an elite soldier nowadays.

'You're a fine wine, Lina. Better every year.'

'Eventually wine turns rancid,' I joke.

'That's true. You're not there yet though. Speaking of which. Wine, beer?'

'Not for me,' I say. 'I got called in. Shift starts at eleven.' Again, the nerves rise all the way to the base of my throat. I feel like I could be sick.

'You're joking,' Claire says now. 'It's been so long since we got drunk together.'

'I wish I was,' I say, exhaling.

'You work too hard. Unlike this one.' Axel gently jabs Cain's shoulder.

I could blurt out, *We're broke*, but it's hardly what they want to hear.

'Do you want a glass of juice then, or we've got ginger beer?' Claire offers.

'I'm fine really,' I say. I'd tried so often to cut back on my drinking. It wasn't until we began trying for a kid that I really got on top of it. And now I barely touch alcohol at all. The only people I seem to drink around are these two. Black belts in peer pressure, both of them.

When we sit down to dinner a little while later, Claire has set the table with placemats and coasters.

'Really?' Axel says, grinning. 'Do we need these old things?'

'We do,' Claire says. 'I just want to keep it tidy.'

Axel clicks his tongue, then explains, 'We've got guests staying this weekend.'

'Guests?'

'We're going to head down to Raglan,' Claire says. 'We're renting our place out again on WeStay.'

'It's a pain but it's worth it. You'd do well out of the lake house,' Axel says to me, spearing a piece of grilled broccolini on his plate. These two are born hustlers.

'How do you know?' I say. 'You've never been there. Could be a dump.'

'I'm sure it's not, based on the location alone.'

Claire tips a little wine into her mouth, her black fringe falling to one side. She's exquisite. Small and strong. When we'd holidayed together in Bali a few years ago, Axel and Claire drew stares everywhere we went. Skin as tight as stretched rubber, hard-edged muscles stencilled just below the surface. After a boozy day poolside, I had let my eyes linger on Axel in the water for just a heartbeat too long, more fascinated than anything else, but Cain had noticed.

'I'm sure he wouldn't mind if you took a picture,' he'd said with a tone.

'No,' I'd replied quickly. 'They're just both so bloody fit.'

He'd raised his eyebrows.

'Like you,' I'd added a second too late. 'All three of you are ripped and here I sit, a doughy profiterole.'

The memory reminds me of the app, Cain in the kitchen earlier. His voice. *What are you doing?* Had he seen it? I touch my upper lip and find it's a little damp, not with drink but with sweat. It's not too late to change my mind. *Or is it?* I realise they're all waiting for me to speak again.

'Yeah,' I say. 'I mean maybe we could make a bit of money but it needs a lot of work.'

'So anyone can book this place at any time?' Cain asks, changing the subject.

'Only on the weekends that we make it available,' Axel says. 'We get three hundred a night for it.'

'Three hundred dollars?' I ask, blinking. Their place is modern and well styled, I guess. More comfortable than a hotel room. 'You could stay in a penthouse in SkyCity for that.'

'Not quite, but it means we can have our own holiday down the coast,' Claire says.

It's not like you need the money, I think.

'I've been telling Cain you should do something with that lake house for years,' Axel says.

Cain gives me a look. He knows that the lake house is more than a house to me. It's there for when we start our own family.

'How many times have you rented this place out?' I ask, to continue the conversation and keep me from focusing on the other thoughts in my head, the images of what I'm going to do later.

'Loads,' Claire says. 'We just go away when they're here. We set our price quite high. We've made thousands.'

'I don't know if I could do it,' I say. '*Anyone* could stay. Remember that time someone squatted at the house for months, Cain? The neighbours called us and we had to get the police to go kick them out.'

'WeStay guests are a bit different to squatters, Lina,' Axel says and I detect a note of condescension in his voice.

'Well, you never really know who these people are, right?'

Axel swallows a mouthful of wine and drags his smile up on one side. 'This is the twenty-first century, Lina, you can't cash a cheque or rent a pushbike without a retina scan, a blood bond to hand over your firstborn and nine different forms of ID.'

Cain laughs. They all do. I push a smile to my lips. 'I know but –'

'It's not so simple as just whipping up a profile and making the booking.' He gestures with his wineglass as he speaks. 'We've never had a problem. Hell, I'd even set it all up for you if you wanted.'

I turn to Cain, hoping for backup. 'Would you do it?'

Cain sucks his lips for a moment. 'You know I don't trust strangers,' he says at last. 'But it sounds like good money, and we could do with a little more.' The understatement of the year.

'If you're worried about people going through your stuff, lock it away,' Axel says. 'You could make a fortune. Market it as an artist's retreat, or a quiet family weekend away, then sit back and count the money.'

'I don't know, it needs a bit of work.'

'Cain could do it.'

'Don't pressure them, honey. It's not for everyone,' Claire says.

'What if someone decided to cook P in your house?'

Axel takes a sip of his wine, pauses with the glass close to his lips. 'This isn't *Breaking Bad*,' he says. 'It's the burbs in Auckland city.'

'Or what if they go through your things and steal your passports? What if they cut your keys?'

'And come back to murder us?' His bark of laughter grates.

I want to remind them all about the news story from a few months ago. The murder, somewhere in the States. That was a WeStay, wasn't it? But by the time I've ordered my thoughts, the conversation is moving again and it would seem petty to bring it up.

'Tell them about the knickers,' Claire speaks with laughter in her voice.

Axel covers his eyes with his palm. 'Don't scare them off, Claire, we can get a referral fee if they do it.'

Referral fee. Is that the agenda here? 'I love a knickers story,' I say.

'It's not much of a story. Just something we found,' Claire says, one elegant hand flicking out, dismissing her own story.

'They were tiny, lacy knickers,' Axel says. 'We found them scrunched up down the side of the bed when we were cleaning after someone left.'

'No,' I say, slowly, my hand coming to my mouth.

'We were tempted to contact the guests to return them for a laugh,' he adds. 'Since then, we just pay a cleaner to come so we don't have to *imagine* what took place in our home.'

'People have sex in your bed and leave their knickers behind?' Cain says. 'And pay you for the privilege.' He glances across the table to me, a question on his face. He turns back to the others. 'Do you change your pillowcases and everything?' he asks.

Am I doing the right thing?

'Oh yeah, we keep the spares locked in the cupboard beneath the stairs.'

'Sounds foolproof.'

I try to bring up the incident in the US. 'What about those rumours, people stealing art and replacing it with replicas, or . . . you know. The other thing?' I say.

'What thing?' Axel says, hunching over the table, resting on his forearms, which are covered in black hair.

'A man was killed in a WeStay. Remember? The killer recorded it and shared the footage.'

'Oh that?' Axel blows air dismissively. 'That wasn't WeStay's fault. Some psychopath just wanted to kill someone.'

Cain is looking down at his phone. 'Lina,' he says, pausing the conversation. 'There's a three-bedroom place on the lake for three hundred a night. We've got more bedrooms. *And,*' he says scrolling with his thumb, 'we're much closer to the lake.'

I hold out my hand. 'Let me see.' It's the big house, with the steep driveway, up on the hill. Walking distance from the Landing Cafe but not on the water like ours.

'It's nicer inside but we could easily tidy our place up to the same level,' Cain says.

I see all the other listings dotted around the lakes area. Lots of people are doing it apparently.

Claire interrupts. 'Lina, you've not seen the terrace!'

'It's finished?'

'Come on,' she says. 'Let's have a look.' She leads me outside on to their deck, up a set of steps. The city emerges from beyond the rooftops, an entire landscape before us. All those lights, embers in the darkness. The terrace is on the roof of their house. It's fake grass and deck chairs. Is this new addition in the tens or hundreds of thousands? It's hard not to feel jealous of their lives.

'God, look at that,' I say.

'It's nice, right?' she says. 'Good night for it too.'

'Stunning.' I can barely keep the note of envy out of my voice. I can't imagine where all the money comes from. There's Claire's yoga studio and Axel has one of those gyms that's full of ropes, boxes and tractor tyres. It must be doing well because he wants to open a chain of them, an empire. Axel was the one that put the idea in Cain's head to start his own personal training business. He even suggested the name, Commando Fitness. Cain cringed when he told me. 'I like it,' I'd lied.

He trains people out of Axel's gym. Despite his injuries, the scars and a knee that barely bends, he still manages to keep strong. Suits and yuppies like the idea of training the way the SAS do; they'll pay extra to know they're in the hands of a trained killer – that's the gimmick, but Cain's had a hard time gaining the sort of early traction Axel experienced. He doesn't have the same gameshow-host charisma. He couldn't get a business loan, so he put most of the set-up costs on the credit card, and he was still gambling back then. The debts piled up. And then there were the medical bills.

'The guests must love this?'

'This is the first booking we've taken since the renovation,' Claire says. It's clear from the way she oscillates her wineglass, almost spilling the chardonnay, that she's at least halfway drunk. I had always assumed cool girls like Claire would drink negronis or craft beer, not the wine I associate with middle-aged housewives.

'Have you guys had any bad reviews?'

A long silence, she takes a sip and the air becomes thick and cool.

'Not yet,' she says. Then she turns away from the skyline, facing me. 'How are *you* guys going?'

'Us? We're good,' I say, guarded. There is something off in her tone. Did she notice I've been preoccupied tonight? She continues watching me until I feel the urge to speak again. 'Cain's good. He seems to enjoy working and it's getting him out of the house. Business seems to be picking up for him.'

Her eyes don't leave mine as she takes another gulp of wine. 'Can I talk to you about something that might seem a little . . .' Her free hand dances in the air between us. 'What's the word . . . gauche?' she says. 'Is that it?'

'I don't know,' I say, a feeling of alarm resonating inside me. 'It depends.'

A moment passes, I see her uncertainty.

'What is it?'

'Look, this is a little awkward but I know you guys are struggling. Axel won't bring it up directly with Cain.' A pause. 'It's just Axel's gym is at capacity, and he's giving up some of his own clients for Cain.' I can see the colour in her cheeks. She's holding her glass in two hands but takes one off to twist a finger at the corner of her eye. 'Axel told me Cain has had a couple of arguments with people at the gym, he snapped at one of the regulars. I guess I'm wondering if everything is okay with him?'

I think of the broken handle on the cutlery drawer at home, a stray spoon was lodged and it wouldn't open, he'd ripped it off in frustration. The year he returned from Afghanistan he was going to physio three times a week, a therapist once and taking handfuls of painkillers and antidepressants. Are those old demons from the war back? Has he been going through hell again right under my nose?

'He's doing okay,' I say. 'He might have been a little bit off the last few weeks but he's been training hard and getting in the right head space.'

'Yeah,' she says. 'Well, Axel wants to open a second gym and after this renovation, money has become really tight for us. I'm sure it took a bit of pressure off when he stopped charging Cain for the use of the gym but now he wants to give Cain a loan, to help him get things moving.'

I can feel blood rushing to my own cheeks now. Axel isn't charging Cain anymore? How are we still going backwards when my income is enough to cover the bills? 'But Cain's business is doing okay,' I say. 'What do you mean get things moving?'

She doesn't say the word 'Oh', but her mouth forms the shape, those perfect eyebrows lift a fraction.

'Claire,' I say, my voice firm.

'Shit, I've put my foot in it.' She clamps a hand to her forehead, swings her head away then back to me. 'Pretend I never said anything. Please?' She tosses her free hand as if dismissing the entire conversation. 'Let the boys figure it out, I don't know why I brought it up.'

'I mean, yeah, I knew the business was struggling,' I say, 'but he doesn't need a loan.' I feel sick thinking about it. We've wasted so much money the last couple of years. *No secrets*, he promised.

'Yeah,' she says.

Oh my God, I think recognising the sadness in her eyes, *she actually feels sorry for me.*

'I just wanted to make sure he was okay. You know what those boys are like. It's not in their blood to ask for help.'

I try to smile. 'Sure.' I check my phone. It's almost time for me to go.

The boys look up from an iPad as we enter the house and their conversation stops. 'What's up?' Cain says, the booze melting the hard consonants.

'Nothing, I was just admiring the view out there. Incredible, Axel. You guys have done such a good job with the renovation.'

Claire strides into the room, places one hand on Axel's shoulder and replaces his glass on the coaster with the other.

'Sorry *darling*, we're still talking about WeStay,' he says. 'I've almost convinced him.'

I feel a pang of frustration slap the back of my neck. *Is that the point of this dinner? To help us make money?* Cain once told me Axel was like his older brother, he'd never let Cain get into trouble. But what if Axel sees things differently? What if Cain isn't like a brother, but a liability?

'It's not him that needs convincing I'm sorry to say.'

I can see Cain has already decided, and my objection is the only thing between him and a new way to make money. My husband has principles he lives by. This is one of them: always look after us first. We never should have ended up here, treading water financially, in a place we don't love, doing work we resent. The plan was – *no*, the plan *is* to move to Tarawera, without the big city rent and expenses, to start a family, to live quiet and still as the lake. We'd be there now, if it wasn't for me. If I'd not failed. If I'd not lost the baby. That's how marriages begin to break, isn't it? One tiny thing derails all the big plans and the rot creeps through a once blooming garden.

A knot of guilt in my throat. I check my phone, swallow hard. Certain now that I'm doing the right thing.

'I should probably get going,' I say.

Peephole transmission

Live streams will resume from this coming Sunday at midnight GMT with new precautions in place to prevent occupants of Peepholes from being doxed or harassed. Given the recent events in Colorado we will monitor the situation closely. Our focus is to protect the identities of our planters and subscribers. As always, members of our community in breach of any of the rules will be punished. Streams will return permanently, provided there is no further scrutiny of our service from authorities and investigative bodies.

Please enjoy the show.

TWO

FAVOURS AREN'T FREE, I think, as I drive back through the streets, reach the motorway and set out towards the city. Gifts and favours arrive yoked with obligation – the *giver* will one day be the *receiver* – but also the expectation of gratitude. Axel has been doing Cain a favour, which means he's doing me a favour. And this idea that he might give Cain money, enough money for Claire to raise it with me, sounds like a big debt we would have to cover one way or another.

It's not that I don't trust Axel, it's just that he wheels and deals, and I don't want Cain to end up in an awkward situation with his best friend. You know the guy that would always put you in a taxi if you were too drunk? That's Cain. You know the guy that fed you too many shots? That's Axel.

Cain's a gambler. It's something he inherited from his father. Not that I knew the man. The only time I saw him, it was just his body. A sorry affair even for a funeral, with no family other than Cain and his father's second ex-wife who had come to the funeral home on her lunch break, still in her bank teller's uniform. She'd asked Cain, 'How did you know Barry?'

'I didn't really,' he had said, the conversation ending there.

At least he inherited something of value from his mother. My favourite piece of jewellery, my wedding ring. Which reminds me – at a set of lights I twist the ring off and string it through my necklace.

I pull off the motorway in the heart of the city. *Stay the course*, I tell myself. Could I have rescheduled, thought it over more? *No*, it has to be tonight, it has to be now. Cain will drink himself into a stupor before falling into the back seat of an Uber and somehow making his way up the stairs to bed. That's something I grew out of, but he did not. The occasional binge. I check my phone to make sure I'm heading in the right direction. I pull into a side street nearby, park, then get out and open the boot, fetching my duffel bag. A truck is parked on the road ahead, the driver is leaning against the door looking down at his phone and smoking a cigarette. I climb back into the car. I change clothes quickly with the seat back, slipping out of my jeans and blouse, wrangling a dress over my body. I glance towards the end of the road where the trucker is still standing. He's watching the car. The dress leaves a generous measure of leg exposed. I add heels, tossing my sneakers in the back, then a dark coat. The bar is walking distance from here.

In the rear-view mirror, I apply a little more make-up and then I spray on some of my Le Labo perfume – an expensive wedding gift I've managed to stretch out for five years. I'll have to wash it off later. I open my phone. I'd started downloading the app again as soon as I got in the car, and now I send a message.

So sorry I'm running late, be there in five, don't start without me!

The trucker glances up as I cross the road, watching me in the jaundiced streetlight, before tilting his head back down to his phone.

It's dark and cool out. On the other side of the street is a dimly lit park. I swallow hard as a pulse of fear races over my skin. I think of those faces that pop up a couple of times a year on the news – girls, usually walking home alone. So many murders, so many rapes seem to happen in suburban parks on quiet dark streets with big trees that absorb screams. If something did happen, what would Cain think? Would he work out why I was here and not at work? I swallow hard and lengthen my stride. No stopping now.

Years ago, when Cain was still in Afghanistan, I'd boasted to close girlfriends that we had better sex than I'd ever had. He was indelicate but considerate. I remember when we first met how much I wanted him from the moment I saw those thick lips, the moment he spoke. He was so unlike the boys I'd known.

But things change, especially sex. It becomes regimented, dull. I can't remember the last time it felt fulfilling or genuinely exciting. Who knows, maybe Cain feels the same.

Turning my gaze from the park, I look towards the houses crowded in a row on the other side of the road, some with lights brightening curtains and blinds, some dark and still as the night.

A distant grumble comes from beyond the houses; it could be the sky heralding a storm, or it could be a particularly loud truck on the motorway.

My phone vibrates. I open the app and see his response: a photo of a pint of beer, half gone already and a caption: *Couldn't wait . . .*

I use the selfie camera on my phone to check my teeth for lipstick. I barely look like myself.

At the end of the street, I can see a strip of shops, a couple of restaurants and the corner pub. Anglers Tavern.

We're meeting on a weeknight because I knew it would be quieter, but also because there is less chance of bumping into someone. I have reached a stage in my life where I don't know anyone who would be at a bar on a Thursday night. I've taken other precautions: only use cash, turn off location services on my phone, which I do now. Most importantly: be late, be quick.

The moment I'm inside, I spot him. Not because he looks like his photos but because he's the only one sitting alone. An air of

27

anticipation floats around him like a noxious gas. I make myself move in his direction, smile. Then he glances up from his phone, his hand rises; a small flick of the wrist.

'Hello, Daniel.'

'Hi,' he says, standing from his seat. A hint of a smile on his lips. I see his pint is now empty. *Dutch courage? Booze hound?* Just like Cain, I suppose.

I kiss his cheek, ignoring his outstretched hand. 'Nice to finally meet,' I say.

A flutter in my stomach; a swarm of butterflies. He's not ugly, but he doesn't really look like his profile picture. Most people might be annoyed, but I'm relieved he's not too attractive. He's just what I'm after. He's also wearing glasses, which give him a sort of tattooed Clark Kent vibe. I wonder for a moment if they're an affectation or real.

'You don't look much like your profile pic,' he says.

'Oh,' I say. Is this a neg? Or honesty? To be fair, I have photo-shopped it, so it doesn't look exactly like me, plausible deniability etc. If you reverse image-search my profile photo, you won't find any of my social media accounts.

'I mean that in the best possible way,' he adds.

And you're nowhere near as hot as your profile pic, I think but it's too early in the piece to lance his ego, and despite the fact he's not exactly like the image on the app, he's still my type. The type I'm after anyway.

'Thank you,' I say.

'Oh, no. It's true. You're stunning.'

'Don't flatter me. I wasn't expecting glasses?'

'I inherited my father's bad eyes, unfortunately.'

Noted. I move on and ask him about work, even though I already know the details.

'I've got my own business,' he says. 'I'm like a handyman.'

'So you clear drains for housewives, that sort of thing?'

'Yeah,' he says, missing the joke but smiling properly for the first time. His smile is self-conscious and creeps up from the corners of his lips. He glances back towards the bar. 'What are you drinking?'

'The first round is on me,' I say, pointing at his empty glass. 'What are *you* drinking?'

'You like to be in charge?'

'I do,' I say, forcing another smile. This is all moving so quickly it feels like a form of motion sickness. I know the feeling will be with me most of the night but hopefully it's worth it in the end.

'I'll have another lager.'

'Please.'

'Sorry?' He looks confused.

'Are you going to say please?'

He gives me a knowing look; a slight smile shifts his wet lips. '*Please.*'

The barman is young and sharp cheeked, with the sort of bowl haircut for which kids were once bullied.

'Hi,' I say. 'Can I get a lime and soda, and a pint of lager?'

'Sure,' he says.

I hand him a note, then lean over the bar. 'Can you do me a favour? See that man I'm with?'

'Yeah?'

'Well, if he orders a vodka-soda for me, could you make sure that it's just lime and soda. I'm not actually drinking tonight.'

His pale face shapes into a question mark. 'We've got mocktails.'

'No, you don't understand. I'm not drinking but –'

'You want him to think you are?' He looks shocked, a hand comes to his chest.

'No, it's . . .' I begin, but when he smiles I realise he's mocking me. 'I just don't want to hurt his ego. You ever been on one of those dates that you know probably isn't worth the hangover?' That's the truth. It's not worth the hangover, but more importantly I can't turn up at home stinking of booze.

A knowing smile, he flashes a wink. 'Say no more. Lime and sodas all night for you. Want me to charge him for the vodka?'

I shrug one shoulder. 'If that's cool with you.'

'I don't mind either way.'

I carry a glass in each hand back to our table. Daniel's head is down, staring at his phone, I see only the diamond shape of his back, that neckless look of rugby players.

'You never told me what you do, Anna?'

'Me?' I think for a moment, placing our drinks down and sitting on the bench seat beside him. I had an answer prepared but it's escaped my mind. I improvise. 'I'm actually a doctor.'

'Where?'

'Sorry?' I say, feeling a little flustered now.

'At a hospital? Or a clinic?'

'Middlemore,' I lie. 'I'm a doctor at Middlemore. But enough about work, what do you do for fun?'

'I'm a country boy. I go fishing and hunting a bit. Other than that, I just train.'

'Train?'

'Gym and boxing,' he says.

I pout my bottom lip and give a nod. 'You're a fighter?'

'Not quite, just do it to keep fit and healthy.'

'Your muscles are not just for the girls?'

He's mid-twenties, dark clipped hair and a hairline that perhaps goes a little too close to his heavy brow, which if I were being unkind, I would describe as caveman-esque. But beneath that brow and behind those glasses, he has the most arresting green eyes.

'No, I'm a good boy. I'm not always out chasing girls.'

Why do we call it butterflies, this feeling? Why not moths? Whatever it is, it's *not* a pleasant feeling. Excitement, yes, but with equal parts anxiety. 'Is that right? They chase you?'

He glances down into his pint, at the tide marks of beer foam.

I reach for his glasses. I feel like I'm an actor on stage playing the role of someone with the chutzpah to take off a man's glasses just to try them on myself. When I do, the world blurs a little. But not too much.

'You sure you need these? They're not so strong.'

'They make things clearer, like seeing the world in HD.'

'And they add a hint of sophistication to you, right?'

He just smiles.

I breathe on them, clean them on the seam of my dress, right near the plunge of my cleavage. Then I place them back on his face, feel the warmth of his cheeks. The prickle of stubble. It's going surprisingly well.

'So is your name really Daniel?'

'Is your name really Anna?'

'No,' I admit.

'Well, believe it or not, I actually am Daniel.'

Daniel Moore, I know.

'I'm not Anna, I'm Annabel. You know what these apps are like though, everyone uses an alias. I guess that's why I like Happn, because at least you know someone is *where* they say they are, even if they're not really *who* they say they are.'

'So why did you swipe right?' he asks.

'Honestly? You're good looking, tall and athletic. And you didn't say anything too boneheaded to mess it up.' *And it's unlikely we would ever cross paths again.* We'd already exchanged messages and I knew he was just here for a month doing a labouring gig. He was keen to get back home to the country. We'd sent each other photos too, talked about certain proclivities. Do I feel a little bad about doing this to him? No. Men use women all the time. Daniel is probably using me too. It's all so easy in this day and age to get away with it.

I met Cain before dating apps were a thing, so when I downloaded the app and started swiping, I was shocked by some of the messages I received. Strangers online can be so forward; they move in quick and are entirely comfortable shifting the conversation to the explicit. There was a grey-haired man whose first message to me was a photo of his modestly sized penis. Daniel was the only one I chatted to who didn't send through explicit pictures, or ask if I did anal, or message me at 3 am on Saturday to ask if I was awake, as though I might be some genie who would conjure for pre-dawn sex.

'I didn't realise you were so young,' I say now. 'I feel like a cougar.'

'I'm not *so* young.'

'Twenty-five?'

'Older.'

'Twenty-six?'

'Twenty-nine,' he lies.

We chat, it's earnest and, in a way, disarming. He admits to being a bit of a 'closet gamer' and spends a lot of time online when he's not gaming. I think about the profile of the Tinder Strangler who suffocated his date at his apartment in Wellington – he spent a lot of time gaming, meeting other toxic men in online fitness forums where he discussed his conquests. I shake all negative thoughts from my head like a dog shaking water off. Daniel is different, I have control over the situation. I wonder how many other women have had these exact same thoughts until the night takes a turn for the worse? It helps that I plan to give this man what he wants.

When I first met Cain, I saw a certain charm in his seriousness and occasionally he would say something genuinely funny. He found in me a laugh I'd never even heard myself. Something deep, a sort of guffaw of which I was almost embarrassed. *Stop thinking about Cain,* I tell myself. For a few hours, I needed to forget about him, forget about my marriage and just do what I really wanted to.

'A twenty-nine-year-old bad boy, my mother would blush.'

'I'm not bad.'

'That's a shame.' I'm beginning to relax a little. It's easier for me now to play the part.

'Is that what you're into?' his voice is already wet with the booze. 'You normally go for arseholes?'

I tip the last of my soda water back, then lick my lips. 'Don't most women?' I hate myself for saying it, but it has the desired effect. A hungry smile spreads across his face, the shyness draining as fast as the alcohol.

'Well,' he says, pausing, summoning enough courage to deliver what is likely to be an appallingly awful line. 'I can be bad, I can be *very* bad if you want.'

It's happening so easily now. I feel like I can almost have some fun with this. 'Yeah?'

'If only you knew,' he says, with a wink and a smile that's morphed from self-conscious to suggestive.

'Well, why don't we cut this date short and head back to the house?'

'Is that a test, make sure I'm keen on you?'

'Maybe.'

'I want to get to know you a little better first, Anna.' He reaches for my hand now, rolling his thumb over my knuckles where my wedding band would be had I not strung it through my necklace before arriving. 'Slow down, no rush,' he says, his brow slightly creasing and his wet lips pulling up at the corners. It's so smooth, so natural that I think maybe he really is a nice guy.

'What do you want to know about me?'

•

I invent a backstory as his questions roll in and I fire back a few of my own. Here's what I learn about Daniel in the next sixty-four minutes and four pints: his mother was a nurse but now she's unwell; his father is a mechanic; he went to a small country primary school but a big all-boys high school where he used to get into fights; he wanted to be an engineer but later decided against it. His childhood best friend, Iso, lost a finger in a pig-hunting accident. He's never done drugs before, not even smoked weed. He had one girlfriend until his mid-twenties, and the break-up was messy. He's not sure if he's looking for anything serious but 'could change for the right girl'.

'And that's where I come in?'

'Maybe,' he says. He's adequately liquored and his advances are becoming more overt. 'It's hard to say after an hour of drinking but . . .' Again, that shyness. He continues, 'I think I like you.' I lean a little closer to him. Then his hand is on my thigh slipping higher and my forearm rests over his shoulder, my thumb sliding along the hard edge of his jaw. Despite being seated, he is swaying a little. His eyes half closed. I block out the guilt. Ignore it. I concentrate on my body instead. I'm ready, I *need* this.

'Okay, let's go,' he whispers into my ear, filling it with his hot boozy breath.

I place my free hand on his thigh, feeling the muscle beneath, then I bring it up near his belt buckle.

'Oh, you're ready now, are you?' I say, my mouth moving close to his. Then suddenly, almost violently, he is kissing me. My hand gropes at him and I can feel his blunt fingers force their way down the plunged back of my dress, searching for something to squeeze.

I pull away, breathless.

'Come on.'

'Ladies first,' he slurs, again with that drunken smile.

I feel much safer walking the streets now but wonder if I should.

'Down here.' We walk past the park and those houses, almost all of which are dark now. I act as a crutch, holding him up as he stumbles along until he turns abruptly into a house and leads us up to the front door. He fishes in his pocket for the keys, dropping them, then scooping them back up.

'Let me do it,' I say, opening my palm to take them from him. The anticipation is growing.

He holds them out by the map of New Zealand key ring and I snatch them.

I force the first key into the lock, turn and hear a click, then I use the second key. Inside, we fall back against the wall. His hands hungry, pulling my dress straight up over my head. I push back, directing him towards the bedroom. He unbuckles his belt almost in a frenzy and falls back onto the bed. I twist my arm up my spine to unclip my bra. I thought I wouldn't mind wearing it, but I simply can't do this with my wedding ring around my neck. I feel like it might combust, or sear itself into my skin, so I slip the necklace off and place it in my bag, which I throw on the bedside table. *Would he even care if he knew I was married?* But it's not just that. It's the betrayal, it's the reminder of the vows I took.

'Fuck,' he says. 'You're so hot.'

'What do you want to do to me?'

'Everything,' he says, breathless, sitting up and reaching for me, pulling me down onto him. I think for a moment about Cain, what this would mean if he knew. I think about Daniel, what this means to him. Nothing, a one-night stand with an older woman.

Not even a fling. A conquest who will scurry away with her heels in hand in the morning. I think about what this means for me. I can't keep going on like this. This dull life. I need to be selfish and do this for me. I block out the noise of guilt and doubt. Well, I try to, but the guilt is a growth at my core, spreading to my limbs, weighing them down. Then he takes my face in his hands, kisses me again. I let my body respond in kind.

At some stage, when I'm on top of him, he reaches for my throat and gently squeezes. Then harder. Suddenly, my hand flies across his face and he stops his bucking beneath me. I see a little blood on his lip. The shock registers in his eyes.

'Don't touch my neck,' I say. 'Don't leave a single mark.'

'Okay,' he breathes.

Afterwards, I find my way to the bathroom. I look around when I'm on the loo, see his toothbrush by the mirror, the modern shower and furnishings. It's a nice place he's staying in, clean, sterile. When I get back out, he is asleep on the bed. My phone is on the bedside table near my bag and my alarm set for 5 am. I can't go home any earlier because I'm supposed to be working a shift. I pull my bra on and climb in beside him, avoiding touching his skin. I lie there, eyes wide, thinking sleep will never come.

Peephole
Live Cam Premium
Stream: 029A
Viewers: 052

GeneralMayhem: Oh yes! We have action on Cam 1. Clearly their
                        first time together.

Le_Coq: Il l'a baisée!

TheSpecialist: Holy shit did she just slap him? This slut is wild.

GeneralMayhem: That was quick. Hope they go again.

RonnieJ: Where is she?

Monsterdong3000:   She's on the toilet. Cam 3.

Predator: What's he doing with her phone?

TheSpecialist: Now she's back, hopefully we get an encore
                        performance.

PlatoOf21C: She looks so familiar. I swear I know this slut.

THREE

'YOU'RE ALREADY AWAKE,' I say, pausing at the top of the stairs as Cain turns towards me from the kitchen bench. I didn't think he'd be out of bed yet. My body feels filthy, as though the guilt of last night is a film of grime covering me head to toe but invisible to anyone but me. I'd almost slept through my alarm, leaving in a mad rush this morning with Daniel grabbing at me again for a second round. I pushed him off in my haste to get home.

Stepping out the door right as the sun was pinkening the cloudless sky, I'd found my car, changed into my ambulance uniform and stashed the bag with my dress, heels, make-up and perfume in the spare tyre well of the boot before driving home.

'Yep, I'm up,' Cain says now, putting the iPad he's been looking at down on the kitchen bench. 'How did you go last night?'

'Oh, not great,' I say, hoping the ambiguity is enough to end the work chat. I never ask him about what happened in Afghanistan, despite how much it still affects him, and he doesn't ask about any traumas I might have encountered at work. He sniffs at the air. It occurs to me that I've not washed off the perfume. He doesn't say anything, so I walk past him into the kitchen and fill a glass of water, take my vitamins and iron supplement. He starts the coffee machine. It filters through into an espresso cup. It's 6.30 am. He's always been an early riser, only now he seems to stay up later too. I can see from the dull pink stain in his eyes and the haggard look of his skin that he's hungover. He holds the coffee beneath his nose, then turns back to me and takes it all in one mouthful.

'It's early,' I say. 'Even for you.'

He gives a tired smile. 'What do they say about the early bird?'

'It's grumpy, hungover and fatigued?'

'Sounds about right. Not that you can talk. Out there saving lives all night, you should be straight to bed. I don't know how you do it.'

'A coke habit,' I joke. 'That's where all our money goes.'

'Ha,' he says. 'Seriously, you don't look so bad. You eaten?'

'I can't eat I'm too . . .' I trail off, a yawn overtaking me, 'zonked for food. I just need a shower, brush my teeth and get under the covers.' I think about Cain's training in the SAS. Resisting interrogation is drilled into them so if they're ever taken prisoner they are more likely to withstand torture. Sleep deprivation is just part of it. Are they also skilled at interrogating others? Detecting lies from the subtle cues most people can't disguise?

I start towards the bathroom, pulling my moss green ambulance officer's shirt over my head and tossing it straight into the washing machine, despite the fact it's only been worn for about half an hour.

'Lina?'

'Yeah,' I say, turning back, seeing his frown. My heart pounds as he holds up his left hand.

'Where's your ring?'

Shit. I force a smile. 'Oh, it's still on my necklace from work.'

'Where's your necklace?'

'Good question, must have left it in my locker at the station. I'll get it on my next shift.'

'Right, okay,' he says, smiling. 'I'd hate for someone to think you weren't married.'

I eye him, keep my smile up. 'Oh, I don't think there's much risk of that, Cain.' Then I turn and step into the bathroom. *Shit.* The ring. Where did I put my necklace? It must be in the car or in my bag. I step into the scalding hot water. Thoughts are the master and feelings are the slaves. Now the thoughts come thick and fast followed by a rising anxiety. *I was wearing it last night. I know I had my necklace on at the bar. I took it off at the house but did I have it this morning?*

In the shower, I hold myself up off the wall, letting the water wash over me. When my skin is adequately scalded, I start to scrub at myself, lathering up under my arms, down my body, between my legs. I scrub it all away, the night that was, the man and his odour. The scene runs through my mind, his hands on me, his thumbs finding the base of my throat. It'll be the one and only time. I can't do it to Cain again. *But what if I get desperate again?* No. This emptiness, this regret, it's not worth it.

After my shower, I regard myself in the mirror, scanning my body for any signs of Daniel. I glance down at my inner thighs for evidence of his hands. I turn my head and look closer at my neck, my ears where he had gently taken the lobe between his teeth. I stand there for a moment taking myself in, the sickness of guilt feels a lot like grief. A gut punch that almost brings tears. *Was it really worth it? Do I actually feel better now?*

There's one loose end I need to tie off before I go to sleep. I go to the garage. I find my bag in the spare tyre well. I drag my hand through it, pulling the clothes out. The necklace is not there. I search the car top to bottom, under the seats, in the glove box.

'What's going on?' Cain says. I jerk, hit my head on the underside of the steering wheel.

'Shit,' I say. 'No, just my ring. I might have dropped it while I was driving.'

'It'll turn up,' he says. 'I can look for you? Go grab some sleep.'

'Don't worry,' I say, 'I've searched the entire car, it must be in my locker.'

When he's left the garage, I pick up my workbag with my clothes from last night and take it with me to the bedroom, shove it in the bottom of my wardrobe, and then climb into bed, sleep mask on, rain sounds coming through my headphones. I close my eyes, become still and pray that Cain never finds out what I did. For hours, I lie there, running it all over and over in my mind until eventually I fall asleep.

•

When I wake, what seems moments later, the clock on my phone insists it's the afternoon. I get up and find Cain in his study. It's a small room. On one wall is an image of him in full sand-coloured military gear, with his wraparound sunglasses and a rifle slung from his shoulder. Beside the photo is a similar image of five men, all in the same fatigues, with their rifles and their big grins beneath those sports-style sunglasses. One is Axel, another I know is the infamous Trent Skelton. A set of drawers sits beneath the window that looks out on the backyard. 'Sultans of Swing' plays through the tiny computer speakers. He doesn't look up until I'm halfway across the room. On his screen is the WeStay website.

'What are you up to?' I ask.

He reaches forward, minimises the screen, lowers his music. 'I'll tell you, but I don't want you to get annoyed.'

'What have you done?'

'I've made a profile for the house,' he says, without further hesitation. 'No one can see it, but I just wanted to play around with it, so it's ready if you changed your mind about doing it.'

41

'Sorry?'

'The lake house.'

'Wait,' I say, my head still a little foggy from the sleep. 'You've put it online?'

'I've just set up the profile. It's not live.'

I catch my face in my hands, draw a long breath. I have no right to be angry at him, not after last night.

'You put it up before I'd agreed? My place?'

'*Your* place? What happened to *our* place?'

It's ours, yes, but technically I own it. He doesn't have memories of rushing up and down the ladder that Grandpa built between rooms or sitting for hours out in the dinghy, hopelessly sinking fishing lines into the murky depths, or helping Grandma turn buckets of feijoas into jam. All those good memories but among them, loudest of all, is a bad one. Mum turning up, eyes bloodshot, haggard. The screaming. Grandma sweeping up the broken glass.

'Cain, I'm not entirely comfortable with strangers going there,' I say, with an even tone.

'I know but can you consider it? We need the money, Lina, and we have outgoings for that house. We've got rates, insurance, utilities. We're treading water as it is.'

'Do we need money that bad?' I press him, remembering the conversation I'd had with Claire the night before. I know the answer. Things are dire. We're behind on rent, we may have no choice but to move to the lake house soon, find new jobs down in Rotorua.

'I see it as a project, something to do while my business is getting off the ground.' He spins around on the chair now, faces me. 'I'll manage it all, you won't even know it's happening.'

'How will you manage it? Tarawera is three hours away.'

He smothers a yawn with the back of his hand. 'I'll make sure we only let people stay who have good ratings and reviews. I'll organise a cleaner, lock our stuff away.'

'Some things are more important than a quick buck.'

'It's not just about the money,' he says. 'I want to do something that makes me feel useful. I'm in a rut.'

'I know, Cain,' I say. It's not just the money; the nightmares are back. He's drinking a lot again. It's the secrets, it's Afghanistan. It's the void of combat that almost nothing, no amount of love or care, can fill. Family is the only thing that can help, I think. A caring, interdependent network.

'When summer comes around, I'll be fully booked with work, but until then . . .'

Just a touch optimistic. Last summer, he raced to get the business started in time for all the 'resolutionists' who sign up for boot camps after Christmas. 'Then,' he had told me, 'it's just a matter of locking them into contracts.' If only it had been that simple. His point of sale system malfunctioned, the website had the wrong phone number and for myriad other invisible reasons it never took off like he anticipated. I'd even helped him with his emails and booking in clients.

In the months after he returned from Afghanistan, Cain had occasional speaking gigs for office workers, politicians, sports teams and schools. He had been in the newspapers, on the morning shows. Still walking with a crutch, bruised and bandaged, but alive. A survivor. This was before the war had soured like old milk in the public's mouth. Before the inquest. Cain and Axel had been there when Skelton slaughtered that family. I'd never got the full story from Cain – he closed up whenever I tried to talk about it – but the media stories made it clear what had happened.

Axel had said with Cain's profile and experience he would have clients on a waiting list. He'd said Cain could take large classes. Given the fact he'd basically talked Cain into starting the business, it's no wonder he props Commando Fitness up financially now.

'Remember our promise, Cain. No new secrets?'

'Yeah,' he says. 'Why do you mention that now?'

I pause, swallow. 'I think you've kept a couple of things from me. I've never asked about your nightmares, about your time in the unit, but I know you're not yourself lately. I need you to tell me if your business is struggling.'

'What do you mean?'

'I mean you've stopped paying Axel rent. I mean you never seem to be training anyone and Claire told me Axel wants to give you money to help us out.'

A flash of anger sweeps across his face. 'Axel insisted I use his space rent free until I'm turning a profit. If he had an issue, he would mention it.'

Maybe, I realise now, it's Claire who has the issue. Maybe Claire thinks Cain is taking Axel for a ride. 'Sounds like he's doing us a favour.'

'It costs him nothing.'

'Except it's costing him customers. Why did you snap at someone there? That's not you, Cain.'

He clicks his tongue, his cheeks have a hint of colour. He's keeping secrets from me. 'Claire shouldn't have said anything. I feel like a leech. Of course I'm going to pay Axel, when things pick up. That's all it is.' He heaves out a sigh.

'And the nightmares?'

'It's fine.'

'It's not, you're not yourself.'

He swallows. 'It happens sometimes. I remember things from over there. Same old crap.'

I can't say why, but I'm not sure if I believe him entirely. I need him to talk about it, to squeeze out the poison so he can move on, so he can get his business on track and start to feel good about himself again.

'I'm always here to talk about it with you.'

He shakes his head.

I step closer now, rest a hand on his shoulder. Even seated in his office chair, he's almost as tall as me. 'Alright. Show me the listing.' Maybe it will be good for him, good for us. Maybe by giving him this, it will take some of the guilt from last night away. 'I'm not saying yes yet, I just want to see it.'

'If we try it just once or twice and you're uncomfortable, we can take it down. No questions asked.'

'Sure.'

He swivels back to look at the screen and brings up the browser. There are photos, a long description of the house with a set of rules, a check-in time, amenities.

'Sleeps seven?' I say.

'Two queens, the bunks and the couch.'

'The couch?' I ask. 'No one wants to sleep on that old thing. Change it to six. The bunkroom gets a cool draught from the ladder too.' Grandpa had built the ladder so I could rush up and down between my room and the rumpus room but it always let the cool air in over winter.

His head tilts. 'Okay.'

'You did all this yourself today?'

'I managed to figure it out. Used old photos,' he says. 'I'm thinking two-fifty a night, plus cleaning. It's cheaper than most of the other places in the area.'

I recall one of the last times we were down there. Cain had taken me to a spot near the lake house where teenagers jump from a tree hanging over the water. Despite all those years with Grandpa and Grandma on the lake, I'd never known of it. The tree looked half rotted, treacherous. Cain leapt first into the blue–green depths of Lake Tarawera, then I'd climbed up the ladder, out onto the branch. Every time I looked down, my legs began to tremble, my gut became an icy soup. It was ten metres but it felt like hundreds.

I knew the easy thing was to jump, to let myself spear through the humid air into the water. It would be easier than climbing back down but instead I just squeezed that branch beneath me, my body tense. This feels a little like that now. I know it's safe, I know it would only take a small commitment from me – acquiescence, a loosening of my grip. Cain would handle it all, but like that moment before my fingers came away from the soft bark and I plummeted, I draw a breath.

'Alright.' I exhale. 'Let's do it. Push it live.'

He tilts his head back, looks up at me. 'You sure?'

'Go, before I change my mind.'

I watch as he activates the listing, opens up all the dates on the calendar to 'Available' and clicks 'Save'.

'Done,' he says, taking his hands from the mouse and keyboard, gripping my own where they sit on his shoulders.

'You did good with the listing, Cain. Might have found your calling.'

Casa Tarawera: Mid-century retreat on Lake Tarawera.

Two hundred and fifty dollars a night and one hundred for cleaning.

'Anyone can book it as early as next weekend.'

'And what will we do if someone does?'

'I will race down, get it all set up. We need a new lock, new sheet sets, a few other bits and pieces.' He pauses, lets out a yawn. 'Bit of paint, tidy the lawns up. Also, the old stereo could do with an update.'

This all sounds like more money wasted.

As if reading my mind, he adds, 'We've got room on the credit card, and it will pay for itself after one booking.'

'Okay,' I say. 'You win.' My hand slides down his chest, and I place my lips on his neck, kissing softly. It has the desired effect. He turns, pulls me down, his hand working the buttons of my top.

I slide onto him. It's quick. Methodical, even. I do exactly what I know works for him. After last night with Daniel, I could almost cry but I want this. I want my husband.

'You're not into it,' he breathes.

'No,' I say. 'I am.' I turn back to him, half-close my eyes and exhale, with the hint of a groan. 'Keep going,' I whisper. He's right, I'm not into it. I'm somewhere else entirely but it has to be this way.

I'm thinking about the lake house, about WeStay. I can't take back my permission now and it does assuage a little of the guilt to do something that clearly means a lot to him. There's so much history in that house, but its old closets have skeletons too. No one is perfect, least of all me. I'd said no new secrets, but sometimes we need to do things to keep each other safe, to keep the relationship well-greased. The tension in his body loosens beneath me, his hands slide down my back and he seems to fold against my body. He kisses the back of my neck.

Some things we simply can't share, address or talk about. They just happen and we move on. Silent but knowing. That's the key, I think now, to a long and happy marriage.

FOUR

THE TRAILER WE hired rattles behind the car as Cain takes a bend. He's the better driver. If better equals safer, not faster. Ambulance officers are all fast drivers; the best are *very* fast. Cain seems to enjoy it on the open road out here. Never aggressive or racing to pass the handful of campervans we see on the trip down. He's like me, made for small towns, a rural transplant in the city. He's generous with a courtesy beep and a small wave when cars give way to him.

As I watch the world passing by outside, I think about the last seven days. Slowly but surely, I've managed to enclose the memory of that night with Daniel in mental scar tissue, partitioned off from the rest of me like the shrapnel in Cain's body. Now and then, the pain of the guilt returns, but it's never as sharp as the last time and eventually it will blunt to a dull ache I can live with. There is just one bridge left to cross. My ring and my necklace. What if that man, Daniel, has them? The ring belonged to Cain's mother – it's one of a kind. I check the rattling trailer in the rear-view mirror, then scan the scene through the window.

'Every view is a postcard,' my grandpa used to say of this country. Beneath an unblemished sky, it's all rich New Zealand green fields and name-on-a-map towns. Each with a corner pub, a bakery and a cafe. Some towns have gimmicks – sheets of corrugated iron bent and bolted to form gumboots or farm animals, a fence of jandals, or murals painted on every wall. This nation has always been obsessed with *character* and without something to distinguish it, a town out here might simply cease to exist. *Every view is a postcard*, and Grandpa chose one of the best views to set up his life. The picture-perfect isolation of Lake Tarawera.

After a couple of hours driving, we begin to see the steam of Rotorua. It crawls out of drains and sweeps across the roads. It rises up out of the muddy pits of Kuirau park. Rotorua's appeal can't be simply replicated with a few sheets of iron or by tethering jandals, bras, hats or beer bottles to an otherwise naked fence. It's geothermal. It's *volcanic*. The tourists say the smell is rotten eggs, but to me it's richer than that, earthy with an ammoniac sting. Cain steers us the long way around Lake Rotorua out near where he grew up as a kid. The sun is high, and the lake is flat, jewelled with sunlight. I spy that knuckle of land, Mokoia Island, at the centre of the lake as Cain slows down to pass over a narrow bridge where a river feeds the lake. Boys are lined up in the sun, looking down at the water, their brown skin glistening.

Cain indicates, pulls over into the gravel at the road's edge.

'What's up?'

'Quick dip,' he says, reaching for his towel on the back seat.

He peels his t-shirt off, places his hei matau, an intricate fishhook of Pounamu greenstone he wears around his neck, on the dashboard and climbs out of the car. He starts back towards the bridge, leaving his towel on the boot. I move my thumb to roll my wedding ring around my finger and remember it's missing.

I watch the boys. One turns, nudges the others then they're all watching Cain, grins lighting up their faces, eyebrows rising. The constellation of scars, the coils of traditional tattoos spilling down over his shoulder to his forearm, his Tā moko, it's all on display.

I quickly download the dating app again and sign in with my fake credentials.

Looking up, I see Cain climbing the rail of the bridge with the ease of a professional wrestler preparing for an aerial manoeuvre. He leaps as best he can with his knee, takes flight for a moment, suspended at the peak of his arc then he's falling. The splash reaches up over the rail and the boys collectively hunch away from the spray.

Right then my phone chimes. It's a message on the app. A bubble rises up from my chest and settles in my throat.

I've got something for you.

I knew it. Dread washes over me as my eyes dart back up to the bridge, searching for Cain. The message is oddly cold. He has my ring and my necklace. I must have left them at the house.

Cain emerges at the river's edge, starts back towards the car. Walking just a hint taller now. The kids adequately impressed.

I delete my photo from the profile, but I can't close the account yet – I will need to contact him to get my ring back. Cain approaches. I delete the app and lock the phone, shoving it in the glove box. It was supposed to be one night. Traceless and perfect. I could always take down the profile and sever the tie. As soon as the thought comes, I realise how heedless it is. It was Cain's mother's ring; I can't just lose it. But the idea of having to see Daniel again twists my stomach.

Cain towels off and climbs back in.

'They're happy,' I say, nodding towards the boys.

He turns to me with that crooked smile. 'Just needed to cool down.' He screws a corner of the towel into his ear. One eye is closed, the other is watching me. 'Are you alright?' he says. 'You look pale.'

'I'm fine,' I say. 'Just exhausted.' I try to smile, but my cheeks ache.

He drives again, now with his shirt off, the towel around his waist. Soon enough, we're rolling past the other smaller lakes until we reach Lake Tarawera. I look out at the cliff over the water where all of the trees have grown back over the years, a steel rail has been installed.

I know we are close as we pass the blue letterbox at the end of the road on the eastern side. When I used to run these roads, I always knew I was about five hundred metres from home here and, if I had the energy, I'd pick up the pace. We come to the opening of our driveway, pulling in between the trees down the familiar gravel track to the house. It's always the same when we arrive these days. Silence, climbing from the car gingerly as if stepping into a graveyard. We were here the day we lost the baby. The blood. The pain. *Knowing*. All that trying, all that money, then emptiness. The trees all around, as green as a rainforest and as wet and thick. That's the thing with this country – even the best photos of the view miss the smell, the air. Even here, only twenty kilometres out of Rotorua in the middle of native bush, far from the beaches, glaciers and southern mountain ranges, the air has such a distinct feel in your mouth, clean and wet. Like a palate cleanser.

Opening the door, the dusty house breathes. Memories flood me. My grandma making banana pancakes, getting to the end of a summer-long 5000-piece jigsaw puzzle to find it was actually only 4999 pieces. Grandpa's laughter as we searched for that final piece and never found it. There's a magic room hidden from view where all the lost socks, remotes, jigsaw pieces are tucked away. Somewhere in the house no one can find. For everything else you can check the basement, the shoebox of old keys, remotes and batteries under the workbench.

'How long has it been?' Cain says. 'A couple of months?'

'No,' I say. 'Longer than that.' I step inside and everything is preserved just how it was. No break-ins, no fruit left out rotting on the kitchen bench or trees fallen through the new tiled roof. I run my eyes up the dividing wall between the kitchen and the lounge, counting back the years marked by all those colourful notches.

Cain returns to the car and backs the trailer up close to the house. I watch him from the kitchen window for a while as he crosses the yard carrying fallen tree limbs in his gloved hands to load up the trailer. He pulls a mossy car tyre attached to two feet of decomposing rope from shin-length grass. He looks up, sees the other end of the rope tied around a limb of the tree at the lake's edge. He holds it up. 'Do we still need this?'

I smile, then he heaves it into the trailer.

I step outside now. 'Want help?' I call.

'No,' he says. 'I'm basically done out here, just need to mow the lawn, but I might wait for the grass to dry fully.'

The property is its own world. All you can see is the lake, the mountains across the other side and untamed native bush. So isolated, so private. Invisible to the rest of the world.

Cain carries a box up the steps to the front door, with its faded red paint. He crouches down and removes the old lock and then sands the whole door down, wiping the wood smooth with a cloth after each stroke. He then retrieves a small tin of paint from the box and pops its lid open to reveal a dark liquid. I just lean against the balustrade and watch as he rolls the black gloss up the door. I'd resisted this but against the stained timber of the house, the result is striking. He has a good eye, I'll give him that much.

'Is there a blow dryer here?'

'In the bathroom.'

He disappears to grab it, then dries the area around the lock before he installs the new one he'd picked up at the hardware store. We've changed the locks before. After the police had kicked the squatter out, we'd driven down and found food still in the fridge and one of the beds looked slept in. Cain took to calling the squatter Goldilocks. He changed the front door lock and installed deadbolts on the other doors. Now, just two years later, he's installing another.

The lock is a smart lock. We can change the passcode from anywhere in the world provided we have an internet connection. He's also bought white paint from the hardware store to touch up the walls, and stain for the back deck that he'd built the summer he returned from Afghanistan, when we decided it was time to start a family and move down.

He's testing the new lock out now; it's shiny black like a giant beetle halfway up the door.

He doesn't bother fixing the back door, a jammy old thing that scrapes when you close it. We need only one lock to get in, then guests can open the other doors from the inside, and with a digital lock we never need to worry about lost keys.

I fill a teacup with hot water and watch him as the tea steeps. His shirt off again in the warmth of the early spring sun. He's sweeping away woodchips from around the door.

'It looks great,' I say, outside. I step back and gaze out over the lake, take a mouthful of tea. 'I was thinking about getting some wine to leave for guests, what do you think?'

'As a gift?'

'Yeah, a welcome package. Wine, a nice bar of soap and maybe a candle.'

His dark eyebrows rise. 'Sounds like a waste of money.'

Unlike your fancy new lock.

'I read online that it'll help us to get good ratings and more bookings. So we could eventually charge more.'

A short nod, a thoughtful *hmm*. 'Okay. Good idea.'

I tip the last of my tea back and set my cup down on the porch. 'What can I help with?'

He turns his head up to me, a crooked smile among his stubble. 'You relax, I can do it all. That's a condition of us renting it out. Go find a sunny spot to read your book.'

'Thanks,' I say. 'I might head for a run instead.'

He rubs his thumb along the top edge of the lock, blows away the dust. 'Good idea.'

I grab my running shoes, start my audiobook on my phone and open my running app, MyTrack. I check out the recent activities, the runs and bike rides of the people I follow. I give an old school friend's half-marathon effort kudos. They've managed to gamify exercise; another app to get addicted to. The map loads; there's a blue dot isolated in the square house by the lake. It moves when I move.

'Alright,' I say, back out on the deck now. 'I'm off.'

Right then, a message comes through from a random number. It's simply an emoji of a pair of lips.

I stop abruptly, staring down at the phone. Could it be Daniel? No, impossible. Then who?

'What is it?' Cain says.

I clear my throat. 'Nothing. Just a . . . meme on Facebook. A dog up for adoption.'

'Right,' he says. 'You don't mind if I sand back and paint the door frames, trimming and that sort of thing. Those old marks by the kitchen.'

'Sure,' I say, barely registering his words.

I send a message back.

Who is this?

•

I steady my breath before starting out on my run. My running shoes strike the gravel as I begin on a familiar trail through the bush to the lake's edge. I try to block out the message. Daniel couldn't have my number, but what if he does?

Long before I get home, I can hear the shriek of the power sander. By the time I get to the base of the steps, my dusty calves are aching and my chest burns. Cain is sanding with the doors and windows ajar, that's why it's so loud. I get halfway up the steps to the door when I see him through the glass panels. I see what he is sanding, and a new energy fills my tired limbs. I burst through the door but it's done, he's finished, the wall between the kitchen and the lounge is bare wood now. He's sanded it right back, erased those colourful marks.

He's moved on, pressing the sander to the door frame at the entrance of the hallway.

'Cain,' I yell over the racket. 'Cain!'

He kills the sander, turns back and lifts the clear glasses from his head. He's covered the furniture in drop sheets and I know he will clean up after but my eyes are fixed on him.

'What's wrong?' he says, his voice muffled by the dust mask.

Stupid, pointless tears. They're pressing at the backs of my eyes, squeezing out at the corners. A stone in my throat.

'What, Lina?'

I rub at my left eye. 'What are you doing?' I say. 'The marks?'

He puts the sander down and is coming towards me but I raise my forearms as if guarding myself from a blow.

He breathes deeply through his nose, lips compressed. 'I asked you before your run,' he says. 'You said I could sand them.'

I shake my head to clear it. He's right but I was distracted by the messages. 'It's fine.' A tremble in my voice betrays me.

'No, you're upset.'

'No.' I swallow, meet his eyes. The marks are gone forever, another relic destroyed. I'm struck by a memory. Standing with my back against the wall, Grandpa resting a ruler on the crown of my head.

'Why are they all different colours?'

'Because I just use whatever marker we have handy.'

'What are the numbers?'

'They're dates. That way we will know how old you are each time so we can see how much you've grown.'

'Oh.'

'See, you used to be this tall when you were four, then you were this tall at four and a half, then this tall when you turned five.'

'Then I grew a lot. Look how big the gap is.'

'Well, we didn't see you for a couple of years here. Then again up here.'

'Why?'

'Because you were with your mum then.'

Cain's voice breaks my memory. 'Lina, I asked you.'

'I know,' I say. But still the sadness grips me. It's not just the marks. It's also those messages. I fear the worst. My emotions are short-circuiting. 'It's nothing, don't worry.' Cain didn't know the significance.

'That's why I asked if I could sand,' he says, frustrated.

•

The road out towards town undulates through the lakes area. Cain is silent as we pass by the Green Lake, Lake Rotokakahi. It's tapu, forbidden to swim in and remains mostly undisturbed, flat and much smaller than Tarawera. Once, Cain had pulled over when tourists were paddling in the emerald waters. He'd whistled and waved for them to come in. I had listened from the car as he calmly explained this was the only lake in the area where swimming was forbidden. Without complaint, the tourists took their towels and their van and moved on. Perhaps if it had come from a less imposing figure, they might not have listened but that's the effect of the tattoos, the scars.

Next we come around beside the Blue Lake, Lake Tikitapu. Small and round as a coin. Picnickers fill the crescent of sand at its side. I glance at Cain, see the lines of tension in his brow, his focus on the road.

We stop at the lake store with its unreliable opening hours and equally unreliable manager, Henry, who sells fishing flies and tackle beside pick 'n' mix candy. He has a teddy-bear face and an accent a long way from home; my guess is Bulgaria, Cain's is Denmark. Hard to say now; two decades in New Zealand will begin to flatten even the hardest of vowels.

When the bell over the door chimes, he looks up from the freezer.

'Look who is in town,' he says, closing the glass lid and handing an ice-cream over the counter to a waiting child. A squawk of delight.

'Lina. Haven't seen you guys in a while?' he says, rolling the sleeves of his plaid shirt back down. 'And . . .' he pauses, searching his memory. My phone vibrates. A sharp prick at the back of my neck.

'Cain,' Cain says beside me. 'My name's Cain.'

I glance down at the message on my phone.

Why don't you guess?

I feel sick. It can't be Daniel, how would he have my number? 'That's right, Cain. Welcome, welcome. Down for the weekend?'

'Yeah,' I say. 'We're just setting our place up for WeStay actually.'

Henry jabs at something stuck between his molars with his thumb before speaking again. 'Mm, a few people doing that with their places these days.'

There's a snort of derision from someone at one of the tables in the half of the store that functions as a cafe. I turn back, see an old man sitting alone. Fishing hat on, paper opened in front of him. His shirt hasn't seen the inside of a washing machine in some time. When I meet his eyes, he doesn't look away. His lips are curled down in a snarl beneath his long, hooked nose. I glance away to a couple at another table, who are looking down at a map on their table. She's white blonde and he has that backpacker fuzz over his cheeks and jaw. Do they leave their warm European countries with scraggy beards or grow them when they arrive here?

'We might grab a bite,' Cain says. I turn back.

'Yeah, go for it. Take a seat.' Henry flicks a hand towards the tables. 'I'll bring over menus.'

The eyes of the old man in the bucket hat keep falling on us. Cain has his back to him but if he could see the looks being sent our way he would say something, I'm sure. I turn my attention back to my phone, rereading the messages before deleting them.

A little while later, Henry places our food before us. 'Bon appetit,' he says, giving a tiny bow.

I can barely eat. Cain finishes my salad. The old man gets up from his table. As he is paying at the counter, I overhear him speaking to Henry, his voice deliberately raised. 'More pricks from the city buying up houses and renting them out, eh?'

'Easy, Russ. No one's breaking any laws.'

We didn't buy the house.

'Did you say something?' Cain calls, turning back. A moment of eye contact. The old man raises his hands as if to say, *nothing to see here*, then folds the paper under his arm and leaves. 'Rude bastard,' Cain says, his eyes fixed on the man's back as he departs. The tourists are watching on, quietly passing comments between each other in another language. Henry collects our plates and we head into the groceries section. My mind is still reeling from the messages, my heart thumping from the confrontation. Cain asks me which red to buy.

'Pinot,' I say. 'A nice red to have by the fire.'

''Bout fifty percent higher prices here than in town,' Cain says out the side of his mouth. I can't smile or react. I just grab a few bottles while Cain picks out some handmade soap and scented candles.

'Why are you so uninterested?' he says abruptly. 'This was your idea.'

'Sorry,' I say, puffing out my cheeks. 'A little under the weather today.'

'Yeah,' he says. 'Seems it.'

When we climb into the car, Cain places the paper bag of wine and soap on the back seat. I reach for my phone again, no new messages. But there is something else chewing through me like a parasite. I think about it now as Cain reaches over and squeezes my hand, those brown eyes fall on mine before he starts the car. I'd been careful, I used a fake name, gave all fake details and only ever contacted him through the app. I never gave him anything that could connect him to me. So if it is Daniel, how does he have my number? And what else does he know?

DEADLY SAS RAID IN AFGHANISTAN UNDER SCRUTINY

Pressure is mounting on the New Zealand government to call an inquiry into a botched special forces raid in Afghanistan that left a family of three civilians dead, including a six-year-old child. The raid was planned by NZSAS and carried out with US helicopter support.

A report published this week alleges the NZSAS staged the raid to retaliate for the death of a New Zealand soldier earlier that week. No insurgents were killed in the raid. The NZ military maintains the killings were justified and in self-defence.

Elders from the village, along with insiders within the military community, have expressed dismay at the needless killings. Many have suggested it heightened tensions and undermined trust for foreign agents operating in the war-torn country.

Amnesty International has also called for a probe and five New Zealand human rights lawyers announced this Friday that they were representing affected Afghan villagers. They supported the idea of an independent investigation and have publicly called for anyone within the special forces community to speak up about what they may have witnessed.

Another prominent lawyer called the killings 'a textbook war crime with no ambiguity whatsoever'.

FIVE

THE DIFFERENCE BETWEEN a house and a home can be something as insignificant as the smell. New, sterile places don't have their own smell. The lake house does. It's something I barely noticed growing up; it was a scent that belonged to me. Old pine, musty carpets. A scent I'll always associate with the happy moments of my childhood. But now the paint fumes have chased the smell away. I know it will come back, but what if it's like those marks showing my increasing height, gone forever?

The large house echoes as Cain closes a cupboard in the kitchen downstairs. It's still light out, and he continues working to get the place ready. It's becoming a house, not a home. All traces of life sanded down, polished away. He'd already cut down the snapped rope from my old tyre swing, the rotting tyre was already in the trash. He'd found new rope in the basement, hitched it to the branch and used an old piece of timber from the basement to fashion a seat. 'It's not a tyre, but it'll do,' he'd said.

My mind is still reeling from the messages. Keeping busy, distracting myself by cleaning doesn't seem to help; new linen sheets go on the beds, pillows stacked against the headboards in each room. I tie the curtains back so far that sheets of light pass through the windows and drape the bed in the master bedroom. I flatten the duvet with my palms, snap a loose thread with my fingernails. While I reach up to sweep the spider webs in the corners, I can hear Cain drilling into wood, attaching a lock to the basement door. Grandpa's old dinghy sits dusty and unused out in the padlocked shed. That's where it will stay – it needs a bit of work to get it running again so we won't be letting the guests use it and it saves us searching for the key to the shed.

The guests. Those invisible, idealised travellers.

After tidying, I sit downstairs at the kitchen bench, my phone nearby, never out of reach now. I'm thinking about the text message, I'm thinking about Daniel and what I did. I'm thinking about my ring. There's a tension in my chest. Guilt? Yes. Fear? Possibly. It feels like I'm bracing for a blow. The moment that will destroy my marriage.

The growl of the lawnmower fills the yard and enters the house as a low hum. Cain bought a new spark plug down for it.

My phone vibrates on the kitchen bench, it might as well be a fire alarm given the way my heart leaps. I rush to it. Another message from that number.

Sorry to text like this out of the blue, I was trying to flirt but it's not working. I'm away this weekend, down in Rotorua actually. But I will be in Auckland next week. I've got something for you.

Rotorua. A short drive from here. Is that a coincidence? There is something mildly threatening about it. I'm so focused on the words on my screen I fail to notice the absence of sound coming from the backyard. Not until the door opens and Cain steps inside. I jam my phone in the pocket of my jeans. He goes to the sink for a glass of water, gulps it down before turning back to me.

'What?' he says, with a funny smile.

'Nothing.'

'You're staring at me with that odd look again.'

I shake my head. 'I was daydreaming.' I glance through the doors, across the mowed grass and over the flat lake. Mirror-still, blue sky reflected; the distant mountains and the valley running between, it almost opens up enough for the sky to touch the water and form an hourglass.

'Yeah,' he says. 'I can see that. You're not yourself today, Quin.' I used to love it when he used my maiden name, like I was in the military too. It's lost its charm these days.

What would he do if he saw the message? What would he do if he knew where I was last Thursday night? It was selfish, of course it was, despite how much I tell myself otherwise. I think about Trent Skelton, who served with Cain. I recall the media images of the siege when he'd barricaded himself in his house with his family. How he turned his rifle on himself before the police could reach him. War does strange things to people. Cain has changed in the time I've known him. Death, seeing death and killing would change anyone. He once told me about the Australians he served with, how those without a kill were forced to execute captive insurgents to 'blood' them. My instincts tell me Cain has killed before. He saw enough combat and came back a different man to the one I met at the student bar in Auckland city all those years ago.

He didn't fit in there with his military clipped hair and his tight, unsmiling mouth. He was also older, much older. In his late twenties. A man. I was ready for someone different after those clumsy, privately educated boys in medicine. Grandpa had recently died, it was around the time I dropped out of medicine and started studying for the ambulance service instead. My ID was stuffed down my bra and at some stage during the night it slipped out, through my dress to the floor. Cain had spotted it. He'd walked the bar until he found a face that matched the one on the card. The cover band had just started a version of 'When You Were Young' by The Killers, the snare sizzling, the rasp of a distorted guitar. Punters flooded to the dance floor. 'I found you,' he said, holding up my ID.

I patted my chest as if the ID might impossibly still be there. The lines about waiting for a beautiful boy and being saved from your old ways were playing.

'Apt, this song,' I yelled, taking the ID from his hand.

'What?'

I leant close to his ear, could smell him, not his cologne, but him. This alone set him aside from the crowds of boys soaked in body spray and perfume. 'I'm going to buy you a drink to say thanks.'

Then the singer sang about closing your eyes and seeing the place where you used to live and I felt suddenly effervescent. I can see now why they call it falling in love. It was as though I'd stumbled and found myself wanting to spend every waking moment with this man. That's how sudden it was. Maybe I was already in love that night. If that's possible. Just the idea of him. A soldier in the army. Training for the SAS. Elite, fit, someone who could protect me. So utterly different to my mother's men. He grew up outside of the city, down near where I'd spent so much of my childhood.

We stayed together through his first deployment, committing to long distance – late nights and early mornings with a pixelated version of my boyfriend in a dusty war-torn country on the other side of the world. Then Cain proposed. It was on a call. He stepped back from his laptop, and dropped to one knee. There was no engagement ring, we were supposed to pick it together but by the time he got back it seemed like a needless expense and he already had the wedding ring, his mother's wedding ring. When I said yes, when I burst into tears, his unit busted in cheering and hugging him. It was a special moment. I called Claire first. Then everyone else. A few months later came that other phone call. Over five years ago now. I can still hear the clipped no-nonsense voice. I knew from the moment I answered that it was about Cain.

In my head this phone call had come countless times but now it was really happening. I couldn't move.

'At approximately zero four hundred this morning a patrol including Lance Corporal Phillips was targeted by a troop of insurgents. A rocket-propelled grenade was directed at the vehicles, one of which was occupied by Lance Corporal Phill –'

'He's dead,' I said. Gravity intensifying, my stomach contracting. The one person who could conceivably replace my family, the love of my life and he was gone already.

'Your fiancé was in the range of the blast and has sustained serious injuries. He is currently at the NATO Multinational Medical Unit in Kandahar Airfield undergoing treatment.'

He's alive, I thought. *Thank God.* The man was still speaking but I interrupted. 'Is he . . . will he survive?'

'His condition is serious but stable. He has sustained injuries to his left side with some glass fragments and shrapnel cutting through his protective gear, he also suffered a fracture to his left thumb and has sustained a ligament and bone injury to his right knee. Medical staff are working on him. We are hopeful that he will regain consciousness in the next twenty-four hours and be back home in the coming months, if not weeks.'

'I . . .' No words came, my head was swimming.

'He's lucky to be alive, but he *is* alive and that's the most important thing. In the ensuing firefight he was pulled away to safety.'

I knew two things then: one, Cain's military career was over; and two, he would never be the same man again. I would later learn it was Axel who had dragged him to safety. An act that earned him the New Zealand Gallantry Star. How different things might have been if it was Axel riding in the front vehicle and Cain had saved his life.

•

'When you were young,' Cain croons.

'Sorry?'

'You were humming it, the song.'

'I was,' I say. *Was I?*

He's frowning again. 'I might go see Wiremu and Melissa. Give them a heads-up that we will have people staying.' He scratches a blade of grass from his stubble.

I'd guess only about one in four houses around the lake are occupied year-round, the rest are holiday homes.

'I'll come,' I say. The thought of being alone at the moment makes my stomach tighten. I have this feeling something is about to snap.

We set off together up the driveway towards the road.

Daniel is in Rotorua. He has my number and my wedding ring. I could always change my number, block him. I'll have to explain the missing ring to Cain somehow though.

Wiremu and Melissa's place is a big wooden house, angled out from the hill towards the lake. It's not changed since I was a kid. When Cain knocks, I can hear someone coming towards the door.

'Hello,' Melissa says, leaning her brown sun-creased face out. 'Cain, Lina, how are you both?'

Melissa has wild grey hair and a slightly lazy eye. 'Hi, Melissa,' Cain says. 'We're good, thanks. We just wanted to let you know that Lina and I are going to be renting our place out on WeStay, so you might see a few more strangers on the road.'

'Oh,' she says, frowning a little. 'WeStay, right. Well, that's fine. We'll keep an eye out.'

'Yeah, I'm sure there won't be any issues but if you hear loud music or notice anything amiss, feel free to text or call us.'

'No worries, Cain. I better make sure I have the right number for you both. Did you let anyone else in the community know?'

Cain scratches his stubble. 'To be honest, I think they're all far enough away that they won't notice.'

She bites her lips. 'Sure, well if anyone asks, we will let them know. It's not like you're the first around here to rent your place out to holidaymakers. Sue and Ian Cosgrove across the lake have their place listed while they're in Greece.'

'It's good for the area. Brings tourists in,' Cain says.

'And we all know how much everyone *loves* tourists.' A smile now to let us know there's no meanness in it. 'A bit more money pumping into the cafe and Buried Village doesn't hurt I suppose. We don't mind either way so long as they're tidy and respectful.'

The Buried Village is a tourist spot where a small village once existed. Tarawera was a mountain long before it was a lake. A volcanic eruption one hundred and thirty years ago changed that. The eruption destroyed the eighth wonder of the world – the pink and white terraces, natural hot pools cascading down – and buried a village that's since been partially excavated. That's why everything is so lush here; volcanic soil is fertile, producing a galaxy of greens and browns. Explosions of ferns from ponga trees, and native bush crowding the lake's edge.

Cain and I walk back down the road to our house. The leaves rotting in the shade on the gravel are treacherous slicks. I hide my hands in the pockets of my polar fleece as a southerly tears across the lake and tousles the ferns.

'What should we do for dinner?' he asks.

'There's no food in the house. But I'm not that hungry.'

'I'm starving. Why don't we go to the DT?'

It's on the east side of town. The chance of bumping into Daniel in a town the size of Rotorua is extremely unlikely. I'll keep my head down, be quick.

'Sure, okay.'

'Let me put a coat of stain on the deck then we can head off.'

We don't often cook when we are in Tarawera. The DT, or the Downtown, is fifty percent restaurant, forty-five percent bar and five percent casino. The backroom houses three poker machines that are occupied all night and most of the day. There are signs that warn of the dangers of problem gambling, and a much bigger display with the current jackpot.

Cain has spent time there. Time and hundreds of dollars. He brought home more than scars and a stiff knee from Afghanistan. He still has his own old bank account, but I monitor the business account and our joint accounts closely. It doesn't look like he's been gambling lately.

Soon enough he's finished with the deck. When he comes inside a dark patch of stain sits near his elbow like a birthmark, and blood trickles from above his left eye.

'What happened?'

'The old scar above my eye, just takes a small bump to open it up again.' He cleans it with a warm flannel, holds a folded paper towel to it until the bleeding stops.

'I'd be a hopeless boxer,' he says.

It's a twenty-minute drive back into town. We pass through the east-side stretch of shops. The service station is open, the forecourt brightly lit but the bakery is shut up, the cabinets empty. Taua's Hardware is closed for good, but the sign is still there, the logo a ghost on the fading white paint. Some of the windows are smashed, others covered with graffiti-scrawled plywood. At the DT there's a row of parked cars, a couple of blokes smoking in the fenced-in outdoor section. They're staring at whatever is on the screen inside. I pull up and they glance over, regarding us. Words and smirks pass between them when we climb out of the car, then they turn back. One of the two wears crocs and tattered shorts. On his stained t-shirt I read, *I don't need Google, My wife knows everything*. The other wears a t-shirt that simply displays the label for Waikato Draught.

•

We eat on the bar side, it's cheaper and the food comes out faster. I am a spider caught outside of her lair, shifty, cautious and watching everyone moving around me. If we bump into Daniel, what would I do? Pretend I've never seen him? And if he produces my wedding ring?

I order a salad and Cain opts for the fish and chips. When the door opens, I swivel my head back. It's a couple of old boys. As they pass us one of them pauses, openly staring at Cain. My entire body tenses.

'Cleaver,' he exclaims. 'That you?'

Cain's eyes simply rise from his meal. Then slowly he swings his head towards the man.

The man looks uncertain, then speaks again. 'Coach Ruatara.'

'Oh right,' Cain says, stretching his hand out. 'Been a long time.'

Coach Ruatara turns to his friend. 'Had him as a teenager at Sunnybrook High,' he says. 'Could have been an All Black.'

'Is that right?'

'No,' Cain speaks on an exhale. 'Never had it in me.'

'Chose the army instead,' Coach Ruatara says it like it's the highest praise, a man giving up the glory of professional sport to serve his country. Cain squirms in the heat lamp of public admiration. 'Still got the one hundred metre record at school, most of the athletic records actually. Pretty clever too,' he says. 'You still playing?'

'No.' Cain thumps his knee with his palm. 'Picked up an injury.'

The man looks grave. 'Right,' he says. 'Of course. Tough going over there in Iraq.'

Afghanistan. Cain doesn't correct him, he simply raises his eyebrows in agreement.

'You must be proud.'

It takes me a moment to realise he's talking to me. 'Yep,' I say. 'Very proud.'

'I'm still coaching at school there, always looking for more help with some of the younger teams. And you'll probably have kids of your own coming through soon.'

Cain glances towards me, I try to keep my face neutral but even this innocuous comment feels like a splinter. 'No,' he responds. 'No kids.'

'Plenty of time for that,' the man says. 'Wouldn't mind you coming and having a chat with the current team though.'

'I'm just down for the weekend,' he says, dismissing the idea. 'This is my wife, Lina.'

The coach offers his hand and I take it.

'Come down and say hi at school anytime you're back in town, the boys would love to meet an army hero.'

'Army hero.' Cain scoffs.

They move deeper into the bar, the man's jandals clap as he goes. They find a table to lean on near the screens showing horse racing. Cain lets his eyes linger for a moment on the man's back.

'Cleaver Phillips, quite a ring to it,' I tease, breaking the tension.

He turns to me and smiles, gives his head a small shake. 'It's a stupid high school nickname.'

'Can you at least tell me why?'

'I was good at tackling,' he says. 'At cutting people down.'

'Ah,' I say. 'Makes perfect sense. Pretty clever too, huh?'

He winces.

There's a loud noise. I drop my knife in response and it clatters against my plate. It's just a staccato blast of rugby commentary from the TV above the barman. I turn my head towards the sound.

There's a murmur of appreciation from the three men huddled down the other end of the bar, nursing beers.

'After our first booking we're going out for a nice dinner,' he says. 'That's what we will spend the money on.'

'Won't find much nicer than this around here,' I say, spearing a flaccid prawn on my fork, and scraping it off on the side plate.

'No, back home. Amano, or the Millhouse. Somewhere expensive.'

'Sounds good,' I say. We've got better things to spend the money on, including the eight thousand dollars in credit card debt, but I'm not about to remind him of that.

•

I'm still a little on edge when we get back that night. If I ignore Daniel, he will get the message and leave me alone. If only men were that predictable. If only he didn't have my ring. Moths are beating themselves to death against the security light we stand under as Cain makes a show of punching the code into his new lock, on the freshly painted black door. The lock grinds open, he holds the door for me.

'Seamless,' he says. 'Thought for a moment we might have locked ourselves out.'

'Quite loud,' I tease.

Inside I go to turn the back porch lights off. The light casts a glow out over the lawn, to the water. The stars are out, funnelling down in the negative space between the mountains. It's a magic night, silent and still. My eyes track along the lake then right before I hit the lights, I see something. Some*one*. My heart ceases for a second. Heat on my neck. A prickle at my hairline.

A shape, down near the water's edge. I draw a sharp breath. It looks like a man. It feels like my heartbeat is bruising my ribs. He must have come through the bush, the trees, or by the lake.

'Cain,' I say. 'Cain, come here please.' He doesn't respond. I turn back, searching for him in the house. 'Cain!' I call, louder now, stepping away from the door.

'What's up?' he emerges from the bathroom at the top of the stairs, his toothbrush hanging from his mouth.

I turn back to the window, pointing. 'Someone was there.' But I can't see them now. The shape was right down by the lake, just beyond the reach of the light. Could it have been a trick? Moonlight shimmering on the water? Are my eyes deceiving me?

Cain comes downstairs. He peers out through the back door.

'What did you see?'

'I don't know, maybe nothing.' Doubt coagulates in my mind, blocking my thoughts.

He reaches for the door handle, unlocks it. I clutch him hard. 'No, wait.'

'It's fine, look.' He steps out the door, the cool air rushes into the house. That graceless asymmetrical gait. 'Hello,' he calls. 'Anybody out here?' He turns back to me with a smile. 'Where did he go?'

Where did *he go?* He may have stayed along the lake edge and kept walking around through the bush. It's happened before. People get lost and end up emerging on the property. But at this time of night?

Cain continues further across the back lawn towards the lake's edge. Then he's gone. I squint into the darkness, my heart racing.

'Cain!' I call.

I see him again; he stands up tall and in his hand he has a log he's fished out of the water. He holds it above his head in two hands, then tosses it back into the water.

Cain steps back through the door and slides it closed once more. Locking it.

'I think I found your man,' he says.

I squeeze my lips closed. I was certain I saw someone, not just a piece of wood floating on the water. We go up the stairs together, I insist on being in front of him. I make him come in the bathroom with me when I brush my teeth. I imagine it really was a man out there. *Your mind is your enemy.* One of Cain's tattoos. A mantra when he was training for the SAS and underwent the gruelling selection process. He'd trained almost half his life for selection, knowing the dropout rate was over ninety percent. He ended up with the emblem tattooed over his heart. The sword, the wings, the banner emblazoned with 'Who Dares Wins'. My brave soldier. So why do I feel vulnerable now, even in my own house? I can't tell Cain about Daniel, the texts. Maybe my eyes were playing a trick on me. Maybe there was nothing out there in the night but shadows shifting in the wind, driftwood on the black, moon-tinselled lake.

SIX

CAIN HAD ONE of his bad dreams last night, he was moist with sweat, tangled in the sheets, panting until I gently shook him awake. I'd wanted to go downstairs and get him a glass of water, or to at least turn the light on, but I couldn't summon the courage to venture out of bed alone. This new fear has come on suddenly. My phone, as usual, was on flight mode while I slept, but still I kept thinking about what messages I might find in the morning, or Cain might find while I slept. Each time Cain jerked beside me and woke me, I turned my phone off flight mode to check if a new message had arrived, holding my breath in the dark, waiting. But there was nothing.

Now the morning has come and Cain is already awake. He's sitting there, looking at the curtains as if working out what time it might be by the intensity of the light passing beneath them. 'What's up?' I say.

He scratches his shoulder, turns back to me. 'Oh, not much, I got up early and had a walk. Couldn't sleep and now I've just come back to bed.'

'Mm,' I say. 'I noticed you tossing and turning. You want to talk about it?'

'No,' he says. 'Not really. Same shitty nightmares. They all blend into one, only now sometimes the war is here, in this country in this house and it's you I'm trying to protect.'

I don't know what to say, this is the most he's revealed about his dreams in a long time. 'You're safe now, Cain. You can always wake me, and we can sit up together and talk.'

'Yeah,' he says. 'I'll keep that in mind. You sleep well?'

'Fine,' I lie. 'But I actually feel hungover.' I force a huff of laughter. 'Despite not having anything to drink last night.'

'Maybe it was the dodgy prawns at DT?'

Then we hear something we usually only hear in summer.

'Fuck me,' he says.

I plug my ears with my fingers. A jet ski is ripping across the lake.

'Summer has come.' He feigns checking his watch. 'A couple of months early.'

'It must be cold out there.'

He stands, peers through the gap in the curtains. 'He's got a wetsuit. Mind if I open these?'

I squint in anticipation. 'Sure.'

The light floods the room.

'I need water,' I say, sitting up, turning so my feet find the cool carpet.

'I'll make you a cup of tea.'

He goes downstairs, I follow him.

'Go lie down on the couch,' he says. He's got a grimace and I notice now his right leg won't straighten fully.

'You're in pain.'

'It's fine.'

'Take a tramadol?'

'I already have,' he says. 'I'll be right.' That Kiwi hardman, stiff upper lip nonsense doesn't help. He needs to get back to the physio or on stronger painkillers.

I shower and Cain swims out a few hundred metres then back. Some Scandinavian cold-water therapy he heard about on a podcast to help with his pain. After he dries off he goes about readying the place for the first guests. He spreads one more layer of stain on the deck. He dusts every surface. He restacks the firewood beside the barbecue then deadbolts the back door and locks all of the windows. He lines the tiny boxes of milk up in the fridge, straightens the toaster and kettle. He drops the blinds so they are half down. He sets the fire ready to light. And finally places a single bottle of pinot on the table for the guests, a yellow Post-it note on the neck of the bottle screams 'Drink me!'

I use my iPhone camera to take new photos of the house, now that it's ready for the guests. The mid-morning glow provides perfect lighting, pillars of sun passing through kitchen windows, burning bright squares on the floor tiles, illuminating the entire room.

'Place has never looked so good,' Cain says, watching me move about the room, trying my hand at photography.

When we go to leave, I check the letterbox. Nothing there. I stare up along the road and again the guilt hits me like a wave. I swallow and try to block out the memories of that night with Daniel. Find a way to pretend that woman, *Anna*, was someone else. The apple doesn't fall so far from the tree; maybe I am just like irresponsible, selfish Lianne.

I think about the nights I search my mother's name. Sometimes it feels like I really do miss her, but it's not just that. It's something different. I think about those short spells I lived with her, in old flats in town, carpet swollen and peeling up at the corners like wet cardboard, loud second-hand fridges and moth-eaten curtains that barely closed. Then there was the parade of men. And of course, there was another presence in the house. Those empty casks of wine piling up, the addiction gripping her body and shaking her until only bones and skin remained. It took everything, drained her of love and filled her with spite. I don't blame her, it's a disease after all. But I blame her for running away from her parents' home when she was fifteen and pregnant. I blame her for not seeking help, not accepting the hand her parents offered, and I blame her for trying to take me back even though she was unwell. Dragging us all through the courts. I've come to accept that my mother is a bad person. I told myself I would never become her; I'd be a better mother.

'Cain,' I say now, feeling the weight of guilt pressing down on me. 'I think I've lost my ring. I'll do one more big search at my locker at work, but what if it doesn't turn up?'

He's beside me in the car, as we're about to leave. A knot at the bend of his jaw. He sets his eyes ahead. 'You're going to have to find it, Lina. That was my mother's, 'bout the only thing I've got left from my parents. You're just going to have to find it.' Then the car starts and we're driving.

Peephole
Live Cam Premium
Stream: 016A
Viewers: 011

A family enters the house, a man in his late thirties, wearing a New York Yankees hat, drags two suitcases in and a heavily pregnant woman follows him, holding the hands of two children. She sits on the couch, and opens her handbag, fetching a packet of apple slices for the children, who appear to be twins. She bends forward now as the kids rush about checking the rooms. She reaches and unties her shoes, pulling them off, placing her socked feet on the coffee table. Meanwhile, on camera 3 the husband is removing his clothes. He wraps a towel around his waist and heads to the shower where camera 5 picks him up – 17 viewers. He points to the child as he passes the bunkroom, then points out into the lounge. She rushes out, grabs her bag and comes back into the room. The woman turns the TV on, scrolls through channels. Dissatisfied, after ten minutes, she gets up, goes to one of the suitcases and pulls out her laptop. At the couch she puts a US reality TV show on the screen.

Later, they all bathe, get dressed in tidy clothes. Then when they're all dressed, they leave for dinner, the place falls dark and the numbers drop again.

SEVEN

CHANGE YOUR PHONE number. The thought comes unbidden but once it's there it lodges itself in my brain. Some thoughts are like that. The longer I wait the more likely Daniel will message me again and Cain might see it. This is the only way to ensure I've severed the thread running between Daniel and me. I can control the situation. It would mean a mass text to all my contacts to update them. I would have to explain the decision to Cain – maybe I'd complain about telemarketing calls or say something vague about protecting my identity. For now I keep my phone close at all times, when I'm in the shower, in the middle of the night, when we go out in the car.

Today I keep my phone in the glove box of the ambulance. My partner Scotty is a veteran of the service with receding ginger hair on a slightly pink, ruddy head. Anything beyond about ten years qualifies as veteran status, but he's spent around twenty-five years saving lives. The only times we don't work together is when I pick up extra shifts on my days off.

A suspected heart attack starts the day for us, a 61-year-old male at a golf course. He'd bent to pick his ball out of the hole and when he stood up again, he'd had intense stabbing pain beneath his sternum. His friends said he just stood rubbing his chest, red in the face. Then he dropped down to one knee.

In any ambulance there's the lead and the driver, and between jobs we swap to keep the workload even. For certain calls, a hierarchy instantly establishes itself where the most senior officer will take the lead but for this call, I'm responsible for the patient. Scotty hesitates at the edge of the golf course, looking out over the perfectly manicured grass.

'Go,' I say. 'It's dry.'

He starts driving onto the grass of the course. I see a man rushing out of the clubhouse, waving at us. The wheels spin, flicking turf. My look tells the man to stay out of the way; his lips seal in a pale line.

We see cardiac arrest calls once a month or so but this one sounds more like a garden variety heart attack.

I find the patient lying down with a group of men in conspicuously bright golf attire, their carts parked off at a distance. They've not moved the patient, thankfully. I assess him. Pupils a little dilated, but fine. Heart rate is at ninety-two, blood pressure is low, ninety over fifty. Oxygen levels at ninety-eight percent. Everything else is fine. We've got time to get him to the hospital. I radio ahead. Scotty pulls the stretcher out, running it over. With his skinny limbs and pot belly, Scotty always reminds me of those middle-aged men who play social sport and drink too much beer after.

'We're going to help you stand and climb onto the stretcher, okay?'

One of his friends comes forward, volunteering to help.

'It's fine, we can manage.'

'He's okay?'

'He's doing well, just need to get him to the hospital if you don't mind.'

One of the men says something I don't quite catch but the two others with him snigger. I get it a little bit less now that I'm in my thirties. Years ago, I stopped wearing make-up at work. Now I don't wear any jewellery at all, I keep my nails clipped short and free of polish. When my hair was longer, it was always pulled back tight into a no-nonsense ponytail.

The patient looks sick in the face but gets onto the stretcher and lies down. We load him up and force the stretcher into the back of the ambulance. I notice that Scotty's eyes are a little dilated.

'Come on,' I say. 'Let's get him on the road.'

I climb in the back and keep an eye on the ECG the entire trip. At the hospital I brief the triage nurse, then they wheel him into a monitored unit. I fill out the notes on the call, filing the report. By the time I get back to the ambulance Scotty still hasn't finished cleaning and replacing the equipment and stretcher. He's off the pace today. He can be a little aloof, with a sense of humour some would describe as un-PC and others would call crass or perhaps worse. I'm his eleventh partner but we've been working together for almost four years now. Someone has to work with him, and I find it easy enough to block out the crap. If nothing else, he's always been a hard worker.

The moment we are cleared from the job I expect the next call from the station but nothing comes through.

'Greasy Spoon cafe?' Scotty says.

'Why not?'

You learn early as ambulance officers to order food and drinks in takeaway containers. You never know when the next call is going to come. Scotty has finished his BLT and I'm two-thirds of the way through my salad when our pagers sound. We stride back to the ambulance and head out.

It's another standard call. A suspected broken wrist and possible concussion. A woman tripped and fell while carrying two bags of groceries from the car. Her son called it in.

Scotty should be the lead, but we swapped so he could drive and I could finish my salad on the way.

'Any plans for the weekend?' he says, as he speeds through traffic. The sirens wail above us, and cars part, or shift to the road's edge.

'Nothing really, might head down to Tarawera if the weather is nice.'

A car ahead won't get out of our way, Scotty leans on the horn. 'Move!' The grey-haired woman behind the wheel looks stricken.

'You heading there to check on your WeStay?' he continues to me, the red fading from his cheeks.

'No,' I say, wondering when I had actually told him about it. We're driving through a wealthy inner-eastern suburb of Auckland.

'How's it going?'

'Good, just waiting for the bookings to come flooding in. It's been two weeks without much traction.'

The conversation abruptly ends as we pull up in front of the house.

'Look at the state of this place. Rich bastards,' he says.

It's palatial. Even for this part of town, a few kilometres from the CBD where properties are big enough to have their own postcodes. The garage is open, and I see hundreds of thousands of dollars' worth of vehicles parked side by side. A sports car with a rearing stallion and an SUV with the distinct boxy font of Porsche.

Scotty turns his head to smirk as he pulls into the driveway.

I climb out and knock hard on the door, twice. A man, with impossibly white teeth, a tan he's picked up somewhere tropical and silver-fox slicked-back hair. 'Hi, thanks for coming out,' he says. 'But I think we've got it covered now.'

'I'll just have to see her to complete paperwork.'

His smile falters. 'Sure. Come on through.'

She's a small thing, sharp clavicle and birdlike bones showing through the back of her hands. When she meets my eyes, she tries to smile but there's pain in it.

I kneel down to speak to her at eye level, check her pupils, her heart, her ears.

'Do you still have a headache?'

'Umm, no it's okay now.' The husband is there, right over my shoulder when Scotty comes in.

'Any dizziness?'

'No,' she says.

'Scotty?' The man's voice is loud. I turn. Scotty's eyes are open wide, but he's smiling. 'Rick?' he says. 'Rick Reynolds, is that you?'

They're shaking hands now, clapping each other's back.

'You're a paramedic these days.'

'Twenty-four years now.'

His eyebrows rise. 'Far out. Twenty-four years, straight out of high school. I had no idea. You've lost a lot of weight since high school too.'

Scotty gives an awkward cough. 'I've seen your billboards,' he says.

Billboards? I thought I recognised him. He's the politician. The upstart businessman espousing populist ideals. A NZ Trump, except he's hardly gaining much momentum. A few of the crazies have probably bought in though. 'Hoping to get into parliament and start taking out the trash,' he says.

I try to block out the boys' chat and focus on the woman.

'What's the day of the week today?'

'Tuesday.'

'How did you fall?'

'I, umm, I just stumbled. I wasn't concentrating.'

A sound in my mind like a distant alarm. She doesn't appear to have concussion, but she mumbles the answer as if unsure of herself.

'Who called it in?' I say, turning back to the husband, interrupting his catch-up with Scotty.

'Ah my son,' the man says. 'He's eleven and got a bit spooked.'

I turn back to the woman. 'Alright, let me get a look at that wrist.' I go to lift her sleeve, but her left hand flies across, holding it down.

'Sorry, I just need to get a look at it,' I say.

Her eyes go to her husband, then back to me. My senses are tingling. Something is not quite right here.

I peel the woman's fingers away gently, then lift the sleeve and hold the wrist up, supporting it. Then I see what she's hiding away. Those four grey spots, finger marks leading up her forearm. I look into her eyes; she looks away. The boys are laughing about something now, reminiscing.

Examining the large kitchen we're in, I see no sign of groceries, so unless this man, *Rick*, put them away while his wife was in pain, there never were groceries. I spy a fruit bowl on the marble benchtop, limp bananas and soft apples. Not fresh produce.

'Does that hurt?' I say, gently testing the wrist.

She winces. 'Yeah.'

'And that?'

'Yep.'

'On a scale of one to ten, how painful is it?'

'Seven or maybe eight.'

'Well I'd say there might be a break in there. You're going to need an x-ray. We can drop you at the hospital, if you like, or you can organise to see a radiologist through your own doctor.'

'I'll go later,' she says.

I administer fentanyl for the pain. Scotty chooses to complete his report inside, so he doesn't need to stop talking to Rick. I go to the ambulance and come back a moment later. 'Hey, Scotty, can you give me a hand finding something?'

He glances up from the iPad. I give him a look that says, *don't ask*.

'Sure. Be right back.'

Outside, tucked out of sight from the house behind the ambulance, I stop him. 'I think she's got signs of abuse.'

He frowns, his ruddy cheeks pinken. 'You're joking.'

'I know the signs, she's hiding bruises.'

'They're from the fall, surely? You might be jumping to conclusions.'

'She might have been pushed or hit.'

'Hit,' he says, and the word tumbles into incredulous laughter. He's a bit off today. If we suspect domestic violence, we have a duty to report it. Even if it turns out not to be the case. 'He's a politician, Lina. He's a good guy and there's nothing to suggest he has hit her.' He has an odd, serene smile – is it possible I'm overreacting? 'Come on, Lina. I'd be the first one to phone it in, you know that, but there's no real evidence of abuse here.'

He can't be serious. The guy who's called the cops on every potential domestic violence situation we've seen. But those cases were almost always lower socio-economic homes. The violence was obvious. Children with black eyes. Women with cigarette burns. Scotty knows this man.

I shrug. 'I've got to ring it in. If there's nothing to hide, it won't hurt them at all.'

He touches my arm as I reach for my radio. 'Let me speak to him, please. I'll get to the bottom of it.'

'Scotty, no,' I say. 'We don't warn them, we don't let them get a story straight. That's how men like him get away with it.'

He pulls his hand away, shows me his palms as if to say, *your call*. 'Alright. Can you wait until we've wrapped it up at least?'

'Okay,' I say.

Scotty goes back inside to finish the report. When he comes back, I add to it. Noting the bruises, the wife's demeanour. Police don't need the wife to confess to what has happened, they need only to suspect abuse before they intervene. The eleven-year-old son probably called 111 before he knew what he was doing. How will that man punish the kid if that is the case? Or it could all be a mistake. Those finger bruises could be from some adventurous role-play. Or a judo class she takes. There's no certainty, just a balance of probability. Scotty is at one end of the scales and I'm at the other.

Rick comes out to the ambulance. 'What's going on?' he asks, that smile gone now. 'What's taking so long?'

'Nothing,' I say. 'We've almost finished up the paperwork here.'

'Right.' He looks to Scotty, raising his eyebrows as if this is one of those women things. *Thoroughness, am I right?*

'Sorry,' Rick adds now, zeroing in on me. 'Have we met before?'

'Me?' I say. Feeling a sudden flush. 'No, I don't think so.'

His eyes narrow just a touch. 'I could have sworn I recognise you from somewhere. Maybe not.' He stands uncomfortably close, hands on hips, forcing his suit jacket open. 'No, I have seen you somewhere. It'll come to me. Or maybe you've just got one of those faces.' Then he lets out a laugh and slaps Scotty's shoulder, before retreating to the house. I radio for the police and we stick around outside the property until they arrive and I explain what I saw. Then, Scotty insists we clear off. He doesn't want to see his friend's face when the officers knock on the door.

I back out of the driveway, look once more at those vehicles, that house, then ease my foot down on the accelerator and head towards the station. Scotty is quiet, unreadable. He's playing on his phone and barely speaks for the rest of the shift. I've ruined his little catch-up with an old school friend who appears to be doing well for himself. Maybe Scotty could see a friendship re-forming before I snuffed it out. At six-thirty when we get back to the station, he simply says, 'See you next shift,' signs out and takes his bag to his car without another word.

•

'How was work?' Cain asks. He's got his tattered light boxing gloves on and has been hitting the bag in the yard.

'It was okay, had an odd call this afternoon. Have you heard of Rick Reynolds?'

A spark of recognition. 'Yeah, I have actually. I think I've seen him at Axel's gym. Tallish, Pākehā fellow? Pretty lean.'

Everyone in Auckland is connected somehow. 'That's him. He's running for prime minister with about zero point one percent of the population behind him.'

'Careful, there is plenty of looneys that will probably vote for him in the next election.'

'We got called to his house. His wife had bruises.'

I see a vein near his temple. This is one of Cain's rules: men should never hurt women or children. They shouldn't hurt other people at all unless it is *completely* necessary.

'You sure?' he says.

'No, but my intuition with this stuff is normally pretty good.'

'So what happened?'

I pinch the bridge of my nose, massage my eyelids. 'I called the cops, Scotty wasn't too pleased about it.'

'You called the cops on him?'

'Of course.'

Peephole
Live Cam Premium
Stream: 019C
Viewers: 009

A man in his sixties is nude in the villa's pool as seen on camera 3. The stone Balinese statue behind him spurts a stream of water into the pool and he swims to it and lets the flow splash over his head – 9 viewers. On camera 2 a grey-haired woman is mixing pineapple juice with vodka in tall glasses with ice. She does a small dance in the kitchen to whatever music is playing. Then she carries the drinks over, puts one near the pool's edge and the other on the low table beside the banana lounge. She steps out of her sundress, wearing a bikini now – 11 viewers. Puts on a large straw hat and lies down on the banana lounge, taking up her drink. They pass most of the day like this, moving in and out of the pool, in and out of the house. Two masseuses arrive in the afternoon. In the sun, the couple get massages.

EIGHT

IT'S ONE OF those weeks of sulky New Zealand weather. Rain that comes down slowly, consistently for days. Halfway through my next shift Scotty says, 'Heard from Rick.'

'Rick Reynolds?'

'Yeah. He didn't say anything about the cops but he asked about you.'

'What'd he say?'

'Nothing really. Just wanted to know how long we've worked together.' He laughs. 'Haven't seen him in twenty years and he just wanted to talk about some ambo he met for five minutes.' A stitch digs in at my side. I don't want to push him any further about it, but it doesn't feel right. He might just be winding me up as payback for calling the police. The shift passes slowly, it's a quiet night and when I get home I can barely sleep again. Every night I think about Daniel, I wonder when he will try to get in contact with me again. I relive that night we spent together, the guilt pressing down.

The next day after my run I get back to find Cain standing there waiting for me. He's beaming. 'We have a booking,' he says.

'A booking?' I swipe my forearm across my brow. 'A WeStay booking?'

It's been weeks; I was beginning to wonder if it was going to happen. Cain had tweaked the photos, lowered the price and, voila, we have contact. 'Come have a look.'

Cherry has requested to book Casa Tarawera – mid-century retreat. That's what I see on the screen of Cain's computer when I walk into his study. $432.60 for two nights. The first money we've made from the property. It feels odd. Strangers will sleep in our beds, they will sit on our couch looking out at our view of the lake.

'That is so cool,' I say, as he lowers himself into his desk chair. 'Go on, check them out.'

He turns back to the screen and clicks the profile. A small maple leaf flag suggests they're Canadian. Home town: Vancouver, BC. Cain scrolls through the reviews from other hosts: 5.0 stars average rating. Perfect. Six reviews.

Left our place spotless.

Easy to communicate with and very tidy.

Loved hosting Dan and Cherry, very friendly and flexible.

'Look at the other places they've stayed.'

'How?' Cain asks.

'Click the profiles of the people who have left reviews.'

He does, we see the listings and go through them one by one, checking out the places they've been. They've got good taste by the looks of it. Always big houses from different parts of the world: Portugal, Morocco, Japan. They seem to be working their way around the globe and Lake Tarawera is next on their list.

'Anyone could follow them around,' Cain says, 'stay at the same places after them, relive their trip.'

'Why would you bother?' I say.

'Well, there are some freaks out there.'

It's four hundred and thirty-two dollars we wouldn't otherwise have. Money for nothing really and easily covers the costs of setting the place up.

Cain opens Google and he punches their name in, strikes enter and results flood the page.

'What are you doing?'

'No one is going to be honest on their WeStay profile. Let's see if we can find their Facebook page.' He's scrolling as he talks.

'Really? This feels a little like stalking.'

'It's harmless, Lina,' he says. 'Plus what if they were neo-Nazis or child abusers, you would want to know, right?'

'Probably not. And who would list that on their Facebook anyway?'

'It's not hard to tell something is off about someone just by looking at what they choose to share. Couple of guys from my unit constantly post borderline neo-Nazi propaganda.'

Their social media profiles are easy to find. Cain finds the man's twitter and reads his tweets aloud. Twitter is where you learn the most about people. A couple of hundred characters of anger, or admiration. Dan thinks Trudeau is a puppet. He's a big Maple Leafs fan but will not be renewing his membership if they don't fire the head coach soon. Cherry retweeted a feel-good quote from Chrissy Teigen and tweets about going to the gym almost every day, with images of smoothies, gym shots of her mid squat with a bar across her shoulders. More healthy recipes and #fitspo. She posted an image of an old man I assume is her father, on the anniversary of his death. I find their LinkedIn accounts on my phone. Dan has a much more professional photo than his Twitter account. A shirt with an open collar, a smile that is slightly restrained.

'He's a geologist working in exploration for a mining company,' I say.

'No wonder he hates Trudeau,' Cain says.

'She's an accountant and has worked at the same firm for nine years but is taking annual leave for an upcoming trip to New Zealand. They have a chocolate border collie at home and were so sad to leave him at the kennels while they were away on their last trip. Who calls a dog Donald?'

'A Trump fan,' he says.

'Ugh.' Four hundred and thirty dollars, I remind myself. 'Might need to burn sage after they leave.'

Cain, who is, as far as I know, politically agnostic, stands now. 'They'll be fine.'

'Maybe we don't do this with each guest,' I say with an uneasy squeezing feeling inside. 'I don't think it makes me feel any better.'

'Really?' He laughs. 'You don't find this interesting? Kind of fun? It's harmless.'

I swallow. 'Fun? Really?' It doesn't feel like we are looking into the internet at them but rather they're looking out at us. I shudder.

'You like it,' he says. 'I can tell.'

•

When the weekend comes around, he does it again. Only this time I catch him in the act, at his desk in the study. I head in to ask if he needs anything from the grocer and see he's on their social media feeds. I lean against his desk.

'At it again?' I say.

'Just checking up on them,' he says. 'They're there now at our place.'

On Cherry's Instagram there are photos from in our house. Grinning, sitting around our table, using our Yahtzee set, and drinking the wine we left out for them from our glasses.

'I think you're a voyeur,' I tease.

'Maybe I am,' he says. 'I'm not going to pretend I don't find it interesting.'

'Am I pretending that I don't find it interesting?'

'You seem to be.'

He opens up the electricity app. Bar graphs spread on the page showing time of usage for the day.

'The information is out there, *they* are putting it out there. And it's important for us to make sure they're looking after the house. Like this,' he says, looking at the power app closely. 'They've been using power since yesterday afternoon, so we know they arrived and made it inside.'

'The power peaked this morning for an hour at ten,' I note, looking closely at the bars.

'It must have been the oven, or the heater,' he says. I can see why some people like to watch others, just for a short while; inhabit them in a way as if they're watching their favourite TV show, or reading a familiar book. They can be that person for a while to escape themselves. But there is a line, and when you cross that line you're no longer *doing due diligence* but stalking.

'Don't overthink it,' he says, turning back to me. 'It's natural to be curious.'

'What if they have sex in our bed?' I say, trying to make light of it all.

'They probably *have*.'

I let out a huff of laughter. 'That's gross.'

'I'm more worried about them breaking something or getting into the basement and going through our things,' he says.

'Surely we've got some protection against damage from WeStay.'

'They've left a thousand dollar security deposit.'

'Is that enough?'

'What sort of damage could they do?'

My phone vibrates and I almost leap. I leave the room before opening the message. Something clots near my heart.

Hey Anna, Daniel here. I know it's been a while but I was hoping to catch up again soon. I've still got your necklace with the ring on it from that night.

I look back; Cain's eyes are fixed on the computer screen. I quickly punch out a message. It's been a month. The ring won't just materialise.

How did you get my number? I never gave it to you.

I see him typing, the three dots dancing on the screen.

I have my ways.

I feel like I can't breathe. This is all backfiring. And yet it feels inevitable, a car crash in slow motion but only I realise the pain is coming; it's a moment or an eternity away but it will arrive. I delete all the messages except that last one, so I have his number: *I have my ways*. Playful, I think. Or threatening? I turn my phone off, go to the bathroom and splash water on my face. That thought comes again: *Change your number.* I will, but first I'll try to get my wedding band back. That ring cannot be replaced. A plan forms.

Peephole transmission

In response to the incidents in Colorado and St Petersburg and the growing Interpol attention, VIP access will no longer include information about the location of streams or information about the guests. This is to protect both the identities of our planters, and the integrity and privacy of our service. Our planters will continue to enjoy full access accounts. If you cannot afford our service, you can always join us.

Enjoy the show.

NINE

A BREEZE SWEEPS in from the sea, between the islands and across the rippling plain of water. We're accompanied by that odd percussion of aluminium tinging and boats knocking the harbour. The viaduct, one of Auckland's social hubs, is a nice walk although it tends to be heaving with tourists. I've not been to a bar in so long, not since that night with Daniel. I think about him as we stroll along.

I have still got to organise the exchange: my necklace for a second meeting. He's suggested a drink, but when boys like Daniel suggest a drink what they really mean is more than *a* drink. At the very least he wants a chance to charm me, get me in bed again. It was so easy for him last time; he probably thinks it would happen as easily as the first time.

Thankfully Cain's had other things to occupy his attention and hasn't mentioned the ring again. But he will. He's been quiet, working hard, a little distant. He was first like this when the media began to follow the story of the botched raid. Skelton killed himself three months and seventeen days after the investigation began. Six days after a document was leaked and published by the Blood,

Sweat and Beers political blog that implicated him and suggested an arrest was imminent. A still from the headcam footage showing the victims reached the media, and the story of a once celebrated, now disgraced soldier metastasized into cautionary tales of war, potential CTE, a man pushed to the edge. Family, friends, old schoolteachers all said the same thing. War changed him. I didn't get this information from Cain but all the others who gave interviews. A letter released by Skelton's mother to the media revealed his attitude towards the leadership in the military. *They trained us to kill but they can't untrain us.* Did Cain hold the same views? Were they let down by those in charge?

After Afghanistan, Cain showed no desire to go back to warzones, until one day he told me how much he would make as a private contractor for oil companies. They needed security, and others from his unit had signed up, making astronomical sums of money. 'I could set us up for life,' he had said. 'If it wasn't for this buggered knee of mine.'

I hold Cain's hand in the pocket of his puffer jacket as another gust sweeps in from the sea. The boats rock, their masts swinging like needles hacking at the twilight sky. His phone sounds. 'Another one,' he says, extracting it from his jeans pocket. 'It's for this weekend.' Once he lowered the price on WeStay, the floodgate opened. I'm growing used to that familiar chime of his phone, heralding a new booking. Dan and Cherry Evans stayed last weekend. Now so many others have booked. The squares of the calendar are filling up. Each one represents more money, greater financial security. One step closer to the life we want.

'I'm still a little nervous about the state they left the house in,' I say. 'What if they stole something?'

He takes his hand from his pocket and wraps it around my shoulders. 'Everything will be fine. Trust me.'

Late afternoon crowds fill the bars, mostly tourists. Our dinner booking with Claire and Axel is for eight. We're not far from the restaurant, Amano, in the trendy central hub of Britomart, but our reservation isn't for another hour, so Cain wants to have a drink first.

'What about here?' I say, pointing to the terraces of a bar overlooking the busiest corner of the viaduct. It's near the America's Cup exhibit showing the black keel of the 1995 winning yacht. He looks up, sees all the knots of young people on the patio.

'Busy for a Tuesday,' he says. 'There's a quieter place around the corner.'

'Sure.'

He takes us to a wine bar, a different crowd. Hipster types, a few suits having a knock-off. We find a quiet booth.

'You want a wine?' he says.

'Maybe just a soda water.'

He goes to leave, pauses and slowly wheels back towards me. 'You feeling alright?'

I find myself subconsciously rubbing my elbow. 'Yeah,' I say. 'I'm just not drinking much.'

He pokes out his bottom lip, regards me for a second longer. 'Soda water,' he says. When he returns with our drinks, he exhales as he sits and the old leather of the seat creaks.

'I'll need to head down and clean the house after the last guests since we still haven't organised a cleaner.'

'I can help,' I say. 'It'd have to be on one of my days off.'

'No, it's fine, I can go when you're working.'

'Why don't we just go tomorrow, or after my shift on Thursday, in the afternoon? I could sleep on the way down.' I don't want him to resent me for not helping, despite it being his idea.

He shakes his head. 'I've got no work on Thursday. I can go early in the morning and get back before dark. I'm only thinking of you.'

'Cain,' I say, reaching for his hand over the table. It's cool from where he was holding his beer. 'Let me help.'

'No,' he says, with the weight of finality that seems to come much easier to men like my husband than women like me. 'It's my project and I don't want you worrying about anything. It's easier if I manage it.'

And with that the decision is made. I'm not going to argue when he's right. The thought of any damage to that house fills my gut with dread, despite the deposit and insurance. I would stress the entire drive down there. He takes a big mouthful of his beer and says, 'So where exactly is the last place you remember wearing your ring?'

I drink some of my soda water and an air bubble seems to be trapped in my chest. It hurts to swallow. 'Oh I forgot to mention,' I say. 'It actually turned up.'

'It did?'

Why did I lie? It came so naturally, so quickly that before I can stop myself more words come out. 'It was in my locker, like I said. Right down the bottom. It's actually getting a little big for me, this whole not drinking thing has not only shed weight off my body but my fingers too apparently.' I try to laugh, but the sound is unnatural. 'I've got to pick it up soon, it's being resized.'

He's frowning. 'How much does that cost?'

Before I can answer, his phone buzzes on the table between us and I see Axel's name. I'm grateful for the distraction. I need to get my ring now. If I can't get it back from Daniel I'll have to get a replica made, find a way to siphon the money from our account, take a photo to a jeweller.

'Kia ora,' Cain says. 'We're just at – what's this bar called, Lina?'

I crane my head to look through the window at the sign. 'A Deeper Blue.'

'A Deeper Blue, mate. Just off the viaduct . . . no worries, I'll order for you both. Pint of lager and a lemon, lime and bitters.'

Axel arrives in a tidy faded black shirt and dark jeans. Claire comes in beside him, winged mascara and a warm smile.

'Hello, hello, hello,' he says, shaking Cain's hand. Planting a kiss on my cheek. Claire comes over next.

'You look gorgeous as always. Love this top. Where's it from?'

Discount bin at H&M. 'Oh, I can't remember where I picked this one up.'

They find their seats beside us and take up the drinks Cain had ordered for them. I hope it doesn't turn out to be one of those nights where we forget about money and live like Axel and Claire, drinking cocktails and overeating, only to get a reality check when the bill comes. Cain laughs at something Axel has said, but I miss the joke, occupied instead by thoughts of the ring. I devise intricate plans to get it back but they all end the same way, with me having to see Daniel again. Could I really risk it a second time? Claire touches my wrist.

'How is work?'

I press a smile to my lips. 'It's work,' I say. 'You?'

'Busy, busy. Classes are filling up and Axel is planning on offering yoga and Pilates when he opens the new gym so we might even work together.'

'Great idea.'

Axel speaks to me now. 'So the WeStay idea, was I right or was I right?'

I smile at him. 'One booking down. I'll admit, it's okay. It's actually paying for our dinner tonight.'

'It's money for nothing and your place looks beautiful. Cain showed me the listing.'

'You'll have to get down to see it in person sometime,' Cain says. 'I can't believe you've not been before.'

'Well, we'll need to get all our travelling in this year.'

A pause. I watch Axel's eyes shift, meet his wife's. He almost seems earnest with a smile beginning at the edges of his lips.

'What?' Cain says. 'What is it?'

I know. Before another word is spoken, I just know. We've talked about it ourselves, Cain and I. When will Axel and Claire start *trying*. I know before she says, 'We're having a baby.' Before Cain gets up and hugs Axel hard, and kisses Claire. Before Cain says, 'Better get you a top-shelf whisky.' Before it all happens, I *know*. I feel sick watching it play out in slow motion before me, trying so hard to smile but feeling like tears could break through at any moment. *Why aren't I happy for them?*

The boys head to the bar for the whisky and Claire's hand touches mine again. 'Lina,' she says. 'Are you okay? I'm sorry I know it's hard with . . .' A pause. She almost looks guilty. Like Cain's non-existent sperm count is somehow her fault. 'You know, I've been so nervous about telling you.'

'Were you trying?'

'It doesn't matter,' she says. 'It just happened I guess. We weren't not trying.' A guilty look. 'I had a bottle of wine that night you guys came over, whoops. But I didn't know then and the doctor said not to stress about it. We conceived a few weeks before that.'

I swallow. Squeeze her hand back. 'I'm happy for you,' I say. My own desperation has mutated, now I feel a roaring jealousy, frustration and shame. I feel it all rushing about my body. Burning the skin at the back of my neck, my cheeks. Drilling down through my sternum. I've not been drinking *in case* I fell pregnant. I've been taking the vitamins for years, forcing Cain to stick to our schedule. We spent so much on IVF and alternative treatments. We've been desperate and now it has *just happened* for Claire and Axel.

'I'm happy for you guys. Really I am.' I've risked everything to try to make it happen for us. *It might have worked,* I think now. *You'll know very soon.*

The boys are coming back and I don't even want to guess how much Cain just spent on the whiskies in their hands, served neat. Their glasses clash then they take a sip. Cain seems genuinely happy. I wish I had that. Loyalty to the happiness of those I care about. Another rule of his: squash envy, kill jealousy, celebrate your friends and family. It's usually such an endearing trait but right now it only makes me sadder.

'I can't believe you guys are going to be parents,' I say. 'It's such good news.'

•

After dinner, when we are home, I'm taken by a sudden fatigue – the compounding effect of shift work – and decide to get to bed. I head downstairs to wish Cain good night and find him in the study. He's not heard me coming, I realise, with his big noise-cancelling headphones on, and he's looking at the guests for this weekend. He's looking at her. The thin sound of rock music escapes the headphones and grows louder as I gently pull one side away. He doesn't jump, but I notice his shoulders rise, a prickle of irritation.

'Don't do that,' he says. It's not a snap exactly, it's three words said slowly and deliberately as if he's holding back.

'Do what?'

'Sneak up on me in here.'

'I didn't sneak, you just looked busy.' I say it like a question.

He draws a breath. 'No,' he says. 'Not really, just . . .' He lets the sentence die in his mouth, he's zoomed out on the image now, but I know exactly what he was gazing at.

'Who is she?' I ask.

'These are the next guests.'

I lean closer, staring. She's in a bikini, sitting up on her husband's shoulders. 'And you're just staring at a photo of them, of her in particular.'

'Of them,' he says.

'You were zoomed in on her boobs.'

'No,' he begins. 'I . . .'

'It's okay,' I say, dragging the spare seat closer. The leather is cool on the skin below my pyjama shorts. 'She's hot. I just find it odd that you'd sneak down here after dinner to have a perv, that's all.' I can smell the three beers and two whiskies from dinner on his breath.

'It's due diligence. It might save us a headache.'

'I thought I was the paranoid one.'

'I'm doing this for your benefit, Lina. So you can have peace of mind.'

Maybe he's telling the truth, he just wants to check them out, make sure they're not suspicious. Then he saw her and decided to get a closer look. Why else would he search them? 'So what did you find out about them, you know, other than how many abs she has?'

'The wife, Lucy Swallow, booked it. She's a recruiter. She works for a small HR company in Ponsonby. She has a sizeable network, over five hundred connections but she isn't overly active on LinkedIn.'

'Mustn't be a very good recruiter then.'

He continues running through the profile of the two guests. Somewhat predictably – given his muscles – the buff husband, Phil, is a tradesperson. Rain slaps against the steel roof outside.

'She's made the same post on Instagram as well as Facebook.'

He brings it up now.

Eatery suggestions near Rotorua/Tarawera . . . and go!

Dozens of responses on Facebook, a few on Instagram.

You're going to Tarawera! Great. Check out the Downtown, excellent pub food near the turn-off outside of Rotorua.

You've got to check out the redwoods.

Go to Lucky Egg. Try the pan-fried gnocchi.

'Lucky Egg,' I say, jabbing him in the arm with my elbow. 'Your favourite.'

The message is accompanied with two thumbs-up emojis.

'It's just a little odd,' he says.

'What?'

'I'm sure it's nothing. It's just they both started Facebook profiles less than a year ago. At around the same time.'

'Is it any weirder than the couple who booked for next month who had a shared Facebook page?' A yawn seeps out of me.

'I suppose not,' he says, but the way he says it, still staring at the page, makes me think he's not sure at all. He turns back to me. 'Most of her followers on Instagram have private accounts.'

'You checked out her followers?'

He shrugs. 'I've been conditioned to be suspicious of strangers.'

'I know,' I say. 'But this is paranoia now.'

'Alright, bedtime.'

I can see through his neutral expression to the uncertainty beneath, a strong current somewhere deep, despite the stillness of his face. 'I actually came down to say goodnight,' I say. 'And to say good news about Axel and Claire. They'll be great parents.' The words have a bitter quality, artificially sweet. When we're in bed together, for what seems the first time in weeks, I forget about Daniel, my necklace, the predicament. I'm simply myself, present in that moment as I reach for him. He seems to anticipate it and before we've kissed, before we've had time to do anything else, he's inside of me. I need him now, I need his support and love. He's breathing close to my ear and his fingertips dig into my hips. It's how it was all those years ago, how it used to be. His blood is running hot. Just for a moment Lucy Swallow rises through the sensations, I look at my husband's laboured face behind me. His muscled, scarred body, rocking. His eyes are barely open and it occurs to me that he's imagining me as her. I groan with him. I imagine I am Lucy Swallow, just how he's picturing. It's odd to admit but as that deep rush comes on, I like being her.

Peephole
Live Cam Premium
Stream: 033C
Viewers: 013

Fruitdrop: What did I miss?

Whiteknight: wife and husband were going at it. Child is in the
                       bath now.

Fruitdrop: I can't see the bath.

Thefinisher: Cam 7

Fruitdrop: ah there we go. what a sweetie, might stay here
                       for a while and get a look at him.

Thefinisher: Is there anything happening on any other streams?

Fruitdrop: Big girl was in Stream 32B, they were fucking all
                       day but they've checked out now. No one else in

there yet. There's a new channel, Stream 37B, old house by a lake. Nothing live yet but we will have a new peephole soon.

Thefinisher: Mmm, goodie.

TEN

'IT'S FINE,' HE says now down the phone. Cain is at the lake house cleaning up after our first guests, Dan and Cherry. 'Nothing broken or stolen, dishes cleaned, sheets stripped.'

It feels like a miracle. My fears of the house disappearing in an inferno and taking every memory of my grandparents were unfounded. Sometimes things aren't nearly as bad as we expect them to be.

'Cherry left us a lovely note,' Cain adds, 'and the recycling was all out too.'

'Make sure you leave them a positive review,' I say, eyeing Scotty beside me as he takes a bite out of his burger. He gives a small nod of acknowledgement. We've been talking about my anxieties about the guests and the house all day, in between calls.

'Seems too easy now, doesn't it?' Cain says. 'I'll quickly set it up again and hit the road.'

I hang up and take up my chicken wrap. When we've finished I turn to Scotty.

'Can we quickly duck to the post office?'

'Which one?' he asks.

'Mount Eden?'

He screws up the wrapper of his burger, puts it in the paper bag on the floor and starts the ambulance. *Too easy.* So why do I feel this unease? I think about the way we're using the lake house, hardly what my grandparents had in mind when they left it to me. We've scrubbed any trace of them from the house.

'Here we are,' Scotty says.

The Mount Eden post shop, like everything these days, has diversified their offer. It's easier to find books, toys, *As-seen-on-TV* merchandise than it is envelopes and stamps. I wait in the queue, inching forward. When I get to the front the man simply raises his eyebrows.

'Hi,' I say. 'I'd like to open a PO Box.'

'What size?'

'Sorry?'

'What size? We only have letter size left. Is this for packages or letters?'

'Letter size is fine.'

'Right,' he says. 'It's two hundred and forty-five for the year and you'll need to fill out this form.' He bends, searches the shelves beneath the register, extracts a sheet of paper. 'And I'll need a copy of some ID.'

'ID?' I say. 'But PO Boxes are anonymous, right?'

'To the public, yes.'

I turn back. Scotty is a couple of people behind in the queue with a roll of stamps in his hand.

Two hundred and forty-five dollars, I think, *and it's not guaranteed to work.* But I'm desperate. Why else would I do this with Scotty? I need to do it today.

'Right, so no one could know it was me?'

'No one except us,' he says. 'And, of course, the police, if you were to use it for illegal activity.' His eyes seem to narrow slightly.

'Nope,' I say. 'I've got a crazy ex is all.'

'Right. If you wouldn't mind filling it out over there so I can continue.'

'Sure,' I say, stepping away. The queue moves forward.

After I've filled the form, paid and collected my new key, the man takes me to the side of the building where the rows of PO Boxes are and shows me which is mine.

'Great. One last thing,' I say, as he's turning to stride back inside. 'Do you sell sim cards?'

•

When we get back to the ambulance, Scotty says, 'So what's all that about?'

'Oh,' I exhale. 'We've just noticed some of our mail has gone missing, no big deal.'

'Right,' he says, with a small smile. 'And the sim card?'

'I'm changing my number. Telemarketing, you know how it is.'

He gives me a look. He's not buying it. 'You're not making a run for it?'

I conjure my best fake laugh. 'As if,' I say. The radio bleeps. We accept the call. Scotty reaches forward and starts the ambulance, hits the siren and lights, then we are moving again.

On the way I take my mobile phone out and find that message. *I have my ways.*

As Scotty races through traffic, siren blaring, I draft the message, deliberating over each word before hitting send.

Hi Daniel,
Sorry I haven't gotten back to you! my father is very ill and I am going to care for him over the next weeks or possibly months. I'd love a drink and catch up when I get back but I won't have the time or energy to do anything until then. That necklace and ring are family heirlooms and if he took a turn for the worst, I'd like to have it with

me so I need it urgently. For now would you be able to send it in the
post? This is my mailing address.

I add my brand-new PO Box and a series of x's at the end of the
message for good measure. He may not send it to me, he may insist
on waiting and giving it back when I return, but it's worth a shot.
I don't know how much longer I can lie to Cain about it. What if
he offers to pick up the resized ring from the jewellers? How long
does it take to get a ring resized anyway?

The ambulance lurches as Scotty presses the brake hard, I look
up and find we're parked outside a tiny brick flat.

'This is the one,' he says.

I shove my phone in my pocket and climb out, striding towards
the door.

The call is an elderly widower. Every paramedic has these cases.
Lonely elderly people who call in for emergency assistance for false
ailments, whether they believe them to be false or not. Some have
other issues – mental health conditions, chronic pain – but almost
all of them are simply lonely. Today I'm the lead. I find the woman
lying alone in her living room. She had triggered the emergency
alarm she wears on her wrist.

She's eighty-seven and has lived alone for twenty-one years. Most
of the people in this block are elderly. The flats are single level, most
single bedroom by the looks of them. Ramps installed out front.

'Hello, Anne,' I say, crouching down on the floor. 'What's
happened?'

'I've had a spill,' she says. I check her over then gently help her
to her feet and run through her vitals; nothing is amiss. We get
her to the couch. She's not moving entirely freely but she's doing
well for her age.

'Everything looks okay, you be careful in the future.'

'Before you go,' she says. 'Would you put the kettle on for me?'

Scotty and I share a look. 'Well,' he says. 'If you're having a cuppa, mind if we stay for one? We've been run off our feet today.'

He's got that big grin going now and the light through the door illuminates his ginger hair. There's something about the way he talks today, the care he takes with his consonants, speaking slowly like they might shatter in his mouth. And he completes each small task, like pushing his torch back into his belt, with exaggerated care.

'We've got time, don't we, Lina?'

It seems like a kindness, but the cynic in me suspects it's laziness. We can't accept another call until we are done here and Scotty might be killing time to bring about the end of the shift faster. I give him the benefit of the doubt. 'Sure.'

'Oh that would be lovely,' she says. 'I've got some biscuits somewhere here too.'

I'm there on Anne's plastic-wrapped couch beside Scotty who looks ridiculous with his saucer and tea rested on his thighs, when my phone vibrates again. I pull it out to find another message from Daniel.

Yeah, I think I can do that. When would you need it by? It might be easier for me to drop it off to you. Are you out at work or are you off today? It gives me pause. 'Out' is a curious word to use. I told him I worked at Middlemore hospital, so why would I be *out*. Does he mean out as in 'unavailable'? Is this yet another coincidence like the Rotorua connection, or something else? He never told me how he got my number.

Something feels off but I can't fixate on it. I've got work to do.

Yes I'm working and I've got long shifts until I go. It will probably be too difficult to meet up and I'm really not in the mood for company, sorry. Let's catch up when I get back. xx.

Scotty quickly uses the bathroom, then we head back to the ambulance. It's late in the afternoon when we leave but another job comes through. A family barbecue. The father's birthday. Suspected stroke, paralysis on his left side. I sound the siren, racing through traffic. It's just starting to rain and on the windscreen specks of water appear, grow tails, slide up.

The family is at the bowls club, the flat manicured greens are empty as the rain comes down but I can see masses of people inside. Scotty climbs out, rushes to the entrance as I park the ambulance. I run towards Scotty who is kneeling down beside the man. A woman, I assume the wife, is sobbing while another man holds her. Children are nearby, little brown-headed things with thunderclouds passing over their faces.

'Thank God you're here,' says a burly man with muttonchop sideburns coming forward through the crowd. 'He just collapsed; he was on his way inside to get a beer.'

The patient can't be any older than fifty. Scotty is focusing intently on his stethoscope as he unwinds it to check the man's vitals, while I chat with the burly man. *Come on, Scotty, hurry up.*

'How long did you wait before calling us?'

'Someone called straight away,' he says, without pausing. 'The moment he collapsed we knew something was wrong.'

'Did he do anything before he collapsed? Did he hit his head or stumble?'

His eyes find the ceiling as he thinks. 'Shit, what did he do? He sort of reached up like this.' His hand comes to his sternum.

The observations suggest a stroke, the fact the left half of his body is frozen supports this. He's conscious but can't move. One half of his face is screwed up as if in agony and the other hangs, frozen and melted. But why did he reach for his heart?

'Definite stroke,' Scotty announces. 'Let's load him up.' He's not even finished checking his vitals.

I turn back to the man. 'He grabbed his chest?'

'Yeah,' he says. 'Right before it happened.'

'Scotty, what was the blood pressure?'

'Eighty-five over ninety-seven. Not too bad.'

'Check again,' I say, the urgency in my voice springing tears from the daughter, who can't be older than seven. The mother moves to the children, her hands gripping their shoulders. I turn back to Scotty.

'That doesn't make sense,' he says as the reading comes up, his eyes slowly rise to mine. 'Eighty over seventy.'

'Heart rate?'

'Ninety-two, I think.' A tiny shake of the head.

'Get the stretcher, I'll take over.'

'What?' he says.

Scotty's still not right, I saw it at that woman's house. A slowness about him, a silly smile he almost never wears. He's missed the signs here. 'I'm taking the lead. I've seen a case like this before.'

I remember it from medical school before Grandpa died and I dropped out. The patient's blood pressure is falling because he's bleeding somewhere. If I'm right then this isn't a stroke at all. I lower my ear to his mouth, he's hardly breathing. Triple A. Abdominal aortic aneurysm. It comes to me like an elbow to the throat. His right subclavian artery is torn, it feeds blood to the left side of the brain which is why he's frozen down that side as if from a stroke. We've got minutes at most to get him to surgery.

I turn to the wife. 'Get the kids out, now.' The hospital is close. I radio, brief them for our arrival. Scotty is running the stretcher back. I've got to get the patient breathing again by releasing the blood that's filling his chest, pressing down on his lungs, before the pressure impedes his heart.

'Ventilate him, Scotty,' I say. Then again to the mother. 'Get them out now.' Finally she pulls the children away. They don't need to see this.

Scotty gets the tube down his throat, starts the ventilator. I take a scalpel; this is the part these children would never forget if they were to see it. A lifetime of nightmares. I cut his shirt away, insert the scalpel just below the ribs to make an opening. Finger thoracostomy. I've not done one in years, but when I move the tip of my finger in through the gap in his skin and feel the hot rush of blood spray out, I know it's worked. The pressure slowly eases as the blood continues to drain from between the chest wall and lungs. Scotty, eyes wide now, rallies a second man to help us get the patient onto the stretcher. My finger is still there, holding the gap open to allow the blood to escape as we get him into the ambulance. He won't die of asphyxiation now, but he's a very high chance of bleeding out. I climb in, close up the doors and Scotty shoots us out through the parting traffic, the siren screaming, the wheels humming over the wet road.

The man's blood pressure is still crashing. I peel his eyelid back, see the black ring, all pupil. That familiar sinking feeling inside me. The brain pressure has collapsed the iris. Brain death is now the best-case scenario. As we're pulling into the hospital, I think about the children and feel the heat at the back of my eyes, unwanted tears forcing their way to the surface, but I won't let them. A parent gone. I sniff, scrape my eyes across each shoulder before Scotty opens the back doors and pulls the stretcher out.

I know he's a goner before the surgeons even start. I know that if we were faster today, if we picked it earlier and got him here sooner, he would have a chance. Not much chance, but *a* chance.

After we've finished at the hospital, we climb back into the ambulance. In the dark of the car park before I set out, I say Scotty's name. He turns to me. I raise my flashlight and aim it at his eyes, he brings his hand up to block the bright light but it's too late, I've seen what I expected. He was slow to blink, his pupils slow to contract and slow to dilate when he blocked the light. He's medicated.

'What are you doing?' he says, irritated.

'What have you taken?'

'What?'

'You're on something,' I say. 'You've been off the last couple of weeks but it's worse today. We missed our shot with him.'

He scoffs. 'Come on, let's go. Nothing would have saved that man and we don't have time for this.'

'I don't care what you do at home, that's your business, but you can't have *anything* in your system when you turn up for work.' I feel like my entire body is vibrating with anger. 'Whatever you're on, it needs to stop.'

'You don't know what you're talking about,' he says, again that narcotic smile, only now it's touched with menace.

'Oh I know. You can lie, but your eyes, your irritability don't. You're on something.'

'You've got the wrong end of the stick. We all have our off days, Lina.' He shows me his teeth again, his eyes widen, and those light eyebrows climb up his forehead. 'And I happen to know for a fact *you* are not so squeaky clean yourself, are you?'

My stomach drops, the radio crackles with a new call and I shift the ambulance into gear.

'Just try to keep it together.'

ELEVEN

AFTER MY SHIFT, I run to clear the tension in my body – my calves, clenched fists, my hips aching to move. I think about tomorrow, my next shift: twelve hours in one vehicle with Scotty. I could always ask to switch – it's not easy but possible. Sometimes if you change stations, you end up passed around different partners on different shifts until something permanent opens up.

I start my run on the MyTrack app and set out down the stairs, under a pink twilight sky, with my headphones in and my phone strapped to my upper arm. I pick up the pace. Everywhere I run is well lit, but whenever I see someone, particularly men, nearby I pause my podcast and my senses peak.

Grandma was a firm believer in motion for unlocking stress, clearing illness and bad moods. Cold? Run it out. Headache? Run it out. Butterflies? Run it out. She died when I was fifteen. Grandpa died when I was twenty-one. The two most significant moments of my pre-adult life. Mum gave me nothing, other than a penchant for dark spirits which haunted me through university and my early twenties. I never knew my dad and she gave me up to my grandparents, then left home or was kicked out. I never got the full story. Then, when I was around eight years old, a short custody battle ended in favour of my grandparents. The times Mum was around she was either drinking or mean. I'm *nothing* like her.

My shoes strike the pavement as I recall those tough years. I take my usual trail down towards the harbour, lengthening my stride out beneath the streetlights. There are almost no other runners despite the fact it's still early – my usual runners' group has been and gone today. On the road nearby, cars pass. I don't venture from the footpath, never veering too far into the shadows. I run at a level where I can still think clearly and breathe in through my nose. I think about Daniel.

I deleted the dating app. I'd not given him my number or met him near my place. I concealed everything that could have identified the real me. I found someone who didn't live in Auckland full-time, someone outside of my social circles, age group. Someone who seemed normal. Funny, he probably thought the same thing about me. But obviously I'm not normal.

My purse was on me at all times. Well, sort of. It wasn't on me when we had sex, and I suppose when I got up to go to the bathroom or when I slept. In his drunken state could he have gone through my things and seen my ID for the ambulance service? Could he have taken my necklace as a way to organise another meet-up?

What if he turned up at the house? What if he met Cain?

And there's something else. I feel *different*. It feels how it did last time. But now the knocking in my chest grows fierce. The emotions have been deeper, much more sudden. The loss of the father today had brought tears, something that hasn't happened since my first few months in the ambulance. And my energy levels have felt a little low.

I'm close to home. I feel like if I keep running I'll faint, so I walk briskly towards the house. Dizziness swirling the streetlights. It's unfamiliar, this feeling. A new drug. A sort of motion sickness but it's not quite the same. It might have worked. It might have *actually* worked.

Cain's car is there. He's home from Tarawera.

I find him in the study at his desk. Despite how much I slow my breathing, my heart continues to pound. I just stand there and watch as he opens a window and a horse race pops up, the rapid voice of the announcer comes through the speaker. He leans forward on his forearms, while I observe him.

'Come on,' he says. 'Come on, get up!' He leans closer and closer. 'Oh shit.' He clicks his tongue when the race ends. He gently knocks his fist against the table. 'You lame bastard.'

He must be gambling again. But I have my own secrets. And if this pregnancy lasts, if I am pregnant then none of this will matter. Our lives will be back on track.

He closes the window and pulls up a spreadsheet. I've not seen it before and have no idea what it's for but it's clearly something to do with his work.

'Knock, knock,' I say.

He turns back. 'Lina,' he says, trying to smile. 'How long have you been home?'

'I just got in,' I say. 'I've been out for a run. Is the house all ready for this weekend?'

'Yep. Still can't believe how spotless it was.'

'That's great.'

He narrows his eyes. 'What's with the smile?'

I can't tell him yet. I can't get ahead of myself; I need a test and it might not last. I'll need to wait until I can get to the doctor. 'I'm fine. Just went a little too hard.' I try to laugh, he's not buying it.

'Right,' he says. 'How fast?'

'Sorry?'

'How fast did you run?'

'Oh,' I say, taking my phone from the case strapped to my arm. I open the MyTrack app. Six kilometres in 25.41. I notice then that I have six new notifications on my running app. I never get notifications. I try to swallow the stone growing at the base of my throat, but it only seems to make it heavier. It feels like I can barely draw air down into my lungs.

'Well?' he says.

'Four minutes ten per kilometre,' I say.

'Pretty good,' he adds, dropping down onto the leather couch and taking up the remote. We used to run together before Cain's deployment. He once ran a marathon in a little under three hours.

I click the tiny red number six in the app. Someone has liked all of my runs from the past month. *Daniel Moore.* It's as though my body knew this was coming. And yet this can't be happening. But it *is* happening. The runs start and end at the same point so he knows where I live. He knows my real name, my full name. Does he recognise a pattern? Every second or third day at around 5.30 pm. Or at midday when I'm working night shifts.

Cain is close, I could just tell him. He would help me, after the storm of rage, the explanation, the regret. If he doesn't leave me, if I can hold on to him, he will help. But that's a big ugly *if.* The sort of *if* I'd never risk. He won't understand why I did it. My desperation to save *us,* what we have.

I change my runs to private, that way no one can see them but me. *Breathe slowly, Lina.* I'm still gaping at the phone while Cain strides past me out towards the kitchen, the lounge.

'I'm going to have a shower,' I say, feeling the sweat running down my cheeks.

'Sure, I'll get dinner on soon.'

The room shrinks. *This is everything you wanted.* Not like this. This could all blow up. *Cain will never know, you can protect him. You will have a child. You can move to Tarawera and start a family.*

You can delete all your social media profiles, go offline. The doctors had always told us it would take a miracle and now, for the second time, we have the miracle. There is a long way home from here, I know, but if I can just escape Daniel, and keep this secret, we will be a family. Our problems will evaporate. I'll give the baby everything I never had. Two loving parents. A quiet, happy life.

But we lost the baby the last time I fell pregnant. *It will all work out*, I tell myself now, *it will be worth it in the end*. The planning, the choosing, the deception and guilt. Cain told me he could never raise someone else's kid. *I couldn't do it knowing the real parents were out there in the world.* One of his rules, I suppose. It hurt to hear, it seemed so out of character and shut down the conversation about sperm donors. But this way he will never know our baby might not technically be *his*.

I close my eyes for a moment, just standing there. 'Oh also I was thinking about getting a new number,' I say. 'For my phone.'

'Why would you do that?' he says, without looking up from the couch where he's sitting.

'Telemarketing calls, happens all the time at work.'

'I've not noticed,' he remarks.

'Yeah, it's just gotten bad the last couple of weeks. No big deal but it's the easiest way to make them stop.'

'You'll have to message everyone, let them know.'

Stay the course, be vigilant. Cain and I will get through this, we will be a happy family just how we had planned all those years ago before it all went wrong.

Peephole
Live Cam Premium
Stream: 031B
Viewers: 017

There are three of them in the room as seen from camera 9, angled down at the bed. He has brought the bottle of wine up with him, almost empty now. They've been drinking most of the afternoon. Flirting on the couch, passing a joint between them in the candlelight. Polishing off a couple of bottles of wine, they sway and hold each other, laughing as he falls against the wall halfway up the stairs – 19 viewers. Now in the bedroom he falls back, his arms come to rest beside his face, bending, cradling his head – 40 viewers. The woman with the long dark hair climbs on him first. She pulls her top over her head and tosses it towards the door. She scrapes her hair back away from her face as she bends, folds over the man to kiss him – 51 viewers. His hands move to her waist, pulling her hard against him. The second woman climbs onto the bed beside him now. She unbuttons his shirt, and quite suddenly he sits up, his hand knotting through the woman's dark hair. His lips find her throat – 63 viewers.

TWELVE

THERE IS A silent peace treaty between us for the next two shifts. Scotty is lucid, much more switched on than before but also much less chatty. Probably for the best, I try to tell myself. I don't need a friend in this job, just someone I can rely on. And that's how it is now, all business again, as it was when we first partnered up years ago. I work with a little more caution, always thinking of the baby.

After my last shift for the week, I head home. We're off to Tarawera this weekend to tidy up after the last guests. Cain was going to do it alone, but I insisted on heading down this time and making a weekend of it. I'm going to tell him about the baby at Tarawera; I'm going to raise the issue of his gambling and begin to plan our future. I'm not angry but I am concerned about the fact he's betting again. And that he's kept it from me. How much has he lost?

I can't blame him. He's always looking at ways of making a little more money. There are no SAS privileged payments for injuries incurred in conflict. His pension, when he was still receiving it, was for eighty percent of his wage for three years. That's all they gave him. Now he's only eligible for a general disability benefit of a couple of hundred dollars a week. That's quite a fall from grace when you think about the money he used to earn. He'd told me, with a bitter laugh, he would never take the dole, and he shouldn't have to. But he's not making any more money working.

When I check the mail I see something that freezes the blood in my veins. It's in our letterbox. A few bills, junk mail. And something else. An image. I feel like I could throw up. It's of me . . . and Daniel. The ground oscillates beneath me. He took a photo of us. Together. Then he printed it on this card, found out where I lived from my MyTrack account and delivered it. But the image is from inside the house, shot from the ceiling as if from a surveillance camera. I turn it over and see five words written on the back.

Does Cain know about us?

I search the street with my eyes, every window and door all the way to the end. *Where is he? Did he put this here?* I shove the photo in my bra. Marching straight to the bathroom, I lock the door, rip it up and flush it down the toilet. What if Cain had found this? It could end my marriage.

'Lina,' Cain calls from somewhere in the house. I go to the basin, splash water on my face and eye myself in the mirror. *He doesn't know*, I tell myself. *He didn't see it, otherwise his voice wouldn't be so light.* But he could have seen it. And what then? Our marriage would be over. My life would be over. Another surge of guilt, it feels like grief. But there's nothing to grieve. Nothing has happened. I could contact the police, does this qualify as harassment?

'Lina,' he calls again.

'One moment, just on the loo.'

A few deep breaths, I flush again then I open the door and head towards the kitchen where I find him sitting on a stool at the island.

'Hey darling,' he says, rising and kissing my forehead.

'Hi,' I say, relieved to find he's normal, nothing amiss.

'I want you to see something.'

He has his laptop open and he shows me a Facebook page, it belongs to one of the last guests.

'What is it?'

'Read this.' His finger lands on the screen, a review.

Stayed at the best WeStay on the weekend on Lake Tarawera. Would recommend it to everyone.

How can I feel pride, how can I feel anything other than this sickly anxiety? It's the photo, the fact an image like that exists. Could I claim it was photoshopped if Cain ever did see it?

Cain scrolls down. *Dream retreat and we have the place all to ourselves.* In another photo, the woman is in our bathroom. I wince seeing how dirty the mirror looks in the camera flash. Next is a man in our bed, his scruffy hair poking out of the sheet, flattening the pillow. In the background you can see the lake.

He continues scrolling through the images. Two glasses touching in front of the fire. The glasses are full of white wine.

These photos are getting twenty to thirty likes. Low numbers but then again Lucy Swallow doesn't have *that* many followers.

'So should we leave them a review?' I say.

'Wait until after we've seen the state of the house,' he responds. He changes the subject. 'How was work?'

'Good,' I say, trying to smile. Trying to block out the rising siren of panic. 'Actually I'm a bit worried about Scotty.'

'What do you mean?'

'I mean he was off at work, I thought maybe fatigued but now I'm certain he was taking something.'

'What, like smoking pot before a shift?'

'Yeah maybe, or painkillers. We had a call the other day, he misread it as a stroke. If Scotty wasn't high I feel like we could have saved him. I mean the chances go from zero to maybe one percent, but that's still a chance.'

He closes his eyes for a moment, gives a slow nod. 'Mmm, sounds like he needs to pull his head in.'

'I could report him. I *should* report him. I made it clear that I knew what was going on and he's been better these last two shifts since then. It's always awkward with guys like that. He's more senior. But if it happens again, I'll have to report him. Otherwise I'm culpable too.'

He turns back to his laptop. 'Not your job to babysit him if he's getting high before work. Maybe just keep an eye on him to see if it happens again. That's odd,' he says abruptly, checking his phone.

'What?' I say, moving towards him.

'The last guests used almost no power. Just a little spike in the morning by the looks of it.' He's on the power app.

'That is odd,' I say, distracted.

'Maybe they ate out, used the candles when they were home,' he says but I'm barely listening.

Changing my phone number wasn't enough, I need to do something to block Daniel permanently. Cain looks up at me now, really looks at me. 'If you're worried about it, maybe ask to change partners?'

I realise I'm frowning. I feel sick, lightheaded. 'It'll be fine,' I say. But it's not. I finally have what I've wanted all these years, I'm finally pregnant. But there's a photo of me and Daniel together out there. Everything is wrong.

THIRTEEN

WE'RE ALMOST AT the house now. Axel was over last night, he and Cain had a couple of beers and graduated to whiskies at around 9 pm. The old stories came out, while they watched the rugby. Cain took some waking this morning, then was grumpy for not getting away earlier.

'Why do you want to stay so bad? There's supposed to be a big storm tonight,' he says to me now.

'It's nice down here,' I respond. That's not the only reason. After finding that photo I've been terrified in the house, like someone is out there waiting to spring another surprise on me. Down here it's isolated, quiet, *private*. And I want to tell him about the baby, talk about our future, practise being a family in a home we actually own. I know it's early and I know we can still lose the baby but I want him to feel the excitement. Our plans are back on track.

My period hasn't come, it's days late. I can finally let go of all the doubt, all the fear that it's just in my head. I feel like I should be wrapped in cottonwool, buried beneath blankets, mindful of keeping myself and this cluster of cells inside me safe. It's growing. It's mine.

'Why don't you want to stay?' I ask him.

He shrugs one shoulder, his other arm is straight out before him holding the wheel.

'I guess it's just a pain to change sheets twice and clean up after ourselves. And like I said, it's going to bucket down tonight.'

'It's nice sleeping out here when it's raining,' I say.

'Maybe you're right. I guess it would be nice to stay.'

Along our road, with the swaying ferns and native bush on one side, glimpses of the shimmering lake through the trees on the other, I get that same feeling I had last time. I'm silent as we pass the spot, at the bend where the cliff drops away to the lake and the new rail is. The house could be in any state. I imagine it trashed, scratches deep in the floorboards, burn marks on the rug, stained sheets. WeStay holds the bond for ten days after checkout but that doesn't help when it's only one thousand dollars. You could lose tens of thousands of dollars in one weekend. Flood the upstairs bathroom, rot the floorboards, steal the furniture. Burn the house down and leave the country. Not for the first time this week I think about my grandfather, his silver ponytail, skin spotted but eyes still sharp all the way to the end. How would he feel knowing the place was being filled and emptied with strangers every week?

Cain parks beneath the deck, and cranes his head up. 'You can't see anybody from here?' he says, grinning.

'Don't joke, Cain. It's not funny.' Ever since that night I thought I saw a man near the lake, he's taken every opportunity to remind me of my paranoia. If only he knew that I have a real stalker, someone who knows my secret, my phone number and address. *What would you do then, Cain?*

We climb out and I follow him inside. It should be special, this moment, being back at the house, my grandpa's home as a pregnant woman once more. It should be exciting, imagining the life we will soon have here, but it's not. It's tainted by my fear of Daniel, and the memory of losing the last baby, the blood and the clot on the bathroom tiles. That slow drip over the following days, emptying me out. It's still so raw it might have happened yesterday.

The place is . . . spotless. It seems almost as clean as we left it, the floors mopped, free of shoe prints. A few dishes sit on the drying rack. The table is clean with the bottle of wine we left out at its centre, unopened. It's as though no one was here at all.

'I feel like it's too tidy,' I say.

Cain raises his hand, focusing on something on the dining table. A slip of paper. He crosses to it and picks it up.

'What is it?'

When he holds it out, I see messy, rushed handwriting. Almost as messy as a doctor's scrawl.

We just loved our time here. We will definitely be back.
Thank you.

They haven't left us a review yet, but they wrote us a note.

'Odd,' I say.

'It is.' He drops the note. It falls through the air, swinging back and forth with the languid cut of a cello's bow pass, then comes to rest on the floor. 'Let's get tidying.'

'Tidy what? It's tidy already.'

'We should still vacuum, and we will have to do the sheets for the guests coming next weekend.'

He goes to the kitchen, pulls the fridge open. 'They've used the milk.' He holds the open carton up to me.

'I'll do upstairs,' I say.

'You can relax if you like.'

'No, I came to help. I insist.'

Cain's phone pings. 'Speak of the devil,' he says. 'Their review has just come through.'

He hands me his phone and I read it aloud.

'*A gorgeous house on the lake. Great amenities and very tidy.* That's nice I guess. A bit formal.'

'Hard to please, aren't you? Do you want to write them a review now?'

I click their WeStay profile, to see what other reviewers have said about them. The reviews are all great. Every single host has mentioned their cleanliness.

It's like they never stayed, one review says. Then I see something that causes my heart to stop. A room I recognise. I swallow, but when I do, an itch starts at the back of my throat. I cough, and my eyes water. I feel sick.

'You alright?'

I pat my chest and Cain goes to the kitchen. When he returns he rests his hand on my spine and holds a glass of water out for me. I take it, and sip. My eyes are fixed on his phone in my hand. It's the same place, I can tell by the photo. That house Daniel took me to. But I've changed my number, I've deleted the app and his messages. There is nothing to trace me back to him. *But obviously there is, he has my address, someone stayed both here and at the WeStay he took me to.* It occurs to me now, if he saw my runs on MyTrack in the city, he must have seen them down here too. *He has this address. He was in Rotorua the last time we were here.*

'Just an itch at the back of my throat,' I say. I pull my shoulders back, run my hand down my face to straighten it out. He takes the phone from my hand.

'I can write the review.'

'Sure.'

Nothing makes sense, everything is wrong. I thought I was safe here, hidden away, but I'm not. *He knows.* A weight presses down on my chest. Or could it be a simple coincidence?

'*Left our place clean and tidy. A pleasure to host and would recommend.* How does that sound?'

'Good,' I say. 'Fine.' I thought I was playing Daniel, but I'm beginning to see he might have been playing a different game altogether.

FOURTEEN

I CLIMB THE stairs, check the rooms. They're all . . . perfect. It's almost as though no one has been here at all. All of the bedrooms, with one exception, are tidy. The covers on the queen bed in the master are ruffled and there is something else: a single black hair lying across one of the pillows. It's so odd, because neither of the guests had black hair in their photos. I have black hair but there is no way my hair could be on this pillow.

I open the wardrobe and, as the doors swing, something nails my feet to the floor. I'm looking at a dress. Black, knee-length and long-sleeved. It's Witchery, I know this because I've seen this dress. I've *worn* this dress. I reach out and touch it. It's hanging there like a body before me. The dress I wore the night I met Daniel. The same one I had folded up and left in the boot of my car then stowed in the bottom of my wardrobe. *But did I check it was definitely in that bag?* I realise I've been holding my breath. I let it out but there's nothing there, just a tightness. Is it possible Cain found the dress? Decided to hang it up and forgot to tell me? I can hear him coming up the stairs. Daniel can't have taken the dress that morning because I saw it in my bag at home. I quickly slam the wardrobe closed. Turn so my back is against the door.

'How do the rooms look?' he says.

'The beds are made, except this one is a little messy. The rooms are perfectly tidy too.'

'Easy money, eh?'

'Yeah, kind of. Just feels like something's off.'

'Off?'

'Look.' I point to the pillows.

Cain leans over the bed, looks down at the hair.

'So?' he says.

'Remember their photos? Neither of them had black hair.' It doesn't make sense. A blonde woman and a man with a shaved head. This is a black hair.

'I think you're overthinking it.'

'It's not their hair,' I say.

'Maybe someone else stayed with them, it's not the end of the world.'

'This isn't a joke.' The dress in the wardrobe, the stay at the other WeStay, it's making my head spin and my heart race but I can't let him know why this hair is so significant.

'Maybe there were two couples and they didn't want to pay for the extra guests. Is that a possibility, Lina? This is why I should do these cleans myself. So you don't get paranoid.'

'Two couples, but they only used one bed?'

He sighs, long and slow.

I continue speaking. 'How would you miss a dark hair on a white pillow if you wanted to tidy up after yourselves?' Would he recognise the dress as mine? He'd just say that I accidentally left the dress here.

'Forget about it, Lina.' Cain plucks the hair with his finger and thumb. He goes to the window, opens it and casts the hair outside.

'Let me manage the house so you don't have to stress. Just remember we're now four hundred dollars better off.' Cain takes my upper arms, looks deep into my eyes. 'Everything is fine.'

I try to smile, but it ends up more of a sigh, like letting go of something heavy. I slip into his embrace, feeling safe. 'You're probably right.'

'I *am* right.'

Outside the window, I see someone rowing on the lake, dragging himself through the water. It's the old man from the cafe. A green boiler suit and a bucket hat. He turns, aiming his dark eyes at the house. He continues on.

I twist around in Cain's arms and we stand looking out over the landscape in the shadow of the mountain. I'm still watching the man paddling along as Cain rests his hands on my shoulders, digs his thumbs in and rolls them up to the base of my neck.

'We can go down to Lucky Egg,' he says. 'Make a night of it.' He places his thumb tips just below the occipital bone.

'Okay,' I say, tilting my head. 'Right there.' He presses a little harder. The landscape outside darkens as a cloud moves before the sun. 'Why don't we take that bottle of wine to Lucky Egg tonight?'

'It was for the guests.'

'Their loss,' he says. 'I feel like we need a good drink and a night to unwind.'

I nod but I feel like my emotions are tripwires that I'm going to get snagged on at any moment. Someone is doing this, someone is trying to scare me. It's Daniel. If he has been in the house, hung my dress up like this – what else is he capable of?

FIFTEEN

AS WE HEAD out in the early evening towards Rotorua, I turn my eyes towards the jumping spot; I can't quite see the ladder but I can see a group of boys moving through the trees towards it. It'll be cold, especially in the late afternoon shade, but it's always been a ritual for boys that age out here in the lakes area: rugby on the weekends, driving dusty old cars, drinking at the ski lane and jumping from heights into icy water. It's a particularly Kiwi pastime. Occasionally my mind wanders away from the photo, from the dress, but always my body knows, the trembling energy inside is like an illness, something terminal.

Cain navigates between the lakes all the way into town. We drive past the skatepark, in the twilight there are kids on bikes near the corner, talking, each with one foot on a pedal and one on the ground, others roll by on scooters. I follow Cain's eyes to an old shopfront, long since empty. Above it the latest coat of paint has flecked off and you can make out the block letters that read 'TV Repairs'. Next door, second-hand whitegoods crowd the footpath in front of Billy's Electrical.

They're a different breed in town. Tarawera is surrounded by homes for retirees and weekenders built to accommodate Auckland millionaires. Rotorua is much more working class – tourism operators, loggers, hunters and hospitality workers catering to the constant flow of tourists. The town is big enough to have its own hospital but too small for a professional sports team. Then there are the suburban pockets you know not to venture to, particularly in the evening. The areas described in *Once Were Warriors*. Roads that belong to the gangs, places even the police avoid.

Cain rasps his hand back over his shorn hair. His hairline is tongue and grove, and if he grew his hair out, you'd see how thin it had become. 'Always weird coming back here, things seem to change every time we visit.'

'Like what?'

'The KFC has closed,' he says. Then we both laugh. It's a relief, but once more I remember the dress, the messages, the ring and the flare of joy fades. 'I don't know, it's just the streets. It's like an old friend; we've grown apart and now it's hard to recognise the place.'

I sense it too. Especially at the lake house. In the summer the lake buzzes with engines. More homes dot the water's edge. The old floating boatsheds have all been painted. Everything changes. *What if we went somewhere else? Truly off grid for a while to let things settle. Where else could we disappear to?*

We reach Lucky Egg and grab a table outside, looking over the quiet street. Lucky Egg is quiet for a Saturday. Maybe the weather forecast has scared everyone away. It's on Eat Street, a strip of restaurants near the lakefront in the heart of the town designed, I suppose, to create a carnival dining atmosphere. On weekends it's normally packed with tourists and locals out for a *nice meal*, but the weather's been threatening a storm all day. The restaurant is in an old fire station with vaulted ceilings. Those high, leaning panels of glass keep the rain from hitting the cobbled street. Instead it spots and collects, ripples the sky above, and runs in rivulets to the gutters.

'Storm's coming,' Cain says.

A couple on the table next to us pop a bottle of sparkling wine; he's in boat shoes with one too many buttons undone, and the last remnants of his white hair combed forward.

'Going to be a wet walk back to the hotel,' the man says to us. 'At least we've got champagne.' I don't point out the difference between twelve-dollar sparkling wine and champagne. My mother had the same habit of confusing the two. *On the champers tonight.* It was always excitable, a gleeful grin, a war cry. She probably never tasted a drop of champagne in her life. Only when I was an adult did I realise how sad that was.

The waiter comes over and opens our bottle of pinot, the one the guests left. I raise my hand. 'None for me.' Even if it wasn't about the baby, I don't think I could stomach alcohol.

I note the disappointment in Cain's eyes. 'Oh, you want a cider?'

'No,' I say, just a little annoyed he hasn't realised the significance of why I'm not drinking at the moment. 'Water is fine.' He will understand tonight, when we get back and I give him the news. Will it be the same as last time? Weeks of effervescence, boiling over with plans of the future, endless speculation about what the baby might look like and planning the perfect combination of our traits? *My nose, with your skin and eyes. Definitely your ankles.* Or will it be dulled by the reality of what we went through, what we lost? What if it happens again? Most marriages don't survive the loss of a child. What about the loss of two?

The waiter collects my glass.

'Still or sparkling?'

'Tap is fine,' Cain says.

I raise a finger, turn to the waiter. 'Do you work here every Saturday?'

'Sorry?' he says.

'Were you working last Saturday?'

'Last Saturday night? Yes.'

I smile. 'Oh right, you might have served a couple we know, Lucy and Phil. In town for the weekend from Auckland.'

Cain gives me an incredulous look.

The waiter frowns, thinking. 'Lucy and Phil.' He brings a tattooed hand to his jaw, scratches. 'I think we did have a couple from Auckland. Blonde woman.' He's squinting now as if seeing them.

'That would be them. Phil has short hair.'

'Yeah,' he says, nodding.

'They said they had a lovely meal,' I say.

'I'll pass the message on to the chef. Are they your parents?'

'Parents?' I look to Cain, who closes his eyes now with the tiniest smile. 'No, they're our age, maybe a little younger.'

The waiter holds his cheek, glancing up. 'I must be thinking of a different group.'

After the waiter has left, Cain says, 'And I thought *I* was the stalker.' He tries to make it a joke with a smile, but his brow is furrowed in concern.

I can't tell him what I know, the coincidences that are lining up like dominoes, because I would have to tell him when I last wore that dress, why I stayed at the WeStay in Auckland and where my ring really is. And there's the small matter of the photo.

I notice a group rush in off the street, their jackets held up over their heads to keep the rain off. They look like a family, making their way towards the long table nearby.

I'm not obsessed, I tell myself. *I'm terrified*. The dress. He's been to the lake house. It's not paranoia. Cain is still watching me. He's always been hard to read, but even more so lately.

When we first met, I didn't think he was that into me until we were out with my friends one time. He was taking it slow, too slow, until in a dark, crowded bar full of mostly over-forties swilling wine, 'Go Your Own Way' came on. People filed on to the dancefloor. I said, 'Come on, let's have a boogie.' I took his hand and that contact was enough. Just my hand squeezing his. His self-consciousness seemed to evaporate, he trusted me. Then we were dancing and before long he was kissing me, pressing me against the wall outside the bar. It started to rain but we didn't stop at first. His body so tense and powerful. I remember my hands sliding over the hard muscle of his back. 'Come back to mine,' I said. It's what he was waiting for. No taxis would take us, being drenched like that, so we walked in squelching shoes through the city back to my flat.

'I just want to feel safe at the house,' I say now, 'that's all. And something feels off about the last guests.'

'We can change the entry code if that's what you're worried about.'

'Yeah. Can we do that?' My voice is unnaturally tight.

'Sure. I'll do it tonight.'

I realise other diners are quieter now, listening to us. Cain turns his head, his eyes wandering the street. 'After dinner, I'll check the house properly. I'll make sure there's nothing to worry about, okay?'

I give him a smile. 'Thank you, that would be nice.' I'll need to hide my dress or tell him I hung it there when we arrived.

Cain sips from his glass of wine and screws up his nose.

'No good?'

'Putrid. Lucky we didn't let the guests drink it.'

I take the glass from his hand, sniff it. 'Doesn't smell too good.'

'No,' he says. 'Tastes even worse than it smells.' He takes another sip. 'I'll get through it.'

Cain orders the pan-fried gnocchi in an oily white wine sauce. I go with the lamb bolognaise.

He takes his phone out of his pocket, looking down for a moment, reminding me I've left mine in the car – part of me wanted to put some distance between me and the messages. Now

I wish I had it so I had something to look at too. I need to distract myself from these thoughts about Daniel.

'Maybe I should go get my phone,' I say, 'I haven't received my roster for next month yet. I'm starting to think there's something wrong with my emails.'

Cain looks uninterested.

'Actually, can I use your phone?' I say. 'Just to check quickly?'

He slides it over the table and I sign into the mail app. My roster is still not up and it's a new month in less than a week. It never takes this long.

'Thanks,' I say, handing it back.

When the food eventually comes, Cain is onto his second glass of wine. The taste doesn't seem to be slowing him down too much. 'It's actually much better now, maybe it just needed time to breathe.'

'Sure,' I say. 'Or maybe it's singed your tastebuds with its bitterness?'

'Suits me,' he says. Then he takes another small mouthful.

The wine seems to be getting him drunk quickly. He doesn't even notice I've barely eaten any of my food, I've just moved it around with my fork. There's no way I could keep it down. I can't stop thinking about the dress. Someone at the house. What are they planning to do? The waiter clears our plates.

By the time he comes back over with the menus again, Cain's eyelids are lower and he is breathing heavily.

'Can I interest you both in dessert?'

Cain looks up now, his eyes a little unfocused. 'Um, I'm okay.'

'And for you?'

'No,' I say. 'I'm fine, thanks.'

Cain checks his phone and when he puts it away it takes him a few attempts to get it in his pocket.

'Are you okay?' I ask, peering forward.

He frowns now, blinking rapidly. 'Yeah, I'm just feeling a little sleepy.' The booze is making his consonants wet and slow. *How much did he drink?*

'Cain, have you taken any medication, anything else?'

He shakes his head, closing his eyes as he does so. I know the signs of anaesthetic, he's got something in him, a narcotic. It can't just be the booze.

'Let's get the bill then,' I say, turning back towards the door, searching for the waiter.

I go inside and pay.

'Alright, let's get going.'

Cain stands, turns, stumbles. He slams into the neighbouring table and I clutch him to keep him upright.

'I'm so sorry,' I utter to the diners, my face flushing. 'He's unwell.' Then I say quietly into his ear, 'What's gotten into you?'

I hear the waiter behind me asking, 'Did you want to take the rest of your bottle?'

Cain turns back, his elbow bumping the bottle from the table. It tumbles and explodes on the floor.

'I'm so sorry,' I say. 'Let me tidy it up.'

'No,' the waiter cuts me off. 'It's fine, just leave.'

He must have had some painkillers or something at the house before he drank. He falls against another table. A woman in a dark dress stands abruptly, moving away from her meal and the glass of wine spilling towards her.

'Watch it!' her husband says. Someone else is there, the bartender gets under Cain's other arm and we carry him out into the rain all the way to the car.

'Thanks,' I mutter to the man's back as he rushes towards the cover of the dining area. Then to Cain, 'What's the matter? How much did you drink?' But I know how much he had. It was less than a bottle. I get him into the car; rain runs down the back of my blouse, it drips from my nose. By the time I am in the driver's seat, he is blinking slowly, like a newborn.

He swallows. 'I'm okay,' he says. 'Drank too quickly, that's all.'

'No, it can't be that alone.'

I can look after him, I just need to get him home.

I reach across, buckle him in, then start the car.

SIXTEEN

AS I NAVIGATE through town towards the lake house, the rain thickens, drumming down hard on the roof and bonnet of the car. Blades of water keep passing before the headlights. Cain's cheek is pressed against the passenger-seat window and his breath casts an amoeba of fog that grows and shrinks on the cool glass. I don't want to go back to the house, I want to go home to Auckland. Why didn't I listen to him earlier when he said he wanted to go? Reassured by the soft, rhythmic press of his exhale, I place my hand on his forehead. No temperature. I reach, peel his eyes open. Glance away from the road on a straight. No dilation. He keeps them open for a few seconds, blinking, before closing them again. I take the wheel in both hands. The wine, I realise, is the bottle we left out for the guests. The one they didn't drink. Could the wine have been bad? Could the wine have been open? We simply handed it to the waiter at the restaurant to open and pour.

The storm is swelling, ratcheting up to a feverish lashing of the car. Whipping across the road. I notice headlights behind me as I begin the ascent over the hill towards the smaller lakes, with the redwood forest sprawling out on one side and farmland on the other. I shouldn't go any faster in this weather but with the itch of

143

fear, I urge the car on, pressing the accelerator. We reach the summit and descend now. The headlights behind are bright, then off, then bright again. A car flashing me. It gets close, so close I'm forced to flick the rear-view mirror away, to keep the light from blinding me. Still it's so bright, so close. I squint, my heart pounding. Am I going too slow? Or is it something else? Is it *him*?

'Cain,' I say, panicked. 'Cain, wake up!' I swerve at the last second into Okareka Loop Road, the long way out to Tarawera. For just a moment it feels like the wheels won't grip the wet road. The car skids a little. We swerve. My knuckles ache around the wheel but I don't overcorrect. The car stays on the road.

The other car has stopped following us. A flash in the distance then moments later the rumble of thunder. I exhale. The headlights were just kids messing around, I tell myself. I reach across for Cain's phone, feeling in his pocket, but when I get it out, I find it is flat. I let my breath out and continue on, descending the hills, then around Lake Okareka. My own phone is in the glove box, it might be tricky to get at without stopping. We emerge on the road towards the Blue Lake and finally on around Tarawera towards the house. I slow down, always silent and careful at the cliff bend. It would be easy to go over in this weather, a little too much gas, the tyres losing their grip. Maybe that's what happened all those years ago . . .

There are no other cars. The roads are black and silent beyond the fogged windscreen. I lean a little closer to see properly.

Soon enough we are approaching the house. I ease off the accelerator, indicate and pull in. Part of me expects to see that car, the one that had flashed its lights, there beneath the tree. I park close to the steps and prod Cain's shoulder again. I speak softly, begging him. 'Wake up, Cain, please. We're home now.' Rain is flooding out from the drain beside the house. Another crack of thunder sends my nerves fizzing. The steps and deck are wet. There is no way I will get him inside without waking him first.

'Cain,' I say louder now, gently slapping his face. His lids peel back. 'Come on, up you get. We're home.'

'Home,' he says, dazed.

He looks down as if realising for the first time that he's in the car. I unclip his belt and reach across to open the door. The cool air rushes in and it seems to wake him a little more. When he stands, rain pounds the seat through the open door. I rush around beside him and feel the rain soak through my blouse. Taking him by the arm, I drag him along, up the drenched steps and beneath the eave at the front door. I punch in the code for the lock. It beeps three times. It doesn't work. I try the code again. But once more it beeps three times and doesn't unlock.

'Shit,' I say. 'Wait here.'

The backup key is in a key safe under the deck. I rush to it now. This time the code works, the key falls out and I take it back to the front door. The lock opens with the key and we move inside, dripping on the hard wood. Could the rain have gotten into the lock and caused it to malfunction or has something else happened?

I strip, removing my blouse right there, dropping my shoes. I even unclip my soaking bra. Cain, oblivious, steps forward.

'Wait,' I say. 'Get your shoes off.' He looks down. I go closer, on one knee I untie the laces of his boots, pull them off and toss them back beside the door. 'Stay here a moment.' I rush to the linen cupboard and find towels for us both. Patting his face dry, stripping his jumper, his t-shirt, his pants, I take his clothes and dump them in the washing machine before helping him up the stairs to bed. He falls on the covers in his underwear. There's a glass of water on the nightstand, and I decide I'll take him activated charcoal and a bucket after my shower. I know by the rhythm of his breathing he is already asleep before I even turn the light out, but I'll wake him through the night, check his breathing, his heart rate and feed him water.

Back downstairs I lock the door. The shadows in the corners and my reflection in the glass send my heart racing. I approach the back door slowly, eyes fixed on the lawn outside, and check it is locked. I turn the lights off, before rushing towards the glow coming down the stairs from the bathroom. The darkness presses me on faster, and when I reach the foot of the stairs, I'm almost running.

I stop at the bedroom on the way to the shower. Cain is still now. I fetch warm trackpants and a sleeping shirt to put on afterwards, still aching with fear but pushing through. *There's nothing to be afraid of. It's in your head.* I peel off my underwear and climb into the shower, letting the warmth rush over me, washing the chill from my skin. It almost stings, a good slap of heat. Despite the age of the lake house, the plumbing has always been fine but this shower is fickle, an all-or-nothing hot tap. I twist it a little to cool the water. I just stand there for some time, before reaching for the face cloth to wash my face. I've always taken long showers before bed, only now I can barely summon the energy to clean myself. Soon I reach for the cold tap, twisting it. That's when I hear something. A gentle knock out there in the storm. *Could it have been the pipes groaning?* My gut plunges, that sound again. *A branch knocking the side of the house?* No. I know that sound. That is the sound of footsteps near the front door. Someone is downstairs, I think. *Impossible.* But then I hear the mechanical beep, the grind of the bolt. The front door lock. Despite the heat of the shower, I freeze. Could it be malfunctioning? It has to be because the only other option can't be true: there's someone in the house.

Peephole
Live Cam Premium
Stream: 037B
Viewers: 003

After the man is assisted upstairs, and the woman is in the shower, someone else appears on camera 1. He opens the door gently, then closes it again – 11 viewers. He is wearing a gas mask that obscures his face but you can see him looking up directly at the camera. His hand moves slowly to the small of his back, then when he brings it before him, he is holding a sawn-off shotgun – 29 viewers. He raises his hand, places a finger where his mouth would be beneath the gas mask – 53 viewers. The show is about to begin – 127 viewers.

SEVENTEEN

I FEEL MY pulse in my chest as I turn both taps off and stand listening. The heat leaves my skin, goosebumps rise. I reach for my towel and quickly dry off. I can't call Cain's name, I can't summon the courage to hurl my voice out into the dark, still house. I think about the bunkroom, the ladder downstairs. *Why am I planning an escape? It's all just in my head.* But is it? What if there really was a man at the lake that time? What if someone has been following me?

I pull on my underwear, the old t-shirt I wear to bed and slowly draw the door open. The air carries a chill in the passageway.

'Cain?' I call, softly. 'Are you awake?'

I'm so focused on Cain, I forget about the loose floorboard outside the bedroom. It whines under my foot sending a current over my skin. I press the bedroom door open, the bedside lamp is on and Cain's still there. He has fallen in beneath the covers.

'Cain,' I say, a little louder. I was hearing things. My ears playing a trick on me through the rumbling, pounding storm. Yet it was so clear, I'm sure I heard the lock. Something is on the bedside table, it's so out of place, so absurd as if in a dream. A medical syringe lies on its side, the needle pointing at me. *What is that?* My heart slams, yet still I can barely move. *What is that syringe doing there?*

Did Cain take something? Or – a new thought comes that freezes me – *did someone administer something, someone who is still here?* I step closer, reaching to pull the sheet back. My heart feels like it's bruising with each thud against my sternum. There's another sound. The loose floorboard. My hand is on the sheet but now my heart stops. I brace. I can't move at all.

'He will be fine.' A gasp. My body leaps. I swing around, facing the door and see him. The scream doesn't come; it's a bird trapped in my throat, beating its wings. The shotgun comes up slowly. The barrel stares me in the eye. My feet won't move. Nothing moves.

'Come on,' he says, his voice deep, distorted by the mask strapped to his face. It's a relic from an early war; black rubber, a canister hanging down below the chin. Beyond the two round pieces of glass, like a pair of old coins in a well, I see eyes looking out at me. Deep green eyes. *It's you,* I think. *Daniel.*

'Please . . . Wh-what do you want?' Weakness, that's what this feeling is. A malaise, like falling limp and playing dead.

'We're going to talk,' he says, a voice full of gravel. He's disguising himself, his voice. *That's a good sign.* I'd heard that somewhere. *If they're hiding their face they're planning on leaving you alive.* But what if he's hiding it for some other reason? I'm not prepared to test the theory. He lowers the gun, so the barrel is directed at the floor. He turns, sweeps his arm in a gesture for me to leave the room. My heart is a fist, air is trapped in my throat. How can I move, how can I do anything?

'Come on, little rabbit,' he says. He steps back, and gestures again. In the light of the hallway, his black hood keeps his face and that awful mask in shadow.

'Please,' I say, 'let me go, you can take whatever you want but just don't hurt us. Please don't hurt us.'

'Shh.' A sound like a slow gas leak. I fall silent but my lip quakes. 'I know I can take whatever I want,' he says, showing me my car keys. 'I know that already.' I turn back to Cain, who is still prone, facing away. My phone is in the car, why didn't I grab it? 'He's not waking up any time soon,' he says. 'Downstairs, let's go.'

Impossibly, despite the numbness, my legs respond and I walk past him, my body a struck bell. 'You've been watching me.' Even my voice shakes. 'It's been you.'

'We are all voyeurs, Lina. You included.'

Me? What does he mean? I take the stairs, gripping the handrail tight.

'Up all night, searching your mother's name. Trying to know everything about her. You're just as obsessed as the rest of us.'

I grit my teeth, biting back against the rising anger. It's not due to some protective instinct, but rather the simple fact that this man, this *monster*, possesses my most private secrets. 'How do you know about that?' My head is swimming.

He doesn't answer my question. 'Over there by the fireplace. Sit.'

'No, please just –' The gun barrel comes up to my face again. 'Okay, okay. I'm sorry.' I sit down and see the handcuffs. One end is closed around the foot of the fireplace, the other is sitting loose, open on the tiles.

'Go on, you know what to do.'

'No,' I say, tears coming. 'No, please don't do this.'

'Put it on!' His voice rumbles. I sit down, reach for the handcuff and close it around my wrist. 'Tighter.'

I squeeze it until the cold steel is pressing against my skin all the way around.

He sits on the coffee table near me. Places the shotgun down. 'You're a paramedic, right?'

I just stare at that mask, those green eyes.

'You're Daniel, aren't you?'

'Who I am is not important right now.'

'What did you do to my husband?'

'He's just having a sleep, that's all.'

It comes down on me like a thunderclap. This has been planned. Daniel, or whoever this is, has gone to a lot of trouble. 'What did you do to him?'

'I gave him something, ketamine.'

'How much?'

'I don't know. I put a sedative in the wine, I assume he drank it all. Then I gave him ketamine while you were in the shower.'

Shit. Cain is in trouble. He's mixed anaesthetics. Ketamine overdose is very rare and unlikely but in high enough doses he could choke on his own vomit, or the ketamine could interact with the other sedative and suppress his breathing. 'Please let me help him.'

'You were supposed to have a little each, you were supposed to stay at the house with a mild buzz. Why didn't you drink, Lina? Why did you go out to a restaurant instead of staying here?'

'What was the other sedative?'

He shakes his head slowly. 'I don't know.'

'Tell me, you're going to kill him.'

'That would be a shame, wouldn't it? I know what I'm doing, Lina. I didn't kill him. Not yet.'

I swallow. 'You've not done anything irreversible. You can just let me go, walk out that door. I won't call the police. I won't do anything.'

He pauses, staring out at me, considering it. A hack of laughter now. Then he turns away, picks up the shotgun and strides up the stairs towards the bedroom.

I sit there with my hand cuffed to the fireplace. If I could get my hand free, I could run. There's the front door through the kitchen, or the exit that overlooks the lake. And the third door. Does he know about the side exit? I could slip out through the laundry, past the clothesline and into the bush. Then it's not so far to the road. I pinch all my fingers together, tear at the steel loop over my skin, but it won't go past the joint of my thumb.

He's moving around upstairs. I hear him. Any hope I had of Cain coming out of his stupor and saving me is disappearing. Even if he can wake, with enough ketamine he would likely just sit there, unable to move his legs or arms, scarcely lucid to the world around him.

What does this man want? Why is he doing this?

I hear a tap running then footsteps back down the stairs.

If we buy enough time and Cain comes out of his stupor, he could get to the ladder in the bunkroom, climb down and get out the side door at the back. He could find help. But that's not my husband, he wouldn't leave me here, he would stay and fight. Without a weapon and in the state he's in he wouldn't be too much help. Then I realise this man wouldn't leave him up there without something restraining him anyway, probably another pair of handcuffs.

'Please, just take what you want, I won't call the police, I won't do anything.'

'You'll never call the police about this?'

'No,' I say, a flash of hope. 'No, I promise. Please.'

'But you know who I am, don't you?'

'How could I know?'

He laughs again. Hoarse through the mask. He sits on the couch, places the shotgun down beside him and unclips the keys from his belt, setting them on the table between us.

He holds his phone out so I can see the screen. A video begins playing.

'What is this?'

'Just watch.'

There's something familiar about the room he is showing me. A night-vision lounge room. There's a watermark in the corner of the footage: a small outline of a house with an eye in the centre. Then a flare of light, the camera adjusts, and the scene is thrown into colour. A plunge in my stomach, my gaze leaves the screen, bolts to the man's green eyes again. I take in the shape of him, the bulging shoulders. It is him. It has to be. Why else would I be looking at the house where Daniel took me? I look back to the screen as fresh sparks of adrenaline crackle up my spine. In the video I'm pushing him up against the wall, the view of us is from the ceiling. I'm pinning his hands back, kissing him hard.

'You set it up . . .' He booked the WeStay, he recorded us. What's the end goal? Blackmail? Is it possible that he targeted me somehow? He finds married women and fucks them, then what? The dating app relies on proximity, perhaps he was following me until we matched.

'It looks like you, doesn't it?' he says. 'But it can't be you because you're married.'

'You . . . you were recording? You've been stalking me.'

'Not me,' he says. 'I didn't do the recording.'

'What do you mean? *You* have the footage.'

'I do,' he says. 'Someone shared it with me. When you decided to stop messaging me, I planned this rendezvous, a date you couldn't say no to.'

He taps the screen. Now I see myself afterwards, in the bathroom sitting on the toilet.

'You're a pervert,' I say, staring him in the eye. 'Is this some game? Something you do to women?'

'You did this to yourself, Lina.'

I let out a groan, something deep and atavistic, that trembles through me.

He taps the screen again and I see night-vision footage in the bedroom. I see Daniel. He reaches out and takes my phone sitting on the bedside table. He's doing something, holding it close to his mouth as if talking to it.

'Pretty clever, isn't it? Even when a phone is locked, if Siri is turned on, you can ask it to call a phone number. I asked it to call my phone so I would have your number.'

It makes sense now. On the screen, as he puts the phone back something falls out of my handbag. It's my ID for the ambulance service. He stares at it a moment, then towards the bathroom door and back at the ID before shoving it back into my bag. That's how he got my real name. Did something else fall out? Maybe my necklace and ring?

'Why do this? To punish me for something?'

'This isn't about you, Lina. This is about me. Some people like to watch, but more than that, some people like to control. I *need* control.'

He seemed so normal on the date but it was an act. 'Please, just go. Just leave us alone. I'll forget everything. You can just walk out that door.'

'I'll make you a deal. If you can reach these keys, you can unlock your hands and you can go help your husband. I'll walk out that front door and you'll never see me again.' He nods at the table. His voice is croaky.

I watch him for a moment, dubious. Then I crawl towards the table until the chain is taut. The keys are still far away. Lying flat, I turn and kick my foot out and reach with my toes. They just touch the corner of the wooden table, but I'll never be able to reach the middle where the keys are.

'Go on,' he says. 'Stretch.'

I do. The cuff bites, but I feel no pain. I keep stretching. My body is at its limit, fully stretched out and yet my toes are still two feet from the keys, barely an inch past the edge of the table.

'Too bad.'

I drop to the carpet. Knock my forehead against it. 'Fuck you.'

'I know what you did, I know what sort of woman you are. You think you can have it all but I'm going to give you a simple choice. Him or me?'

I don't hesitate, the anger is coiling in on itself. Growing more intense by the moment like a grudge. 'Him.'

'*Him?*'

'I would *never* choose you over him. He's my husband.'

'Oh,' he says, a teasing note of sadness in his voice. 'That's the wrong answer, Lina. Or are you still going by Anna?'

'Fuck you.'

'I'll give you another chance. Your husband or you?'

'What do you mean?'

'Pick one.'

'No.'

'Lina, please just play the game.'

'I'm not playing your stupid games.'

'Here's what I'm going to do. I'm going to drown *you* in the lake. And I'm going to blow your husband's head off with this gun. I have killed people before. You may not believe that, you may not want to believe it's possible, but I promise you I have. And once you have done it, it changes you. Just ask your husband.' He doesn't speak for a moment. 'Here is what the police are going to find: a textbook murder–suicide. It will only take them a few days to investigate. Your family and friends will assume you were the latest victim of an epidemic of domestic violence and your husband will be just the latest piece of shit to murder his wife. PTSD, they will say. CTE from the head knocks. There is nothing you can do about it. Unless, of course, you choose me. In which case I'll simply kill him. You and I can be together. So let me ask you again. Cain or me?'

The rage swells. 'You'll never be half the man Cain is,' I hiss. 'You're a weak little man. My husband is a hero.'

'A hero,' he says, his voice chillingly neutral.

Then he takes the gun from the couch, strides towards the stairs and climbs them. A moment later there's an explosion upstairs.

EIGHTEEN

'CAIN!' A LONG wretched cry escapes me, stinging everything inside. I try to scream again but anguish clogs my throat. In the seconds after, everything is almost silent except for the static of the rain on the iron roof and the wind tearing across the lake, through the trees, up the hills. And that other sound growing louder now: an animal whining, reverberating from my own chest. The explosion still rings in my head, would anyone have heard it out in the world? Wiremu and Melissa up the road might be close enough if not for the storm.

I scream again, my body contorting against the handcuff; blood wells around the steel. He's coming. Footsteps down the stairs. I kick out for the keys and the table moves a little further away. The shotgun blast can't have hit Cain. My mind rejects it as something fundamentally impossible, an apple falling towards the sky, water flowing uphill. If it did hit him, the shot didn't kill him, he can survive. He went through worse in Afghanistan. He's built to survive.

My next thought comes on as a burning imperative: protect the baby. Kicking once more at the table, my foot impotently passes by without touching the wood. The footsteps come closer. Then he is there, in the room, rushing towards me. 'Stop screaming!'

But I can't. The sound pours out of me. He forces his gloved hands into my mouth, compressing my tongue, blocking the sound. He wraps something behind my head. I'm coughing against whatever he's tied in my mouth but it doesn't move from between my teeth. My words are just a panicked hum.

'That's one of your husband's socks. He's up there, lying in blood.' He yawns, whatever is disguising his voice crackles. 'And now you're going for a swim.'

My head shakes, my body convulses violently, ripping against the handcuff.

'Stay still,' he says. 'I'll take the sock out, but if you scream it's going straight back in and you're going in the lake, understand?'

I nod.

'Good.'

He steps forward again, his boots knocking on the carpet. I draw away, pressed hard against the black iron side of the fireplace.

'Stay still.' He reaches out. When the glove touches my cheek I wince. I eye the shotgun behind him, what I would do to have the gun in my hands, aimed at him.

He unties the sock and I cough, resisting the urge to spit.

My body is aching. I squeeze everything inside. 'Please don't kill me. You – you can't.'

He is so close now, the black mask hovering inches from my face. The leather of his gloved finger grazes my cheek. 'And why is that?'

The panic reaches a crescendo. 'I'm pregnant,' I say, a note of hysteria in the chorus of desperation. 'Please, my baby. You can't hurt my baby.'

Something in his eyes changes, those two green discs narrow. He draws himself back away from me. Hands on hips. 'Pregnant.' It's not quite a question but it's clear he wants a response.

'Yes, six weeks.'

'Six weeks,' he utters to himself. He turns away from me, his hands still on his hips. I can hear him breathing.

'*Six* weeks,' he says without turning back.

I find myself fervently nodding. 'Yes, it's already got a heart.' This detail might make him more sympathetic. I was going to tell Cain tonight, it was going to be perfect, the start of our new life and here I am telling this man instead.

He turns back, tilts his head one way then back again like an owl studying its prey. The hanging canister of the gas mask swings below his chin. 'This changes things.'

A splinter of hope lodges between my ribs. He won't hurt me, now that he knows about the baby. He thinks, or perhaps he *knows* that it might be his. 'Are you sure you're pregnant, Lina?'

'It is you, isn't it, Daniel?' I say. 'Why are you doing this?' The adrenaline, the anger, it's fading now, cooling, forged to a sharp edge. I need to get away. I need to get Cain to a hospital. *Cain.*

'I asked *you* a question. Are you sure?'

'Yes,' I say. 'I took a test.'

A long pause, he studies me.

'I'm the father . . . I'm going to be a dad.'

He rises suddenly and heads back up to the bedroom. I can hear him moving around up there. Then a moment later he returns.

'This place is different since last time I was here,' he says. 'Or maybe it's just a bit different during the day, it seems cleaner, nicer somehow.'

He's been here before. Of course he has. He drugged the wine. He got inside, he must have changed the code to the lock. Rain pounds the roof. Even through the mask, I see a bead of sweat running down into his eye. But it's not hot in here. He's nervous.

'Let me ask you something,' he says, sitting on the couch. He rests his feet on the table near the keys for the handcuff. 'Why did you choose *me*?'

'What?'

'Why did you choose me, on the dating app? My tattoos? My looks? What was it?'

I swallow. 'Why do you want to know?'

'Because I want the truth. Because I am a *fucking* caveman, Lina. That's why. Now answer the question.'

'It was supposed to be one night,' I say. 'I'm sorry if I gave you the wrong impression.'

'Was I not good enough for you?'

I take a breath. 'Please take this off? Then we can talk properly.' I raise my cuffed hand so the chain is taut.

'No. Tell me why you chose me, explain to me why you ghosted me afterwards.'

'Because you seemed normal, you had a good job, you were young.'

'What's that got to do with it?'

'There was less chance we would have friends in common. You said you were a country boy but I didn't think you meant Rotorua. I never would have –'

'You thought you had gotten away scot-free, you'd never see me again.'

'I did.'

'So it was just sex?'

'No,' I say, without thinking. I hesitate. 'Well, I guess it was.' I need to keep him onside.

'Oh, Lina, you're going to have to give me a little more than that. Do you love your husband?'

'Yes.'

'Then why were you cheating on him?'

'It's complicated.'

'We've got time.'

I lean up against the fireplace, my shoulder and hips ache from sitting in this awkward position but I can't turn from him. I don't have the mettle to look away from his eyes even for a moment.

Those years of pain, of trying for a baby. Marking dates on the calendar app on my phone, reminders to have regimented sex. Killing the joy we once took in each other's bodies. 'We've been trying for a baby for years,' I say. 'I thought I could get pregnant, tell him it's a miracle. I needed it,' I say. 'We needed it.'

He guffaws now. 'You selfish bitch.'

'I did it for him, I was doing it for us.'

'Why do you need a baby?'

He's watching me closely. I think about the question; is it because of the fraught relationship I had with my mother? Because some part of me wants to prove I am not her? Or is it simply some hardwired evolutionary trait, an atavistic need to procreate? Cain was the same, so much of his depression spawned from the lack of meaning he had after the war. He didn't have any family anymore either. A child would give him purpose.

I give him the only answer I know is true. 'It was an ache for both of us. I did it as much for him as me.'

'How many times did you do it?'

'Do what?'

'Find men, cheat on your husband.'

'You were the first. The only time. The guilt felt like it was going to kill me. I couldn't sleep, I couldn –'

'Shh. Enough.'

I stop talking.

I had rationalised it in my head. I'd convinced myself through some magical thinking it was for the best, that I was doing it for Cain. I'd planned it meticulously. It was going to work. The night with Daniel fell right in the window of my cycle.

'And what about Cain? Poor cuckolded Cain was going to raise someone else's kid.'

'He would never know. It would be his. It *might* be his.'

'Wouldn't he think it odd if the kid didn't look like him?'

'I was careful,' I say. 'I was looking at people like him.'

'Except I have green eyes.'

'Cain's dad had green eyes,' I say. 'You've got a similar nose, lips, height. You're a Maori boy like him.'

He laughs again. This time he straightens his legs and the table moves an inch, sliding on the carpet. I see the keys jiggle but he doesn't seem to notice or care.

'And your mother, tell me about her, Lina? This is why you want the baby, right? To prove you're not as much of a fuck-up as her?'

I look away this time. 'I just want to be a mother. I want to raise a child with my husband. I never wanted to hurt anyone.'

'But she died,' he says now. It's a blow right to the gut.

'She did.'

'In this lake. Drove her car through the barrier. Awful way to go.'

'Don't,' I say. 'Please.'

'The articles said she was leaving her parents' house, which . . .' A pause. He turns slowly, raising his arms. '. . . Is this place, right?'

'Stop it.'

'So what happened? Because the way it was written about in the news article I read from all those years ago it sounded like the police weren't sure if she deliberately drove through the barrier or if it was an accident. Her blood alcohol was almost zero point two, enough booze to bring down a rhino and yet she drove. So it begs the question, did she do it on purpose? Did you push her over the edge?'

I don't respond. I sit balled up, slowly shaking my head. I've read the same articles. I was young, but I remember it all so clearly. I was in this room when the fight happened. When she turned up to take me away and Grandpa sent her packing. If I'd gone, would we both have died? Or would she have driven away slowly, carefully?

'Oh, Lina,' he says. 'Don't cry. It's not your fault. You can never know what might have happened, what someone was thinking. What secrets they keep. It makes sense to me now though. Your behaviour.'

'Please stop. Just let us go.'

'I think we'd better get on with the action: Give. The people. What they want.'

'What are you saying?'

'Let me show you,' he says. He holds the phone out towards me again. I look at the screen. This time it's not the room in that WeStay. It's . . . our room, our room here. In the corner is that symbol again, the shape of a house with an eye at the centre. 'We're putting on a bit of a show,' he says. 'Smile for the viewers. Almost three hundred people watching this right now.'

'What is this?' I say, turning, looking up towards the corners of the room.

'This is Peephole,' he says. Then he stands again, and goes to the kitchen. Drawers slide open until he finds what he is looking for. 'Ladies and gentleman,' he says, his arms wide, as he slowly turns. 'The main event is about to begin.' Now the mask makes sense. People are watching this. He's protecting his identity. He thinks he will get away with it. My eyes fix on what he is holding in his hands.

In his right is a steel, in his left is the Japanese chef's knife we got as a wedding present. He starts sharpening the knife.

'His name is Daniel Moore,' I scream. 'Please call the police, our address is –'

'They can't hear you,' he says. 'No one is coming to save you, Lina!' Lightning cracks the sky open.

He climbs the steps once more, leaving the shotgun on the couch. I can hear the *shhhiiivd-shhhiiivd* of the knife sliding up the steel.

This is my only chance. If I don't escape, I will die; we will both die – me and the baby. I move again, lying down, reaching with my toes for the table. It is slightly closer from where he had pushed it with his feet and I hook my foot around one leg, just my toes, straining for purchase. It's enough that the table turns, shimmies closer. The keys are on top and now I bend my knee, pulling. The table lurches forward. The feet whisper against the carpet as I drag it closer. There is no time to waste. I keep it moving, the keys are towards the back edge and with each jerking movement they slide a little further, but the table is coming closer now. Soon it is on me and I can use my hands and feet to keep dragging it. The keys fall on the far side of the table, hit the ground. I reach with my foot again, I can just touch the steel ring.

Sounds come from upstairs. A box moving, dragging over the wooden floor.

Come on, Lina, stretch. Every sinew, every cell strives to move my toe closer. The edge of the cuff bites into my wrist. Between my two biggest toes on my right foot, I pinch the key ring and bend my knee. It is close enough to take in my hand. I turn, get the keys, push one in the lock. It doesn't go. I try the next one. And the next. I can't hear the knife anymore, or any movement. I drop the keys, take them up again, keep trying those three keys over and over but they're not working. *Why won't the handcuff unlock?* My breath is frantic.

'Ha, ha, ha, haaaaa,' he says, slowly, clapping his hands. 'Brilliant.'

I drop the keys. The table slides off me over the carpet. Looking up I meet his eyes in that mask. 'They don't work,' I say, desperately.

'Clever girl. They probably enjoyed that.' He looks at his phone. 'Even more viewers. They're flocking to watch you suffer.'

'You're sick.'

'I have to give the viewers something to watch, someone to root for.' He calmly walks over, places the knife and the steel on the couch, then takes the keys from beside me and places them in his pocket. 'I'll take these. For now you can watch this.' He shows me the phone screen again. I see myself on the floor beside the fire, I see him standing over me holding the phone. But the screen is cycling through the various cameras. For a second I'm looking at the downstairs bathroom, then the upstairs bathroom, then the hallway outside the bedroom, then . . . a scream tears out of me.

He shoves a hand over my mouth, the cool leather gripping my cheeks. 'Shh,' he says. But it keeps coming. The scream dying to a whimper. I feel so weak now, as I look at the body wrapped in a sheet on the floor of the bedroom. The camera is in the hallway but it's clear what it is. 'Shh, he's still breathing. But I want you to watch. I want you to see what they're seeing.' The cameras are cycling back through, so for a second I see us there in the living room. At the bottom of the phone screen words keep appearing, then are replaced.

CallMeDaddy: This is the best stream I've watched on here. Incredible.

Silvesterthekitten: I don't know about this at all. It's not what I signed up for, but I can't look away.

'They're watching?' It's coming together now. This is about something much bigger than jealousy, or some feelings he had for me. This is something else completely.

'I'll let you watch, you shouldn't miss out on this.'

Again he rises to go. He leaves the knife, the steel, the gun on the couch.

I scream and scream but the storm has grown outside. No one will hear me, no one will help. I can't unlock the phone, I can only watch. There's no one but me. *Only I can save myself.* He climbs the stairs and I watch the phone screen. He walks to the entrance of the bedroom where Cain lies. Taking Cain by the leg, he drags him up the hall to the spare bedroom. There's no camera there. *What is he doing?* The comments keep flowing. One catches my attention.

PlatoOf21C: Lift the base of the fireplace you stupid bitch. It's your only hope. They're not always bolted down.

I study the fireplace. The foot where the handcuff is attached. It's an old wood burner. Grandpa installed it in the open fireplace. I would only need to get it up half an inch to slide the loop of the handcuff out.

The gun is just there, and I know it is loaded, or it was. Hopefully there are more rounds in it. I try to stand now, bend at the knees. I grab the underside of the fireplace. It moves. It's working. I use my foot, gripping the chain with my toes, sliding the handcuff. It comes free. I breathe. *I'm free.* This isn't a trick. I'm free. Relief fills my head like an inert gas. I might lift off the ground. But it's not over. It's far from over.

PlatoOf21C: She did it! She's listening. Good girl. Now get the gun. He's upstairs unarmed. He went into the end bedroom. Kill the lights, you've got the advantage. You can do this.

NINETEEN

I SCRABBLE ACROSS the floor and clutch the gun to my chest. Then fall silent listening to the house. More footsteps. I try to trace them, focusing my hearing in the direction of the stairs but I can't tell where he is. I look at the phone. It shows me the inside of the bathroom, then the bedroom upstairs. I can hear a knocking sound. My other hand trembles around the gun. The storm lashes the house outside. Could he have worked out I have freed myself? What if he has another weapon? *He's unarmed.* I drag in a breath and step towards the kitchen as quietly as I can. I need to get help, my phone is still in the car but he has the car keys. I could break the window, but what if he's already taken my phone? What if the car alarm goes off? Cain's phone was in his pocket but it had run out of battery. What is he doing with Cain?

There's a little light passing down the stairs from the bedroom; the bedside lamp is on. I imagine Cain, a body with no head, just a spray of blood, bone fragments and that colourless pulp of brain matter. My breath shakes in my chest. *Keep going, Lina. Do something.* I hold the gun out in one hand, the phone in the other. He's not anywhere on the screen. Is he hiding, waiting for me? My experience with firearms is limited to the single time Cain took us to a shooting range in the US. It was our honeymoon and he insisted we go. *Everyone should know how to fire a rifle, just in case.* In case of what? Did he ever imagine this scenario? I wouldn't trust myself to aim, or pull the trigger if it came to that. I could run, through the dark and rain. Where would I go without a car though? *Aim it with both hands, always the centre mass, spread your feet.*

I creep further, heading towards the front door. Gently turning the lock and the handle, pulling it silently. The wind presses the door hard, it whistles past me into the house. Then I hear a scream. Loud, tearing agony. Another gale blows the door from my hand. It slams against the wall. I'm electrified. *Cain is alive.* My relief is suspended because he's in pain, we're not out of the woods. I look at the phone. It's locked on these streams, touching the screen does nothing, there are no buttons to press. With the gun in my right hand, keeping watch over my shoulder towards the stairs, it takes all my strength to close the door quietly against the force of the wind. It clicks shut. *Move, Lina.* Easy steps over the cool wood floor.

I know this house like the back of my hand, I have the view of the cameras, the gun. I have the advantage. I stride to the switchboard near the bottom of the stairs and hit the power for the lights. The house falls dark, a sheet fallen over the canary's cage. Everything is still and silent but for the storm outside.

'Shit,' I hear a voice mutter upstairs. I look at the screen now, the cameras show the rooms in greyscale night vision. I watch for a few moments, then I see Daniel wandering carefully up the hall towards the spare bedrooms where there are no cameras at all, just a terminal of darkness, train tunnel black. Then a flash of something behind him. *Is that someone else?* Maybe a glitch on the camera. I thought I saw movement. The image changes to the next camera.

I go to the fire, feeling my way in the dark, holding the gun out in front of me, and find the long lighter. Back at the stairs I begin the climb, one step at a time, feeling the muscles in my calves tightening and knotting, trembling with adrenaline. On the camera, I see Daniel in the hallway. It fixes on him. He's removed his mask and seems confused by the darkness with his arms out before him, still and silent. He could fall down the stairs. I place the phone on the step, face down, so the light from the screen doesn't give my position away. Rising, my hands ache around the gun and the lighter. I creep my way up towards the top of the stairs. It's muscle memory. He's close, he must be. I know this house so well, know the points where the floor squeaks, the distance from the top of the stairs to the master bedroom. I pause at the landing, holding my breath and squeezing the lighter in one hand, resting the gun across my left forearm. The trigger feels hard and electric against my right index finger. He's there at the end of the hall. A gust presses the house. The windows creak in their frames. I fumble with the lighter and flick it on. A tiny glow leaps ahead. I see him, see terror in those green eyes.

I don't think. I simply drop the lighter. The gun comes up. I hold it tight. *Centre mass.*

'No,' he says. 'Please!'

I pull the trigger. The room explodes. I fly back, a sledgehammer to the chest that hurls me hard against the wall at the top of the stairs. The house falls into complete darkness.

My breath is gone. An ache in the sternum. *What happened? Did it hit him?* I scrabble along the floor. A gurgling sound. Heavy breathing. I find the lighter. A breath, stillness. I click it and the room glows once more. Outside, the storm quietens a little. I slide my back along the wall. There's blood, pooling. The shotgun blast has left a shark bite at the side of his torso. Heavy metal tang on the air, burrowing into my nostrils. I feel sick, a medical compulsion to help. But not this man, first I must find my husband. The light from the lighter only travels a few feet. I glance once more up into the darkness of the hallway, the other rooms. Then slide along until I can see into the spare room at the end of the hallway, the wall first, then I see more blood. A single drip first of crimson on the pale wall, but the further I slide the more I see. An arc of red. A slash. *Cain's blood.* Rain is trickling into the house through a hole in the wall. It must have been from the shotgun blast. But Cain's not there. Daniel had dragged him in a sheet further along to the spare room. I continue deeper into the hallway. Then I see him. He's on the floor beneath the sheet; a bloodied mess where his head is.

'*No, no, no, no, no.*' The words rush out. I drop to my knees, pull the sheet back.

One eye moves. He sees me, shock spreads across his bloody face. His mouth open. I see his hands now, taped together, he's almost got the tape apart, it's torn the hair off his wrists.

He's alive. Relief, a surge replaces the adrenaline with something softer, heavier. I rush forward and pull the tape from his mouth. Tears run down my face.

'Quick,' Cain says, louder now. 'Untie me.'

I drop down beside him and pick at the tape. Over the slamming of my heart I hear that sickly breathless gurgling sound in the hall.

A thought sends an ice pick sliding in beneath my ribs. *What if there is someone else?* I thought I saw movement.

'Cain,' I begin, the tape coming away from his hands. 'Was it just one?'

He looks confused. 'I,' he says, pausing, 'I think so, yeah. Just him.'

My breath comes back. 'I thought I might have seen . . . I don't know, it was hard to see anything on the camera but there looked like movement behind him.'

'Camera?'

'It's a long story.'

Cain shakes his head, stands up and takes the gun from my hands. I light the lighter again. He checks the gun is still loaded before stepping forward into the hallway, motioning for me to wait in the room.

'You shot him?' His words are still a little slow and slurred. He's shocked. I've never seen such a deep look of concern.

'I had to,' I say. 'He was coming towards me, he was going to hurt us. I had to.'

'You pulled the trigger,' he says. It's not a question. He knows what killing does to someone. 'Are you okay? Shit.'

'I had to, Cain. He was coming towards me. He was –'

'It's okay. It's okay. Don't look,' he says. It's obvious he's still heavily medicated by the way he walks, the looseness to his stride. 'You'll be okay.'

I hear him now, dragging something down the hall and I turn away. When I step out of the room and see the blood I feel a sudden overwhelming nausea. I look at Cain instead and notice that blood still silently seeps down his cheek from his eye. Cain steps over the body, holding the gun ahead of him and using the lighter to look in the bathroom. He picks something up, the gas mask, the hoodie Daniel was wearing.

'He was wearing this, wasn't he?'

'Yeah,' I say.

Cain is still wearing just his underwear. 'Doesn't look like there's anyone else but I wonder why he took it off. I can check the other rooms or we can just get the fuck out of here. If there was someone else, they probably cleared out after the gunshot but let's not wait around and find out.'

The wheezing tells me Daniel is still alive. We both look down at the same time.

'Turn away,' he says.

'What are you going to do?'

'He's not going to make it,' Cain says. 'He's just going to suffer and bleed out.'

'What are you going to do?'

He drops the mask on Daniel's chest, turns back to me, his face changes. 'Nothing. I thought it would be right to . . . I don't know.'

'I should help him.'

'No,' he says. 'Not if you think there might be a second man. We need the police. He's not going to make it, Lina. He's a goner.'

I want nothing more than for Cain to grab me, pull me against him. Hug me so tight I'll never be afraid again, but he's making sense. Someone else could still be here. Cain is trained for this sort of situation, but he's groggy and weak. We need to move.

'Come on, let's go.' He leads me into the bedroom. Checks around the bed for some clothes. He pulls on shorts and a sweater. Rain is flooding through the hole in the wall onto Grandpa's old chest.

'He was trying to put me in here,' Cain says, leaning over, peering in. Adrenaline fills me. A spring tightening, ready to snap.

'Come on, Cain, let's get out.'

He leads us downstairs; I'm tucked in behind him, holding the lighter, which is casting a meagre glow. I don't reach for the phone. I don't want to see the streams and the comments, I just want to get out. We get to the switchboard and he opens the circuit-breaker, the lights come back on.

Two people are watching us just outside the door. I leap before I realise it's only our reflection in the glass. The night is black and the storm continues to pound down.

We set out through the front door, over the deck into the hard rain.

TWENTY

'WHO THE HELL *was* that back there?' Cain says.

'I have no idea.' The lie comes instantly. 'There could have been someone else with him. There were cameras. He showed me . . . footage from the house, it was live. I saw him dragging you.'

I follow him down the steps, he's still unsteady on his feet.

'I saw something,' I say. 'It looked like someone was behind him at one stage.' My head swims. I don't know what I saw, it was probably a shadow.

His doubt is palpable. The way his silhouette shakes its head. He doesn't believe it, or doesn't want to.

'We need to get away. We need to phone the police.'

I don't say what I'm thinking, *Someone could be hunting us right now.*

'Can you run?' I ask.

'No,' he says. 'I still feel groggy. We're just going to work our way up to Wiremu's.'

I grab his shoulder, turn him gently. 'I'm scared, what if there's another one?'

Even in the darkness, I see his eyes are wide. 'We will make it. I only saw one and the only choice we have is to keep moving and stay vigilant.' He shakes his head.

I think about those cameras in our house, are they still watching? A chill passes over the skin of my neck. *A ghost whisper*, Grandad would say.

Cain squeezes me against him for a moment, there on the gravel in the rain. I know we don't have time, but it settles my nerves just a little. 'Stay close,' he says. 'I've got us covered.'

He releases me, raises the shotgun so it's hard against his shoulder and continues moving. I feel the effervescence of adrenaline. Epinephrine stimulating alpha-adrenoreceptors. Narrowing blood vessels, filling muscles with oxygen, enhancing eyesight. My body is prepared for danger, prepared to do what it takes to protect this baby.

If there is someone else, who could it be? A friend of Daniel's? Another sicko he met online to help install the cameras? Or . . . one of the guests. The last guests, the ones who also stayed at the WeStay in Auckland. It occurs to me that it might have been Daniel with a fake account. He stayed in Auckland, installed the cameras then took me there. He must have installed cameras at the lake house too.

The gravel cracks underfoot, and another gust of wind tears across the lake, rustling the trees. The rain thins now, needles of it carried on the wind. We reach the road, and lightning arcs down somewhere. The crack of thunder is loud over the rain. It nails my bare feet to the tarmac road. We are too exposed here.

'Come on,' he calls. 'Let's keep moving.'

'I can't,' I say. 'I can't, I'm scared.'

'Just move,' he growls, 'don't think, just act. We need to get away.' He steps back, grabs my forearm hard and drags me along.

I find my feet again, keep moving along the road, continuing to scan the road's edge for movement.

When we get to Wiremu and Melissa's house, the rain has eased. In the security light at the front door, with the gun, the blood, my wrist in a chaffed ring, we must look like we're running from the apocalypse. I think once more about Daniel at the house, dead by now and *I* pulled the trigger. I killed him. I still hear the gurgling sound. I feel the force of the gun when I pulled the trigger. That story Cain told me comes back, soldiers being *blooded* by killing prisoners. You're never the same; I'll never be the same.

Cain knocks on the door hard. He turns back, gun still in hand and eyes the steps down to the road. The rain continues rinsing the blood from his face. He knocks even harder. Finally, a light turns on inside, footsteps and the door opens.

It's Wiremu. 'What's happened?' He swallows, leans closer to peer outside as if searching for someone. 'You guys okay?'

'Yeah,' Cain says. 'We are now.'

'Get inside,' Wiremu says.

He turns to let us through, his eyes moving from Cain's bloody eye to the gun in his hands.

•

Cain shakes his head. 'I don't know what happened, we were at dinner and next thing I knew someone was giving me a hiding, telling me he's going to slit my throat.' I touch his back, rubbing the soaked cotton of his shirt. It seems like weeks ago we were out for dinner, yet it was only tonight.

We hover inside the door. 'Let me get you a towel and Melissa can take a look at those nasty gashes.'

'Oh,' I say. 'I can do it.' It's above his eye, the deepest cut.

'You're in shock,' Wiremu says. He's right. My hands are violently shaking, a cold damp fatigue is smothering the adrenaline now. 'Just go get warmed up.'

'You're right,' I say. 'You're probably right.'

I'm wrapped in a towel by the time Melissa comes through, yawning as though this is a common occurrence for a Friday night. She brings a small first-aid kit to the table and begins cleaning Cain's wounds. I see now beneath the kitchen lights that Cain's left eye is almost swollen closed, and a small transparent red trail of fluid leaks from his nose.

'It was just the one person?'

Cain glances towards me, looks uncertain. 'Just one,' he says, a small shake of his head. 'We didn't see anyone else.'

'Any more rounds in the shotgun?'

'Yeah, a couple,' Cain says. 'We only used one.'

We, but what he really means is *me*. I pulled the trigger. I've killed someone. Wiremu looks up, the creases bracketing his mouth deepen, those weary brown eyes are focused. 'Doors are locked, I'll call the coppers and an ambulance.'

Wiremu makes the call in another room. The clock tells me it's only 1 am, but that seems impossible. I think of the cameras in the house, what he showed me. Those strangers talking about the scene. PlatoOf21C saved my life. They suggested lifting the fireplace and it worked. It *actually* worked. I don't know who or why these people were watching me, but someone actually helped me out of there.

Wiremu has called an old friend in the Rotorua police directly and he's still talking when he comes back into the room. 'Cain reckons the man's toast, took a round of buckshot to the guts . . . I'll keep them here. Thanks.'

•

'There are cameras in the house,' I say. The cop was evidently once good-looking. Mid-forties, balding with dark eyes and sharp rockstar cheekbones. He stops marking his notebook and his eyes fix on me.

'What do you mean?'

'He showed me his phone, he had set up hidden cameras in our house. It was live.'

'What do you mean live?'

'Streaming, I think.' I pause, my mind is fatigued, I can barely express myself. 'Umm, to people. They were commenting as it was happening.'

His eyes narrow so they're almost closed, a look somewhere between scepticism and disgust. He looks down, his breath is audible. 'Commenting? And these cameras were running?'

I nod.

'Right,' he says.

He stands, take out his phone and steps into another room. I can hear the murmur of his voice. He comes back, pockets his phone and sits down again, beside me.

'And you thought there might have been a second intruder?' he says. I pause to take a sip of the tea that Melissa had brewed for me. Police are at our house now. I imagine it wrapped up in tape. Floodlights. Hazmat crime scene investigators picking their way through the carnage.

Ambulance officers are attending to Cain. Given his head injuries and the risk of concussion, he's going to the hospital soon. I want to go with him. I need to stay with him after tonight. It feels a lot like guilt, like I brought this on us. I can't shake the growing knot of unease in my gut. It's my fault.

'Yes,' I say. 'But maybe I'm mistaken. I don't know, it was dark. I just thought I saw movement on the camera stream.'

'Okay, and you have no idea who the first man was?'

177

I glance through the door into another room where Cain is being treated by ambulance officers and interviewed at the same time. They're going to figure out who Daniel is without me pointing them in the right direction. 'It's hard to know, he was wearing the gas mask, then he was all bloody and it was dark. I could know him, but I can't be sure without seeing him properly. Something was disguising his voice too.' It's not a lie. Not really. It could have been someone else behind that mask.

I see Cain wince as they apply saline to a cut. After I've given my statement, I head to Cain who now has butterfly stitches in the gash above his eye.

'We're going to take you to Rotorua hospital for observation,' I overhear the ambulance officer say.

'She's a paramedic,' Cain says, pointing in my direction. 'She will look after me.'

'No,' I say. 'You'd better go. I'll come with you.'

Cain closes his eyes for a moment. 'Alright.'

The police will look into our pasts for suspects, I suppose. Try to figure out the connection between us and Daniel. I was careful, but there was only so much I could do to cover my tracks. Phone records will link Daniel to me. He might have shown his friends a photo of me. If the police discover the connection, which they surely will, does that mean Cain will find out too? The police will look closely at Cain's history; I read somewhere that soldiers who testify, particularly against those in their own units, often go into witness protection programs overseas, but some refuse to. Cain didn't testify against Skelton, but he was going to. Axel was cooperating with investigators as well.

'Mr Phillips,' the cop says now coming back, addressing Cain, 'when you're feeling better we will need to see you to run through a few further details.'

Cain nods. He's holding his Pounamu greenstone in his hand, squeezing it on the end of the cord.

'In fact, it would be best if you could both get to the police station in the morning. I'm sure you will have more to add to your statements, assuming you're okay to leave hospital. If you think of anything else that would aid the investigation, get in touch sooner.'

'Thanks,' I say. 'We will.'

'The spare room is made up,' Wiremu calls from the kitchen. 'You're more than welcome to stay for as long as you need.'

'No,' I say. 'I don't want to be out here tonight. Cain's going to the hospital so I'll go with him.'

Cain lies down on the stretcher and they let me ride in the back of the ambulance with him. As we start out along the road, I glance through the rear window and see all the floodlights at the house, a pink dawn creasing the horizon across the lake, bringing a deep-sea green out of the surrounding flora. A new day is beginning. There are three police cars, one still twirling those blue and red lights, strobing through the trees. They're all down there, police swarming the house. I wonder if they know that people are watching them, somewhere out in the world. Anonymous peeping Toms. Then that word comes back to me, what Daniel had said. *Peephole.*

Daniel. There's a new guilt. It has replaced that rotten feeling that came over me whenever I thought about cheating on Cain.

•

At the hospital, all the fear and anxiety has flooded from me and in its place is something cold and dark. *I killed a man.* Realising it, thinking the words to myself, it's an almost violent bodily response. I'm light-headed. Someone guides me to a seat and I lower myself gently upon it. A glass of water is pushed into my hand. 'She's in shock.'

'Give her space to breathe.'

I look up into the eyes of a nurse.

'I killed someone,' I say. The words do nothing to assuage the heat of the guilt. They intensify it. The rain comes down harder outside, rinsing the world. The black hole grows within and yet I repeat myself, 'I killed him.' *And now I will never be the same.*

Peephole
Live Cam Premium
Stream: 037B
Viewers: 319

They're in helmets and body armour, rifles raised as they enter the house. The armed offenders squad clear each room, one at a time. The photographers, crime scene specialists arrive now. Police are seen outside in camera 2, standing near the front door, three of them talking between themselves. An ambulance is parked in the background beside all the other emergency services vehicles. A photo flash, the photographer in the hazmat suit is squatting over the spots of blood on the carpet at the base of the stairs. They place a marker down, a yellow tab. Then another and another. Slowly working through the house. Collecting evidence to build a narrative of what happened tonight.

The viewer numbers are steady at 319. No one is going anywhere, they're all watching to see what happens next.

A police officer with strong cheekbones and wide-set eyes rushes in. White protective slips cover his shoes and he's got medical gloves on. He's gesturing towards the corners of the room. He snatches a stepladder away from one of the crime scene specialists. He takes it to the corner and climbs up, his face growing as he gets closer to the camera. He's peering right into it, his brow heavy with two vertical creases drawn up his forehead. The camera shuffles, the image blurring in the steam of his breath. Then the room turns, a sickly twirl as the officer shows the viewers the insides of his nostrils. He's found the first of the cameras. The image drops out. One by one, over the course of the next few hours, it happens again and again until none of the cameras remain.

Peephole
Live Cam Premium
Stream: 037B
Viewers: 319

88HH: Wot a fucking show!!

GeneralMayhem: Look at those pigs swarming. They don't even
                      know.

Daddyboy: Oh well it was fun while it lasted. This sort of shit is
                      going to ruin Peephole. Why can't we just watch
                      people? why do psychos have to go and ruin our
                      fun? We've all paid up and now the service will
                      probably be shut down.

DRUMPF2024:   Where is this? Looks like the sun is just rising.

GeneralMayhem: It's New Zealand, I think. I've been watching
                      this stream the last couple of weekends and
                      the sunset times all align with NZ or one of the
                      few islands dotted in the Pacific, but if you see
                      the ferns on Cam 5 it looks like NZ. Plus that
                      looks like the NZ police uniform.

DRUMPF2024:   GeneralMayhem, you the killer?

GeneralMayhem: The bitch is the killer.

DRUMPF2024:   LMAO

Fruitdrop: LMAO, nice. Daddyboy is right though. Admin is going to tighten things up even more now. Less streams, more attention from police. They'll find the cameras and it will be all over the media.

QsentMe: Speak of the devil. Look at Cam 4, they've already found one.

GeneralMayhem: I was convinced it was staged or some kind of role-play, but she fucking blasted him, right in the guts. He must have been a Peepholer, knew where the cameras were all along.

DRUMPF2024:   Do you think they will get banned? Haha.

Fruitdrop: Love it when the good guys win. ;)

DRUMPF2024:   OMG. I've just realised it's the girl from the other stream. I knew I'd seen her before. WHAT THE FUCK

PlatoOf21C: I don't want to see this shit. This is like a fucking horror movie. I just want to watch people, is that so fucking hard?

Daddyboy: Wait, there was another man, right?

PART TWO
AFTERMATH

TWENTY-ONE

CAIN WAS ASLEEP in his hospital bed when I left with a police officer to answer follow-up questions. He has both ketamine and fentanyl in his system which they're flushing out. I head back to the lake house to get the car. Photographers in hazmat suits are still inside, and a pair of cops are walking down near the lake's edge, scanning through the grass. It hurts to be back here, seeing the house in the light of day. That guilt comes again, the scene pressed deep into my brain – scenes that will never leave me. Daniel on the floor, that gurgling sound. The blood.

The window in the master bedroom is smashed and there's half-a-dozen exit holes from where the shotgun had blasted through the wall which have let rainwater inside. It'll take weeks, maybe months, for the insurance claim to be processed, but I see a police officer climbing a ladder to hang tarpaulin over it.

I leave our clothes and things inside, but the police hand over my car keys, which were in Daniel's pocket along with Cain's phone. I take my phone from the glove box. Cain should be free to come home tonight or tomorrow morning. They're going to scan his brain, observe him.

'You go home to Auckland,' he told me. 'No point sitting around here, you need to rest. I'll manage.' I was too fatigued to argue with him, and I knew he was probably right. I did need rest, and I needed to get as far away from the lake house as possible.

The scene plays out again in my mind. Daniel with the shotgun, those fierce eyes, teasing at times, angry at others. When he found out I was pregnant there was a pause, something changed. Is that what kept him from really hurting me?

When I stop for petrol, I see it on the front page of the newspaper. If nothing else, the media is quick. The image is from the road, a long lens shot taken from beyond the police tape in the pre-dawn house: HOUSE OF HORRORS: HOME INVASION ON LAKE TARAWERA.

I turn my head and quickly look away.

'Pump four?' the attendant asks.

'Yeah.'

I can barely meet the man's eyes as I hand over my card and pay.

•

By the time I get home to Auckland the story is running on the midday news and the news sites. I sit on the couch in front of the TV as 'New Zealand's Mum', Paula Cripps, stares down the camera to report that a home invasion occurred at a property in Lake Tarawera last night and one man is dead. I don't know why my heart is racing, it's as though I'm back in the house reliving it. While doctors gauze the cuts and salve the bruises on my husband, I'm morbidly running through each moment of that night in my mind. It comes in a rush. I can't stop imagining the things I might have done differently. A shorter shower. I could have got my phone from the glove box. Maybe I didn't need to pull the trigger, maybe Cain could have stopped him. Apprehended him. I mute the TV.

Cain has survived worse. He might have new scars to go with the others, but he's alive. That's the most important thing – I don't know what I would do if he had died. When my mobile phone rings I almost leap out of my chair. It's an unknown number. I answer.

'Lina Phillips? Constable Stevens here. We met this morning.'

'Hi,' I say. Then before he can speak again, I add, 'I've seen the news. It's all over the media.'

'Ignore them. It's hard to keep things like this secret in a small town. Word was bound to get out.'

Now on screen I see Wiremu talking into the camera, he's pointing down past the ferns that surround his deck, towards the road at the bottom of his driveway. It's muted but I can imagine him explaining what he saw.

I release a sigh. 'I guess it's inevitable.'

'It is, it never lasts long. Anyway, I'll try not to keep you, after what you have been through. Firstly, I wanted to let you know that someone will be in touch from victims support to offer a range of assistance options, including financial support for therapy sessions but also medical, property damage etc. You don't need to take it up but it's there for you both should you choose to.'

'Sure, thanks,' I say.

'As far as our preliminary investigations go, we've managed to piece everything together. We've found the suspect's car, parked nearby on the road, and have confirmed that last night he left his home at Rotorua and drove to your property on the lake. We're waiting for positive identification, and phone records, but at this stage we haven't yet located his mobile phone.'

'I left it at the house, it was there.'

'There was *a* phone. It's possible he had two phones, but the mobile phone registered to his name has not been recovered. We're waiting for records from Spark to confirm whose phone that was at the house.'

'Well, I only saw the one phone.'

'Okay.'

'Do you know who it is yet? Who wanted to hurt us?'

'We believe so but I can't share that information until we've confirmed it with the family.'

Daniel told me about his family, his dad and unwell mum. How much of it was true though? 'And what about the cameras? Did you find them all?'

'We've found them, yes. There were seven in the house, but we don't know where the stream was going yet. We've recovered a mobile device from the property but it appears to have been remotely wiped.'

'So you don't know who those people were who watched it?'

'It's a slow-moving thing,' the officer explains. 'I would guess they wouldn't want to be found. The footage might have been saved remotely. Could be something for the cybercrime team. We're waiting on details about the phone first, then we'll investigate those who have stayed at the property. But we're dealing with an international company and we are requesting access to users' personal data.'

'Would it help if you had our login for WeStay, to see what we can see?'

'That would probably make things move a little faster.'

Soon after the call ends, the doorbell rings. A cluster of anxiety breaks away from my chest and shifts to my stomach. *What now?* I check my phone. No word from Cain yet. I'd dropped his phone to him at the hospital before I left. When I open the door I find Claire and Axel standing there.

'My God,' Claire says. She hugs me, squeezing me so tight my bones click. Axel watches on.

'Bloody scary,' he says. 'You must be shaken up.' He is much gentler than Claire when he takes me in his arms.

'Cain texted us,' he says. 'Told us what happened but we'd already seen it on the news.'

'He's at the hospital still,' I say. Now that I have the support of my friends, I feel suddenly weaker. Being strong comes much easier when it's the only option. The sickly feeling of guilt returns and with it heat presses the backs of my eyes.

'I thought we were going to die,' I say, tears starting with a helpless sob. 'I thought we were dead. I wouldn't have pulled the trigger if I had a choice.' Axel squeezes me, soothes me with his gentle hands on my back.

'You poor thing,' he says. 'Remember you're safe now. It's all over. I'll pick Cain up tonight, you just rest. He's tough as nails so he will land on his feet and you'll be okay too. You did the right thing.'

Easy for others to say.

'Have you eaten?' Claire says. 'You need to eat. I'll order something.'

'I'm not hungry,' I say but when she suggests pizza, I find my appetite responds to the idea. 'I just feel so guilty. I don't know why. I know he was a bad man.'

'It's normal, Lina,' Axel says. 'But it was you and Cain or him. You need to remember that.'

I try to believe it, but I wonder if there was another way.

When the food arrives, Claire goes into the kitchen, finds three plates. The open box reveals a tomato base, melted cheese over salami; it makes my stomach clench. I realise I've not eaten a thing today. The other pizza is a margarita.

'It's killing me that I got you onto WeStay,' Axel says, handing me a plate. 'I feel like shit. I just can't believe this happened to you.'

'He's been beating himself up all morning since we saw the news,' Claire adds. 'He's been trying to think of ways to make it right.'

'Don't be ridiculous,' I say. 'A very damaged man tried to hurt us and it had nothing to do with you, Axel.'

'I still feel bad. I hate to see you go through this. I just don't understand what the hell happened down there.'

'What do you know?' I say. 'What have you heard?'

'Just what Cain told us,' Axel says. 'But he was almost out to it. He barely remembers anything.'

I take a piece of pizza, strings of cheese hang.

'Don't talk about it if you don't want to, Lina,' Claire says. 'We don't want you to relive it all.'

'No,' I say. 'It might help, I don't know, get some clarity. Like therapy.'

I take my plate with three pieces then go and sit on the couch. The other two come over.

My appetite is fading again. 'Someone just turned up with a gun, there were cameras in the house and he was *tormenting* me.'

Claire looks sad for a moment, I see a question taking shape in her mouth. 'And you're *okay*? Like, you know, with –'

'The police have organised for me to see a counsellor.'

'Good, it will help. Given . . . you know.'

Given I killed a man. Lots of people kill and it's sanctioned, defensible. Then some people kill without reason, without cause or permission, like Trent Skelton. I've seen enough death in the ambulance to grow desensitised. But this is different. The fact Daniel was going to kill Cain and me doesn't change it much. I'd had sex with him. I'd chosen him from all those smiling faces on the dating app. I wonder what would have happened if I'd chosen someone else? Among all the noise in my head – the conflicting ideas and voices – is a murmur: if he was a bad man, what does that mean for the baby? Could there be violence and meanness written into the genetic code of our child?

'Do you want a drink? You must need something hard to take your mind off things?' Claire says.

'I'm not going to drink,' I say. 'But you two help yourselves.' I remember then Claire is also pregnant. 'Or just you, Axel.'

'I might pass, I'm going to pick Cain up when he's ready,' Axel says. 'You sure you don't want something? It'll be good to take the edge off. A stiff drink or a glass of wine.'

'No, I'm not touching alcohol today, Axel.'

He glances at Claire. 'If you change your mind it's there. If you need a drink, or another good cry, or anything, just don't hold back. You've been through hell.'

'Thanks,' I say. I reach for one of the other pieces of pizza on my plate, and when it gets to my mouth I think of something. *Salami.* It's on those lists of things you shouldn't eat when you're pregnant. Being a better mother than my own mother starts now. It actually started years ago when I began taking the vitamins and iron, and looking after myself. I take the pizza away from my mouth. Claire is staring at me, she glances at Axel.

'What is it?' she says.

'Oh, nothing.'

'You need to eat, even if you don't feel like it.'

'It's not that,' I say. Given what I went through to reach this stage I don't want to take even the smallest risk. 'I just feel like eating the margarita, I think.'

They're both watching me, their eyes like heat guns. But they're not on my face, they've slid down to where my other hand is resting. That treasonous hand, sitting on my navel. Purely instinctive, but there it is, gently moving in circles over the tiniest bump.

'Lina?' Claire's eyes come back up, meeting mine.

I can see the anticipation. She has guessed it; she knows. It's no secret how much we want a baby, how hard we've been trying. I don't have the energy to hide it from them. 'Cain doesn't know,' I say. 'I've not told him yet.'

A squeal, then Claire drops her plate on the coffee table and races over.

'Oh my God, Lina. Finally some good news!' She squeezes me tight. 'At the same time as me? They're going to be best friends.'

Axel turns his grin on to high beam. 'Our lips are sealed. Congratulations, sweetheart. I know how much this will mean to Cain.'

'I'm going to tell him tonight. I wanted to tell him at the house but that didn't happen obviously. It's really early so just pretend you don't know until we get further along.'

'Of course. Imagine them at school together, at each other's twenty-first birthdays. I'm *so* happy, Lina. It's been a traumatic twenty-four hours but I just know everything is going to go your way from here. I just know.'

'I can't wait to see Cain's reaction,' Axel says, his grin unshakeable. He's not only been protective of Cain, he's always been proud. The big brother Cain never had. 'Last word I'll say on it.'

'Yeah,' I say.

'The no drinking makes sense now,' Claire says, then winces. 'Sorry for the peer pressure.'

'Did you see the newspapers?' I say, forcing the conversation to move on. 'Amazing how quickly they were onto it.'

'Nothing about the guy, though,' Axel says. 'Do they know anything about him?'

'Not yet. They've got to formally identify him, and then I guess they'll notify his family and release more information.'

'And they think it was completely random?'

I shrug. 'I guess. Who knows?'

'He didn't ask you for money, or . . .' Claire lets the question tail off.

'No,' I say. 'He barely touched me. He just showed me the cameras in the house and said he was going to kill us.'

'And he didn't do anything else to hurt you?' Axel says. 'I'd kill him again.'

I turn to him. His gaze is neutral, his thick eyebrows slightly raised and mouth set in a firm line. His protective instinct has always been as conspicuous as a gorilla thumping its chest.

'No. He just said he had been watching us, that sort of thing. The doctor gave me a once-over just in case, but everything is fine. The baby has a heartbeat.' I find myself gently massaging the painful ring on my wrist.

Axel's eyes glance down. 'Sore?'

'It's okay. I kept jerking on it, trying to escape.'

'For what it's worth, I hope you stop feeling bad about shooting that scumbag. You saved Cain's life, you saved yourself and the baby. You should be proud.'

I should be full of relief and love for my unborn child, but I still feel the emptiness and regret of guilt. The home phone rings. My heart leaps and the fright causes the plate to tip from my lap. The sound of the plate cracking on the floorboard upends my precarious mental state.

'Shit,' I say, through the sudden tears. 'Sorry.'

'Let me clean that,' Claire says. 'Axel get the phone.'

'No,' I say. 'It might be the police again.' I sniff hard as I cross the room and take the landline from its cradle. 'Hello?'

'Lina.' It's Cain's voice.

'Cain,' I gasp.

'I miss you, darling.'

'I miss you too, it's been a long day.'

'Are you okay?'

'Yeah,' I say, sucking in a short breath, trying to compose myself. 'Just so tired. Claire and Axel are here. Do you want me to come get you now?' I turn and face Axel and Claire, who are both watching me.

'No, Axel's going to drive down. I'll be home late. I'm going to go to the police station first to give a few more details but maybe send Axel on his way now.'

'Right. How are you feeling?'

'I'm okay. They've given me something for the pain. I'd better go, I should be home by midnight.'

'Okay, I'll see you then.'

'I love you, darling. You did so well last night, Lina. You're incredible. I hope you know that.'

I feel the tears coming again. He's never so candid and it takes me a moment to collect myself before I speak again. 'I love you too, see you soon.'

I place the phone back on the cradle.

Claire has tidied up the mess and served up a fresh piece of margarita.

'So,' Axel says, 'should I hit the road?'

'If that's still okay?' I say.

'Of course it is. Claire will look after you.'

He takes one more piece of pizza before leaving.

'So,' Claire says. 'Tell me about these cameras?'

'Where to begin,' I say, releasing all the air in my lungs. 'The police have found them all now but they're still trying to figure out how they got in there. They're tracking down the people who have stayed.'

'Any progress?'

'I haven't heard anything else. The door code had been changed but he knew it. I think he might have been there before, maybe he was a guest.'

'Wouldn't it be traceable with credit cards? The cops will figure it out,' she adds.

I poke out my lip, shake my head. 'Who knows? I don't want to guess why he did this. Maybe he was . . .' I pause, drag my fingers through my hair and sniff back more tears. 'Maybe he was inspired by what happened in Colorado. The difference is, that footage was leaked.'

'Colorado?'

'Last year, the WeStay murder.'

'Oh, I remember.' She's still frowning, probably trying to think of something comforting to say.

'The guy in Colorado wasn't wearing a mask though,' I continue. I've seen a single screenshot. A grinning psychopath, holding up a bloody knife to the camera. I'm beginning to feel sick again talking about it, imagining Daniel dying in his own blood. 'This guy wanted to hide his identity.'

'And who was watching that then? If it leaked? The same people who were watching you last night?'

'Maybe,' I say, exhaling. 'I don't know. Just creeps on the internet somewhere.' A chill runs through me. 'Guys that get off on it. Anyone who has the footage is obviously breaking the law, so I doubt it will get out. I can't imagine the type of person to watch something like that. It just . . .'

Claire makes the face of someone holding something sour in her mouth. 'God, it makes me mad. But at least you've got something to look forward to,' she says. 'I'm so bloody happy for you both.' She sits close. 'What do you want to do?'

'I just want to forget it. I want to take my mind off everything.'

'TV?'

'Yeah,' I say. 'Put something on.'

Claire finds a trashy reality dating show, a group of singles on a tropical island, add ex-lovers and light the fuse with clear spirits. We indulge in meandering, mind-numbing chat. She catches me up on what is happening on the show, whose ex is whose and which people are enemies.

'So,' she says, getting up to make a cup of tea. 'What's happening with work?'

Work. I'd forgotten all about it. I'm supposed to be back on Tuesday.

I mention Scotty, and the mistake he made assuming a triple A was a stroke. For the rest of the night Claire helps me forget about what we went through. When Cain came home from Afghanistan I took leave to care for him, but when I went back to work, and before Axel returned from his tour, Claire was there, helping out. Cooking and keeping Cain company during the day. She's always been there for us.

At some time around ten, after Axel has been away for a few hours, I doze off against her shoulder and we don't wake until I hear the door close, and see Cain's bandaged head emerge from the top of the stairs.

I stand, and rush into his arms. He bends, squeezes me. He's in a t-shirt and jeans I don't recognise. He has two black eyes.

'It's okay,' he assures me. 'It's over now. I've got you.'

'I know,' I say, hopeless tears pressing at my eyes again. 'Are you okay?'

He steps back, gives me that smile that's all dimples, but it's pained. 'I feel like I've just gone thirty rounds with Tyson Fury, but I'll survive.'

'Gone thirty rounds and somehow come out on top,' Axel says, giving him a thump on the back that might have sent a smaller man sprawling. 'Home now, mate. Safe and sound.'

'Spoke with the police again before I left,' Cain says, thumbing his tired eyes.

'What did they say?' I ask as we move back into the lounge and sit down. Could they have made the connection between Daniel and me? Would they share that information with my husband?

It's late, the fatigue has settled deep into my marrow but my mind is not ready for sleep.

'Not much really. Still piecing everything together. I wouldn't hold my breath.' He winces as he sits, a hint of the pain he's in. The painkillers from the hospital must be wearing off. I want to tell him about the baby, I want to give him good news but I'll wait until we are alone later tonight, or perhaps in the morning.

I kiss him now and speak gently, close to his ear. 'I'm so glad you're home, I've been missing you like crazy.'

TWENTY-TWO

THEY'RE ALL USING the same photo of Daniel. We see it on the news the next night – barely out of high school, clean shaven, free of tattoos, hair a boyish fuzz but with those deep green eyes. It's strange seeing him now, so much younger. Fresh and ready to face the uncertain future. I'll never understand why the media choose to use the most inappropriate photos for victims and criminals alike. I don't want to see this happy photo of him, this *normal* boy on the fringes of adulthood. I just want to see the real Daniel, the one that was going to kill me. I want the world to see him accurately. I don't want to carry this guilt around.

'As much as I hate what he did to us, I almost feel sorry for him. He just looks like a normal bloke,' Cain says, beside me on the couch. 'Doesn't look like the sort of person who would do all this. Mind you, I saw blokes, *normal* blokes, become animals over there.' *Over there* being his favourite euphemism for war.

When he turns to me, he realises I'm crying again – there's been a lot of it lately.

'Sorry, Lina. That was dumb. I don't feel sorry for him. I don't know why I said that. He's a monster.'

'It's fine,' I say. I can't quite place this particular sadness. It might be the fatigue catching up, or maybe new hormones from the pregnancy. It could be everything. I remember the flash of the gun, the gurgling sound. Then I walked away and left him to die. 'Bad people, people like him, don't make their *badness* obvious. They look normal from the outside. They hide it away.' I find my mind inexplicably going to Scotty now. He's the type of guy that can hide something away from the world, his drug use, certain attitudes he has.

I go to the kitchen for a glass of water. From the window you can see the media out on the street with their cameras and their vans. I wonder what the neighbours think. The international media has picked it up too, all running the same footage from down at the lake house.

I go back to the living room and fall into the couch. On the TV a heavily made-up reporter in a puffer jacket traipses about at the top of the lake house's driveway, the blue-and-white police tape rocking against the twilight breeze. They've staked out both our places now. The image zooms over her shoulder to the upstairs bedroom, where the tarpaulin still hangs over the broken window.

'I've organised a carpenter,' Cain says. 'Insurance will cover the bill but we need to get it fixed to keep the weather out. It looks like the rain ruined your grandpa's old chest, along with the carpet and bedding.'

'Thanks for organising,' I say. Cain turns the TV up.

'*The sleepy community of Tarawera has seen little action over the years. Locals talk about the campsite at Hot Water Beach being ransacked once, or the occasional boating accident, or the time a squatter had camped out in vacant holiday homes around the lake, but there has been nothing like this. A home invasion, hidden cameras with footage the police can't locate, a woman handcuffed to her fireplace, then escaping and saving her husband. It's the stuff of Hollywood movies, not small-town New Zealand.'*

I can't even imagine the feeding frenzy that would come if they found out I'd had a one-night stand with the dead man. That I am pregnant as a result of it. Although it could be Cain's. I made sure that it was possible, that afternoon I'd climbed on him in his office chair. I made sure the timing was airtight.

The guilt strikes me again, the sort that bends me in half like an uppercut. I cheated, I killed Daniel, and despite how much I justify it in my mind, the feeling won't go away entirely. Earlier, when I'd taken the rubbish bins down to the curb, the reporters hurled their questions, and one gave me pause.

'Did you try to resuscitate him, Lina?'

I'm sure many are wondering the same thing: a paramedic shoots someone, what next? Do their healing impulses take over? Do medical oaths override other instincts of self-defence, revenge, justice?

'Wonder how long this will go on for?' Cain says now.

'I'm sure they'll move on.'

A news story about a water shortage for dairy farms plays next and Cain changes the channel.

'We've had more requests,' I say, 'to speak to the media. *Sixty Minutes* this time.'

Cain exhales. 'We could do with the money, Lina.' I think about the investigation into Trent Skelton. The media pursuing interviews from Cain, Axel, the rest of their unit. He doesn't yet know about the baby; costs will likely go up for us, but I can't do it. What if I say something wrong? What if they realise I knew Daniel before and the entire story unravels? What if they suspect I planned to kill Daniel, to silence him?

'I don't want to talk to the media about it, I know how they twist things,' I say.

'Well, just keep the money in mind. It's there for us if we need it.'

•

I have the next two days off work. It's hard to get out of bed, it's hard to cook or do anything at all. I just keep thinking about it, seeing things whenever I close my eyes. Cain bound in the sheet, the blood, Daniel's face. And that flicker of movement behind Daniel. Was it another man? Or some trick, some figment of my imagination? What if someone is still out there? Someone who was there that night?

There were all those eyes on me, hundreds of viewers. Who were they? Why were they watching? Did they see a second man? I'm reminded of a film, a thriller I once saw, but the title evades me. There's a scene where the main character arrives at her home. She enters and sees the room is dark except for the trembling light of TV static, then as she rounds the corner into the room she finds a family sitting there all watching the pictureless TV. Their heads are bobbing as if listening to music, then they turn, eyes finding her and mad grins spreading. I don't know why this comes to me now, something about the eyes. Being seen. I have that same feeling I had at the house, the same terror, but Daniel is dead now. So why am I still so afraid?

I changed my number, deleted the messages. No one saw us. There is no evidence of us together, except that one photo he sent. But what about his phone? The one he was contacting me on. They didn't find it at the house. If it turns up and they go through his messages it could all come out. And the app. The police will make the connection. That's the last piece of the puzzle. I deleted the app, but not my profile. I listen out for Cain, he's still downstairs. I download the app again. Daniel's face appears in a ring at the top of the screen, but all the messages have been deleted. So why is he back in my inbox?

A roar from Cain down in his study, those flat knocks as he thumps his desk and lets out his schoolboy laugh.

I don't go to him right away. The horse racing is concerning but not as important as this. I touch the message and see what Daniel has sent.

I'm waiting near the lake . . . when will you be back here?

It's from that night, moments before we got home. It's chilling. I can't tell the police about the other video he showed me. The one of us in that WeStay in Auckland. There will be doubts about the baby, doubts about the story of what happened at the lake house. No, I can't do that now.

I delete the message, deactivate my profile on the app and delete it again. Then I open my WeStay app. I create a new account, this time just for me, using my work email. I go back to the booking and click the listing. I see the couples who've booked our place.

I find the house in Auckland. The calendar suggests it's booked out most weekends over the next couple of months but there are a few free nights coming up in the middle of the week. I don't know why, but I need to understand what happened that night. Why me? Why did he do this? There's also a chance, as small as it is, that my ring might be there, hidden under the bed. The earliest available night is Wednesday. I could go there Thursday morning on the way home after my shift finishes at 4 am. I fill in my credentials, my email and click book.

I hear Cain's footsteps coming up the hall towards me. I slide my phone into my pocket.

'Lina,' he says, breathless, with laughter still in his voice. 'Come look at this.'

'What is it?'

I follow him to his study. It's just what I thought. I can hear the quick clipped voice of the racing announcer, see the betting page in one monitor and the horses galloping along in the other.

'Cain, what? What happened?'

He hunches forward and points at something on the screen. I narrow my eyes, lean a little closer.

'What is it?'

'I just picked up the trifecta. It's twenty-one grand!'

'How did . . .' All other words fail me. I just frown at him, confused.

'I won the trifecta,' he says. 'A big trifecta.' He gives that boyish laugh again. 'Twenty-one grand, Lina. We just won twenty-one thousand dollars!'

I'm too gobsmacked to do anything other than squeeze him. 'You won it?' I grab his waist and pull him against me. A voice in my head nags, *How much has he been gambling? How much has he risked and lost?* But it doesn't matter. It's so much money. Enough to make a lot of our problems disappear.

'I can pay Axel rent, start advertising for summer. Clear the credit card.'

I sink into him, I try to be happy but I still feel a pang of betrayal or disappointment. He promised no more secrets, but this is a secret. His betting. He's so happy, I can't raise this now though. I think about something else, how much we need this money, especially with the baby. Now is the time to tell him.

'Cain,' I say. I feel my chest trembling against him. 'I've got news.'

He stops, his smile falters. 'What?'

'It's happened again,' I say. His eyes go wide. 'It's happening, Cain, I'm pregnant.'

He steps back, his hands gripping my forearms, and stares at me like a man peering into a chest of gold. 'You're serious?'

I begin nodding and by the time his smile breaks I feel tears. Exhausted, happy tears. He seems to have forgotten about the money. He jerks me towards him so hard my face knocks his chest.

'After everything. Finally something to celebrate. It's beautiful, Lina. A *baby*. *Our* baby.'

TWENTY-THREE

HAND IN HAND, we are leaving the maternity ward of the hospital after a positive scan, seeing our baby's little heart frantically beating away. Cain is effervescent, and that wry smile is unshakeable. It reaches his eyes and stays there. The money and the baby.

We eat lunch at a nice, modern cafe to celebrate. He has black coffee and I have a chai latte, while we watch the people moving about the CBD. We eat avocado on toast and reflect on the good news: a healthy foetus.

We've been talking about the baby news all morning and when Cain finally changes the subject it's to explain his betting scheme to me. But I'm not listening, my attention is focused instead on a narrow man with a plaited ponytail, all in black. He brings a camera up to his eye.

I don't point him out at first, self-consciously bringing my hand up to my face, scratching my temple.

'Sorry, I know it's boring,' Cain says. 'It's just I want you to realise it's legitimate. Everyone thinks betting is gambling, but it's not always the case.'

'It's not that, Cain.' I glance up again. He's still there, the photographer. 'I think we were just papped.'

We are still the story as much as Daniel. Daniel's movements from his home in Rotorua, stopping for petrol, telling his friends he's 'going to meet a girl'. Interviews with his neighbours, his old teachers, his ex-girlfriend. He had arrived at our house about fifteen minutes before we got home, waiting out at the road until we were inside. We haven't given the media anything, yet they've still written about us, Cain's history in the military, my job as an ambulance officer. People are most fascinated about the cameras, about the idea of this normal man, this man described as 'shy, friendly, an average bloke' installing cameras in our house. The gun was loaded. He was going to kill us. It's almost as though this information is secondary, ancillary to the fact of his *otherwise normal character*. Every time there is breaking news I shiver and brace for something about the date we went on. Maybe someone at the pub, the barkeeper with the bowl cut who gave me soda and lime sans vodka. Would he remember my face, and would the police put two and two together? That's how I imagine it happening, those sharp-nosed detectives from old movies turning up, asking leading questions, trapping me in my lies.

'They took a photo on their phone, you mean?' Cain says, scanning the passing crowds. I glance over to where the man was but now he's not there. Maybe he was shooting something else?

'They're making me out to be a drunk,' he continues. 'I should have been the one to save you. Then you never would have had to do it. I wish I could have protected you and now the media . . .' His voice trails off.

I check the time. 'I'd better get to work.' I push my keys and my phone into my bag. 'I'll be home in the morning.'

I lean down and kiss his cheek, the stubble rasps my lips. 'We're going to be parents, finally.'

'I know, I can't wait,' he says. 'I'll see you tomorrow morning.'

I move quickly towards the car, striding in my soft black shoes before setting out for the ambulance station.

•

I put my bag in my locker, and head out to the ambulance to wait for Scotty. By five to four, he's still not here. For all his faults he's never been one to be tardy. Then at four o'clock on the dot the ambulance door opens. I have a sigh ready for him. *Buzzer beater*, I'm going to say – our old running joke – but it's not Scotty who opens the door.

'Hi,' the girl says. 'I'm Sara.'

'Hi,' I say. 'You're rostered with me today?'

'Yeah,' she says. 'Sorry, I'm new.'

'How long?'

'Sorry?'

'How new are you?' I keep my tone light and friendly but I'm a little irked. It would have been nice if Scotty had texted me to let me know.

'This is my third month. I'm mostly doing relief shifts but it looks like we're working together a lot.'

I can't be angry at her; it's not her fault. If we're going to be partnered up for a while it means Scotty is off for a while. I hope he's not unwell. There is another possibility. He may have changed stations or, worse, asked to be partnered with someone else. But even after what happened, I'd hope he'd tell me if that was the case.

'Well, nice to meet you Sara,' I say, reaching over and taking her hand. She wears a little make-up and has a sweet, bright smile, untempered by the flood of trauma she will soon see on the job. 'You don't need to apologise.'

'Okay, sorry,' she says. Then a nervous giggle. 'I can't help it.'

'No more today, okay? You've got to be confident.'

'Thanks.'

'All set?'

Twelve hours is a lot of time to spend with someone. Sara's shy at first but, after a little encouragement, she gushes words like a broken water main. By the end of the shift I know where she grew up, what her parents do for work, the fact she was recently dumped, her grades at high school and all about the first time she ate avocado. She mentions *that thing down at Tarawera*, but thankfully doesn't realise it happened to me. I also learn that she caught the bus to work. So when we knock off at four in the morning, I offer her a lift home and she reluctantly accepts.

'You need a car,' I say.

'I'm saving for one,' she says, sitting in the front seat with the heater blaring.

'Do you mind if I quickly grab my mail on the way?'

'Sure.'

Unsurprisingly, there's no one beneath the streetlights at the post office in Mount Eden. I cross the street and use my key to enter the room lined with those small red boxes. I find my PO Box, and push the key in. When the flap opens, I see a small envelope.

Anna is handwritten on the front above the address. It's from him, it has to be. He knew my name though, so why put Anna? Why not Lina? I don't hesitate in opening the package, tipping the contents into my hand. It's my necklace and the wedding band is still looped through it. I check the envelope again, postmarked for last week. There's a short note scribbled on a piece of paper that falls out. I pick it up, unfold it and read.

Sorry to hear the news, see you soon.

It strikes me as mildly threatening, yet if he was planning what he did, why send this at all? If he knew my address, why not just send it to the house? Could he have discovered I was lying about my dad being sick? I never even knew my dad. Something like that might send an unhinged man over the edge. Maybe he realised I only wanted my ring and necklace and never planned on seeing him again. Or he somehow realised I had changed my number. This could also be a way of covering his tracks. If he did set us up to be a murder suicide that night, and if he was questioned by the police, a lawyer could point to this act as evidence of good faith.

I put the necklace on. Then I twist my wedding band onto my finger, close the PO box and step outside. I toss the envelope and his note in a nearby bin.

'What was it?' she says.

'Just a package from a friend,' I say, before starting the car and heading off again.

I leave Sara at her house before heading towards the WeStay, passing the bar he took me to, then along that quiet suburban park and pulling up outside the house: 299 Hillview Terrace. It's still dark but for the streetlights, and the moment I open the car door the cold rushes in. In the empty street memories from that night flood my mind: walking along here alone, meeting him, traipsing back under his arm with his damp breath in my hair. That emptiness inside me surges again and I think about what Cain said, *I should have been the one to save you.* He's seen that violence before, and he wanted to protect me from it. He lives with his own guilt.

I quickly scan the street once more before opening the side gate and heading for the front door. I find the key safe and punch in the pin code: 4139. The keys fall out. Two of them: one modern, stubby and short; the other long and thin with a blade at the end in the distinct shape of a U. The small steel map of New Zealand is cold and sharp in my palm. More memories come unbidden when I open the door: that mad scrabble across the living room, hard up against the wall, stumbling around the couch then finding our way to the bedroom. The memories trap themselves in my throat and my heart is aflutter. Despite everything, I tell myself again that Cain *could* still technically be the biological father.

When I hit the switch, the place lights up, hospital-bright, but without that distinct low hum. It's set up just how it was that night, but now I see a small note encouraging me to enjoy my stay. Curtains open to the tiny courtyard. I close them first. I feel vulnerable with all that darkness outside. My skin prickles, feels the cameras like eyes. *Are they still there, watching me? What if they come for me now?* I feel a stitch of fear. So different being here this time.

Somehow, impossibly, I'd briefly forgotten what Daniel did to me, what he did to Cain and now that I remember, I feel the anger and shame at myself again. It happened here, in this place.

I try to imagine the phone in Daniel's hand again, video footage of us on his screen. We were here, in this room, pressed against this wall. The view angled down from the ceiling capturing part of the kitchen and the doors to the bathroom and bedroom.

I take a chair and drag it out from beneath the table, before climbing onto it to scan the ceiling for the camera. That night we were in such a hurry, but I would have noticed something conspicuous.

There's a great big light fixture, black and baroque. It's tasteless, oversized and doesn't fit here. Reaching up, I use the torch app on my phone, shining it around the edge of the fixture, unsure of what I'm looking for but scanning until I see something. It's a . . . camera? I peer closer, moving the phone so close that the light shines into the tiny cavity. It's nothing. Just a hole. About the width of a knitting needle but it's empty. It doesn't make sense. A camera couldn't fit there could it? It's no smaller than the camera on my iPhone I suppose. He had showed me footage from the bed too. That is where I head next.

I drag the chair from the lounge into the bedroom. I climb up and scan the ceiling, but there are no holes here. It's an unbroken canvas of white except for the smoke alarm. I bend my head all the way back, looking up at it. I move the chair closer, climb up and look right into it. Another hole the same size. It's right where the emergency light should be. It's perfect; you would never notice it unless you were searching for it. I press the button to test the alarm but it doesn't make a sound. Stretching on my toes, I reach up and twist the alarm from the ceiling. It comes away easily. The plastic mount connected to the roof has another tiny hole through to the ceiling. I'm holding my breath. At the lake house, the police found the cameras hidden in impossibly small crevices. Seven in total. How many cameras were here in this apartment? My skin itches, I feel the eyes on me now, like hands touching me, pinching and prodding. Then a sound.

I freeze. Three hard taps at the door.

I can't move. *Someone is here*, I think. *Someone was still watching*. My breathing is quick and laboured. I climb down from the chair, search the room for a weapon, or an escape. I could go out the courtyard, try to climb the fence.

There is another knock at the door. I'm electric, waiting for some heavy blow. I move silently. If I ignore them maybe they will go away. But what if they don't? It's too early in the morning for visitors, but why knock at all? If they mean me harm, why not just burst through the door? A dark thought enters my mind like a piece of glass, then shatters and spreads through me: *what if it's the second man?*

My sneakers make a small squelching sound when I move across the polished kitchen floor towards the door. I lean in close to peer out through the peephole, my heart slamming now. The sun is beginning to rise, but it's still dark out. Where did they go? Who was it? Someone must know I am here, they must have been following me. I can't just wait it out, but then again I can't go into the darkness alone.

Squeezing my eyes closed I'm back in the lake house with that man, he's hovering over me, taunting me. Then I'm holding the gun, it's exploding in my hand, throwing me back. The trigger was firm, then it was water and I flew, sprawling. I'm there, seeing it all as if it's happening to me again.

I survived. I got through that; this is nothing. Inhale, exhale.

In the kitchen I find a pan. It's light but sturdy. I take it back to the door, where I reach for the door handle, and gently twist it. The door pulls open slowly, whining. The crisp early morning air moves in around me, through my clothes, chilling me.

I pocket my phone, before stepping out with the pan in both hands. Through the door, down the first step, then the second. I pull the door closed, locked behind me. I'm prickling with fear as I peer towards the car. No one is there. Slowly, bending my knees, I find the key safe and push the keys inside. Locking it once more. I rise and start towards the gate, the street beyond. The car is so close now. The gate creaks, a horror film sound that sends my heart racing. I'll have to explain I left a pan in the front yard, it might cost part of my deposit to replace if it is stolen but I need to leave. I squat and place the pan down. Through the gate now, two quick strides. I reach the sedan and am vaguely aware of another car door sounding, footsteps. The fear is overwhelming. He's coming for me. I look up and he's on me before I can open my car door.

I find the key between my knuckles. Turn and swing blindly.

'Stop!' a voice says.

I swipe out again, aiming for his throat. He's turned me using the weight of my attack. My arm is up my spine, the key pried from my fingers and chinking against the concrete footpath.

I kick back and twist. Throwing my elbows.

'Stop,' the voice says. 'Calm the fuck down.'

'Let me go,' I say. 'Help!' I scream for anyone on the street. The sunrise is just beginning to tinge the horizon. Joggers will be out soon. Someone will help me. I scream again.

He's too strong, my arm wrenches higher and I'm pressed against the car. He's going to kidnap me.

'Help!'

His voice is loud, authoritative and close to my ear. 'Mrs Phillips, I'm going to need you to calm down.'

'Let me go. LET. ME. GO!' I twist, kick, turn my head. *If I could just bite his hand. If I could loosen his grip.*

'You've just assaulted a police officer,' he says, with a firm, authoritative tone.

'What?' I say, twisting my head back. It can't be. They're not in uniforms. 'You're not –'

'My name is Detective Senior Sergeant Ed Rata.'

'No,' I say, turning back to eye the man. I realise there's two of them. 'You're not police, you've been following me. You're –'

'And this is my colleague, Constable Black.'

Peephole transmission

Given the recent growth in members, it has become clear that Peephole must implement new measures to protect the anonymity of planters, and keep viewers from interfering with streams. Over the past month, there has been a number of robberies at properties that were vacant, and the recent incident on stream 037B has resulted in further police investigations. This stream would not have been compromised if it wasn't for the individual who interfered. The planter's equipment was discovered and removed by police, this may lead to identification through fingerprints or DNA on and around the equipment. We have closed the WeStay account and have safely removed equipment from all other streams associated with this account.

Until further notice all live streams will be delayed by one to six hours to stop those who are using this platform for anything other than watching.

Please enjoy the show.

TWENTY-FOUR

'WE'D LIKE YOU to come with us,' Rata says. He's darker than the younger one, and has a bristled black moustache you could polish a shoe with.

'How do I know you're cops?'

He produces a badge, but I can barely see it in the early morning glow and even if I could, I wouldn't know if it were real. As he opens his jacket to put it back, I see the handcuffs and the taser on the side of his belt.

'What if I say no?'

'We'd prefer it if you came along voluntarily. It would help to clear things up,' he says. A non-answer. 'We want to know why you're here, at this house?'

A clot of something breaks free from where it had grown in my chest, it rises up and settles in my throat. *I have to tell them.* But I know I can't.

'It's not what you think,' I say, pausing. 'Why are *you* here?'

He doesn't take his eyes away from mine. 'We can talk about that at the station.'

I slowly exhale, thinking through the situation. 'Can I follow you there in my car?'

Rata turns back to Constable Black, who shrugs as if he's asking question.

'It might be easier if you come with us. We can drop you back here after.'

'No,' I say, defiant now. 'If you want me to come, I will drive myself.' I still don't know if I trust these two. I can't pinpoint why, but I don't want to be at their mercy. I want to be able to leave in my car when I want.

'Sure. Follow us.'

I climb into my car, my heart thrashing and my palms damp around the key. The car starts with a grumble. Headlights come on behind me. I wait for them to pass then follow on.

They lead me through the streets back towards the heart of the city, as sunrise slowly continues to peel the layers of darkness away. When we park, me tucking in behind their dark sedan, I'm looking up at what could be Orwell's Ministry of Love. A Tetris block of a building, too banal to be considered 'architectural' but the word 'brutalist' leaps to my mind. Ten storeys of concrete, featureless but for the evenly spaced small square windows, sitting in their own recesses.

'This way,' the younger one says when I climb out of the car. He leads, and the other one, Rata, walks beside me. Everything about this situation feels off. They've got control. Giving me the feeling that it would hurt more to defy their commands than it would to simply acquiesce. These two are well versed. They wield silence like a blowtorch, they know how to get people to do and say what they want. Or maybe I'm being too harsh. Maybe it's me, my own guilt gnawing at my subconscious. Maybe I'm afraid they'll be able to unpick the thread and my secrets will all tumble out.

He stops, opens the door for me. 'Come on through.'

I don't acknowledge the gesture, I just stride past. Cain said the media are like vampires, but I feel that way about these two:

never invite them into your house, never accept a gift from them or do them a favour.

'Kia ora, Tabitha,' Rata says as we pass a plate-glassed booth.

The uniformed woman glances up. 'Morning, Detective.'

A buzzing sound and a door opens.

He leads me through corridors of unblemished beige walls. This is not the police station we had visited to give our statements. This is something else. We reach what feels like the heart of the ground level, a small interview room. If you've been in one, you've been in them all: a table mounted to the wall, a voice recorder and camera in the corner. I remember the first time I came to a place like this. Grandpa was with me because I was too young to go alone. We both had to give statements about that night, when Mum had turned up at the lake house, drunk again.

'She's coming with me. She's my bloody daughter.'

'She's not getting in that car. We're her guardians, not you. You can come back and visit her when you're sober.'

The argument growing, Mum rushing at him, a skinny thing with her hands raised like claws, grabbing at her own father.

Then when they called the police, she'd sped off in that old Ford. And Grandpa just stood on the porch, watching her go. Then that sound. Metal bending, the crackle of branches breaking, and the boom and splash of the car striking the water. That corner at the cliff is four hundred metres along the road yet we all heard it so clear. I still hear it now when I think about her.

'Look,' Rata begins. 'This isn't a formal interview or anything like that, we're not recording you. We just want you to help us understand one or two things.'

'What is this place?'

'It was the main police station in Auckland before the move, but the force still owns it, so we make use of it from time to time. For interviews and meetings.'

Interrogations? I wonder. *National security? Cybercrime?*

'Okay. Is there any more news on our case?'

'We're looking at something different. It's broader than that one case.'

The room drops ten degrees. *Broader.* What does that mean? *Peephole?* Rata sits down, private school straight spine, with a muscled neck keeping that large head of his up. 'Perhaps you can begin by explaining to us why you were at that house?' he says.

'Well, I booked it on WeStay.'

A brow lifts. 'Why did you book *that* place in particular?'

'Sorry?'

'Why did you book it? You didn't stay there tonight. So what is it? Trouble at home?'

All the lies flicker through my mind, *I needed a night away from Cain, sometimes I stay near the ambulance station when I'm on call, I stayed at that house before and left something valuable behind.* None seem plausible. The truth is I don't really know myself why I went, I guess I wanted to see if the cameras were still there. I twist the wedding ring on my finger, I don't realise I'm doing it until I follow Rata's dark eyes to my own hands. I stop.

'I haven't broken the law,' I say. 'So I want to go home.'

'Well, that depends.'

'On?'

'Given what you know about the pending case concerning Daniel Moore and the fact you were at a place of interest, this could be seen as interfering in a criminal investigation.'

'How was I to know that house was of interest?'

His smile says cut the crap.

'I'm not answering any more questions,' I say. I eye the door.

He levels his gaze right on me, letting the tension build.

'I'm going to ask you again, why were you at that house this morning, Lina?'

I just shake my head.

'Why are you and your husband visiting a place of interest in a criminal investigation?'

I freeze. Look up suddenly from my hands. Rata cocks the corner of his mouth. *Cain visiting that house?* A swelling siren of panic. I try to straighten my face out but they've seen it.

'Wait,' he says, leaning a little closer. 'You didn't know.'

'Didn't know what?'

A small laugh. My insides plummet. Rata ribs the other cop with his elbow. 'Hear that, Constable? She didn't even know he had been there.'

The constable speaks now. 'Daniel turns up at your house with a fistful of lead in his guts. He stayed at that house you were visiting tonight, and you didn't know your husband had been there.' The image almost makes me gag. The tone has changed. Rata speaks again now, the smile leaving his face. 'Help us understand, Lina. None of this makes sense.'

I just shake my head.

'If Cain was there and you don't know why, I'd be very careful if I were you.'

I can't help but take the bait. 'What do you mean?'

'It sounds like your husband has a secret, Lina. And you have a secret. Things like this tend not to end well. So why don't you help us out? What we are investigating is bigger than you both.'

Bigger than us both. My mind is whirling. Cain must know something, why else was he there? Or could this be some trick the police are playing on me?

'Cameras were installed at that house. Now they've been removed. Who do you think might have removed them?'

'Daniel Moore?' I say.

'Some would say he's the obvious culprit. But people can make a lot of money very quickly doing this sort of thing. Two places in less than one week and they're both linked to you, Lina.'

'I don't know what to say, I had nothing to do with it.'

Rata shrugs now, as if to say, *prove it.* Then he speaks, 'We've had the place under surveillance. I was not expecting you or your husband to show up. I missed him but when they said you were at the house, well that was worth getting out of bed for.'

'Did you bring him here?'

'No,' he says.

'Why not?'

'That doesn't matter.'

'I went there to check for cameras. I saw on our listing that someone had stayed there as well as our place. I went there because I'm still shaken up and scared and I want answers and I thought there was a second man that night. That's all.'

Rata pokes out his bottom lip as if considering my theory that someone else was involved. 'If you're telling the truth about this, I'd be *very* careful if I were you. But I'm not sure if I really believe what you're saying. I think there's more to it.'

•

Rata walks me to my car. 'Keep an eye on your husband, Lina,' he says as we walk. 'We can protect you but you need to give us something. If you have information and you withhold it, we will find out. If you are protecting someone, you will go down with them. *Unless* you come to us first.'

'No,' I say, an impulse to protect Cain taking over. 'I'm sure this is a big misunderstanding. I don't know anything about anyone being involved with this.'

He reaches into his coat and takes out a pen. Then he fishes in his pants pocket and produces a notebook. He tears out a page, scribbles something on it and hands it to me.

'Keep this somewhere safe and call me if you have any other information that might help.'

'Thanks.'

He doesn't say anything else, he just turns to go.

'Wait,' I call.

'Yes?' He turns back, hands on hips.

'How much can these people make? From the cameras.'

In the morning glow, I see his eyes narrow. 'I don't know for certain, but I would guess in the thousands, if not tens of thousands. Depends what sort of material the cameras yield.' I ignore the suspicious instinct tugging at my consciousness like a dog at the end of its chain. The trifecta was in the tens of thousands, this mysterious injection of cash.

'Is he a suspect for any of this?' I say. 'With the cameras?'

He glances around himself for a few seconds as if following a mosquito with his eyes. 'I'm just saying be careful. If it's not feeling right, or you're worried things are going south, get out and call me.'

Then, before I can speak again, he's turned on his heel and he's heading back inside the building.

TWENTY-FIVE

BY THE TIME I get home, morning has broken in a cloudless blue full of birdsong. There is no point entering silently when I know Cain is likely already awake. On the way to the bedroom, I stop at his study and gently press the door open. It's warmer in here but he's not up. There's no sound or movement in the house, so I step inside the room, moving on the balls of my feet towards his laptop, the two curved monitors on the wooden desk. He spends a lot of time at this desk. I reach for the computer, rest my hand on the side of the casing and feel for heat but it's cool. I could turn it on, snoop through his things for some evidence. But now that I'm home what Rata was suggesting about Cain seems more and more ridiculous. If Cain knew about the cameras, he would know what I did. He would have left me. He's not a pervert, not a voyeur. I know him well enough to know that. So what if it was a ploy? Some move to get me to admit to something I didn't do? Or what if they saw someone who *looked* like Cain at the house. It might have been another Maori boy, or the owner, or a Jehovah's Witness. Maybe even the cleaner . . . *at night time?* Perhaps not, but people make mistakes. There's no way to know for sure that it really was him they saw or if they saw anyone at all.

I move now from his study back into the hallway, up the stairs and towards the bedroom before he has a chance to find me snooping. The curtains are closed, I use my phone as a light, crossing the room towards the ensuite. He doesn't speak or move. Teeth brushed, face washed, I strip down, open the covers and slide in. This could be a mistake, coming back here as if nothing has changed but then what other options do I have? A small paunch is now pressing against the band of my underwear. The baby is growing. My chest flutters just thinking about it, the fact I will be a mother. I may never drink again, I will be perfect to this child.

I reach out, touch Cain's chest, feel his warm skin.

'You're late.'

His voice makes me jolt. 'You gave me a fright,' I reply.

He doesn't speak again.

'I know I'm late. I got caught up at work,' I say, stretching my arms but it does little to ease the tension. 'Someone new started and she had a bunch of questions after the shift, so I had a chat with her, then I dropped her home.' Something else occurs to me. 'Then I went to the jeweller. He opened at eight. I picked this up.' I hold up my ring finger. He feels it with his thumb.

'Oh good,' he says. 'Still seems a little loose.'

'Yeah, it's better than it was though,' I lie.

'I thought maybe you were doing overtime, or something went wrong.' His voice is lighter now.

'No,' I say. 'And you've slept in.'

'Arsenal versus Tottenham at 2 am,' he says. 'Had to watch it. I'm knackered now. Suppose I should get up soon.'

'Well, good morning, I'm going to sleep myself.' I pull my sleep mask on and in my head I hear those words. *Be careful.*

•

When I get up in the afternoon, I find him flat on his back, legs in the figure-four stretch, pulled down towards his chest. He wears a pained expression.

'Good sleep?'

A yawn seeps out. 'Yeah. I need coffee though.'

He rolls over onto his front now, starts arching his back, pushing up. His shoulders bulge in his singlet.

I turn the espresso maker on. He comes over, begins grinding coffee beans.

'Sit down, I'll make your coffee.'

'Thanks, I'll make food.' I go to the toaster with a pair of bagels. 'You hungry?'

'A little.'

Right then my phone rings. It's an unknown number. 'Hmm,' I say. 'I'll have to take this.'

'Who is it?'

'I'm not sure, but I think it's someone from work. Maybe the new girl I'm on with.' I slide outside into the backyard and bring the phone to my ear.

'Hello?'

'Lina, Detective Rata. We've heard back from Vodafone. The phone at the property didn't belong to Daniel Moore.'

'I know, the other cop told me that.'

'So, is there anything you want to tell me?' The tone of his voice has changed.

'No, you know it all now.'

'Why is that phone attached to your Vodafone account?'

A chill rushes over my skin despite the heat of the sun. 'My account? But I'm on my phone now.'

'The phone we found in the house was used that night to access a Tor browser and we believe the Peephole servers. Your sim card was in the phone, it pinged the towers near Lake Tarawera.'

I swallow hard, look inside. Cain is watching the TV but at that moment his eyes shift towards me.

'No,' I say. 'Impossible. The sim card is here, it's in a shoebox at the bottom of my wardrobe.'

'I'm going to end the call and you are going to go and check that it's still there. Then you are going to text me, and delete the message, understand?'

I exhale. 'Okay, fine.'

'Don't tell your husband you spoke to me.'

My breath is hard now. I swallow, try to compose myself. I smile in at Cain who is watching me.

'So,' I begin casually, opening the door to enter the house. 'It was just someone from the ambulance service checking that I'm happy to work with Sara full-time for a while.'

'Kind of them to check,' he says.

The bagels pop. 'I'll make those in a moment,' I say before climbing the stairs, trying not to rush. Silently I reach in the bottom of my wardrobe, grab the box with the sim card inside. I open it. And already know what I will find. It's not here. I search, groping through the receipts in the box, pulling them out. The sim card is gone. Daniel knew my address from the MyTrack app. He was in this house. I text Rata.

It's gone. Then delete the message and lock my phone before closing the box, packing it away and heading back downstairs.

'So, have you had any more wins?' I ask taking the warm bagels out.

'Sorry?'

'With your betting?'

'Oh no,' he says. 'Nothing like the other day.'

'How much money are you actually betting?'

It's awkward but it's the only way to start this conversation. I've been wondering how deep into gambling he has fallen once more. But now I've got an ulterior motive. I've become suspicious.

I can feel his eyes on my cheek, but I don't look away from the bagels as I spread avocado.

'What's this about, Lina?'

'I'm just wondering. I mean, we don't have much money and to win thousands, you need to bet a lot, right?'

'I probably bet a few hundred a month and sometimes I lose and sometimes I win. I'm going up though, I was even before the big win.'

I try not to react. Yet the idea of him betting makes me feel sick. It reminds me of years ago when he was losing big, betting bigger, chasing his losses. Stressed and angry without work to keep him distracted.

Those words the detective said are bouncing around in my head, colliding with all the other thoughts. *People can make a lot of money very quickly doing this sort of thing.* 'It's just a shock. You were addicted to gambling once, remember? Does that ever go away?'

'No,' he says. 'It doesn't. But this isn't gambling, it's *betting*. There is a difference.'

I crack salt and pepper now, squeeze a wedge of lemon over the bagels.

Cain takes our coffees to the table. He's reading a news article on his phone.

'What's that about?' I ask as I bring the bagels over.

He has the phone in one hand, he takes his bagel in the other and bites it. While he chews he turns the screen to me.

I lean forward to read it.

Police investigating if Moore had accomplice

He turns it back and reads aloud. 'A spokesperson for the police has confirmed they're looking to see if someone might have helped him.'

A small sound of surprise escapes from me and he glances up. 'I know you think you saw someone else, Lina, but I only saw one guy. Trauma like that messes with memory. What you believe you saw and what you really saw are two distinct things.'

'You were barely conscious.'

'Still, it was just him when I came to. Why wouldn't a second person come out then? But what I really don't understand is why the police didn't contact us to let us know they're looking into this.'

'Probably didn't want to bother us.'

He puts the phone down and chews the last of his bagel slowly.

'What about the cameras?' I ask, watching his face for any hint that he knows more than he's letting on. If Cain were involved with the cameras, it backfired on him spectacularly. *It can't be true*, I tell myself. *It can't be.*

'They found them all in the house.'

'People were watching, Cain.'

I can see by the way he stretches his jaw that he's digging at a molar with his tongue.

'That sicko could have orchestrated the entire thing. The police said that they couldn't access any footage on the phone they found,' he says.

If he's acting, it's convincing.

'People were watching us online,' I say.

He shakes his head, a short snap to dismiss the idea.

I continue speaking. 'Well, what about his phone, it can't have just disappeared? The police said it pinged mobile phone towers in the area.'

'Who knows? Maybe he flushed it down the toilet. Maybe it's at the bottom of the lake. They searched the entire house. If it was there it would have turned up.'

'Unless a second person took it?'

He lifts the phone again in response and shows me the screen. 'The reputable New Zealand Police Force will have answers for us very soon I'm sure.' His voice bubbles with sarcasm.

I don't say anything else, I just get up, clear the plates. 'I know you explained the betting the other night but I would really like to see how it works.'

A small smile, his eyes flick to mine. 'Sure, Quin. Let me show you.'

•

'So,' he begins, when we're both seated in his study. 'People think it's just gambling but it's not. There are two ways to make money with betting.' His computer springs to life, both screens fill. The right screen with a browser, the left with a spreadsheet. 'The first way is to know something that the bookies don't, or to know it sooner.'

'Like what?'

'Say a star player picks up an injury, if you can calculate the difference between the current betting odds and the new likelihood with the injury, and if the risk versus reward tips in your favour, then it's a good bet. You just need to do it before the odds offered by the betting agencies change. Or say the weather report changes favouring one team, or you see on Instagram a star player's wife gives birth and it's likely that player will miss the next game.'

'Right, so what's the other way?'

'The other way is what's called "arbitrage". You can't lose, but if you win too much you get banned.'

'What do you mean you can't lose?'

'Well, if there is a tennis match say. One player is paying odds of two dollars and five cents on one betting agency and the other player is paying two dollars and five cents on another betting agency. Then you put one hundred dollars on both. You have spent two hundred total but you are guaranteed to win two hundred and five dollars.'

I scoff. 'Lot of work for five dollars.'

'So bet twenty thousand then. That's five hundred dollars guaranteed.'

'So you've got twenty thousand to throw around?'

'No, but you get the point. That's a two and a half percent guaranteed return overnight. It's never as clear cut as that, sometimes one player is paying five dollars and the other is paying a dollar and thirty cents and there's more maths involved, but I've got a spreadsheet that works it out.'

'Who taught you this?'

'Someone at the gym. Look,' he says. Taking the mouse now, he slides the cursor over the screen and opens a new spreadsheet. I've seen him working on this one before. 'Here are the winnings in black and here are the losses in red. Each month totalises at the bottom.' He points to numbers in bold font beneath each month's bets. I feel almost proud. There's a level of sophistication to it. But I'm still worried he's becoming addicted again.

I lean closer, reading over the numbers. January $634, February $158, March $112, April $393, May $2136, June $832, July $219, August $512, September $2393, October $22,312. Total: $28,947.

'Cain,' I say. *Why didn't he tell me this earlier?* I never showed interest, but I didn't *want* to know. It still doesn't sit right with me, the stigma of gambling, of addiction. And this is a lot to keep from me, so what else might he be keeping secret? 'Do we have to pay tax on this?'

'Technically not,' he says. 'It's a hobby.'

'And where is the money?'

'It's in the betting accounts.'

'Can you show me, the money going into them?'

The air seems to cool, he bristles. 'You don't trust me, do you?'

'I just want to see it, where it came from.'

He swivels on his chair, regards me for a moment. 'If it means that much to you.' First, he opens a browser, shows me one account, all the bets, the wins and the losses, the balance. Then he opens up a program, and a number of flags from different countries drop down. He chooses one and goes to another website, this time it's an Australian website.

'What was that?'

'It's a proxy server. It just means I can use international betting agencies. Their servers think I'm somewhere I'm not.'

'Where did you learn to do that?'

'Like I said, a mate at the gym. Axel helped as well. He knows more about the proxy servers.'

He shows me a number of different accounts, all with betting histories and different balances. It's thousands of dollars total. Then he closes them, turns back to me and asks, 'Happy now? I'm not blowing all of our money or whatever else you're worried about.'

'Sorry,' I say. 'I don't know what I was worried about. I just don't want you to do this without talking to me. It's our money and our future. And you're going to be a dad soon.'

'A man in Australia, David Walsh, was so successful at betting he opened a museum and is one of the richest men in Australasia. It's a viable way to make good money.' He pauses. 'But I know it worries you so I'll try to keep you in the loop more in the future.'

You also have another secret, Cain. You visited that house and I need to know why.

'The builder is repairing the damage to the lake house this weekend,' he says. 'It's not much, he's just patching up the wall, replacing the window and fixing the rain damage. Your grandpa's chest is with a restorer, he thinks he might be able to repair it.'

'Great,' I say, standing. 'I might try get a quick run in while the sun is out.'

•

After my run, I strip out of my running clothes and shower. When I've dried my hair and got dressed, I go to him. There is something still gnawing at my conscience. I lean back against the island, watching him cook. 'One of the payments from the betting agencies was missing,' I say.

'What?'

'The big win. There wasn't anything for twenty thousand.'

He sniffs, shakes his head. Through his singlet, I see the tension in the ropes of muscle up his back.

'I closed that account,' he says.

'Why?'

'Because I was banned. Professional gamblers are constantly getting banned by betting agencies. You win too much, you game the system and they block you out.' He turns around now.

I nod, but I can't let it go.

Then he grabs my hips and lifts me up onto the bench. He presses his lips to mine. It's forceful, his hands opening my legs, tearing my pants down. My heart leaps, he's too strong but I want it, I want him despite the suspicions Rata has planted in my mind.

'This is a surprise,' I say, against his lips.

His hand covers my mouth and then in a second his head is down in between my legs. I'm self-conscious, just for a moment. But it takes only a few seconds for me to fall back on the palms of my hands on the bench. I eye the blinds to make sure they're closed. He's not done this in so long, it's like a stranger is down there. When he stands up, he pulls his shirt off, strips me down and turns me around over the bench. He's inside me in an instant. I feel invigorated, intoxicated by this energy, this lust. It ends quickly, a bright flare. Then I collapse over the bench.

I'm still there catching my breath when he places his phone down in front of me. I see the transaction.

$21,129 INTL TRAN – BetGo Corp

'I didn't rob a bank, Lina.' I can hear the smile in his voice. 'You want your child's father to be a criminal?'

My mind searches for something to say, a balm to soothe the shame. I stand and reach for my pants. There's something a little off about how he phrased that. *Your child's father.* Or maybe not, maybe I will see signs of guilt in everything he does.

He starts serving dinner and I go find my own phone. This feeling is odd. The euphoric sex, but also the shame, the power and control he had.

I search for BetGo. Lots of results come up, all for the same betting website in the UK. He's telling the truth.

Peephole
Live Cam Premium
Stream: 016D
Viewers: 018

From camera 9, through the windows, the scene outside is simply a tall grey building beyond the steel red steps of a fire escape. The apartment is small and tidy. On camera 4 a dark-haired man stands before the mirror in the bathroom – 21 viewers. He has a tiny L-shaped scar beside his eye, and stubble coming through. He runs a face cloth over his cheeks, across his forehead before wringing it out and hanging it over the faucet. He then brushes his teeth, all the while staring at himself in the mirror just below where the camera is set. When he leaves the bathroom, camera 2 in the bedroom picks him up. Another man is lying beneath the sheets of the bed with a book open in one hand. The man from the bathroom climbs back into the bed with his lover. He reaches for his laptop on the nightstand and sets it on his lap before opening the screen. He begins typing away.

TWENTY-SIX

WHEN THE SHIFTS are erratic, day–night–day, I try to adjust as quickly as I can, sometimes relying on melatonin pills to help with the switch. I have a day shift tomorrow but don't take anything tonight to sleep; I just try to go to bed early, playing rain sounds and blocking out the light with my sleep mask. I wonder if there was some reason Scotty changed partners. We did have a couple of shifts after I confronted him about his drug use. It was tense, sure, but not so bad that we couldn't continue to work together again. My thoughts stall and sleep hits me.

I don't know how much time has passed when I emerge from slumber. I know it's late because Cain is beside me, stirring. That must have been what woke me. I lift my mask just a little, see the light. He has his phone in his hand. I could doze back off, but I don't. He makes the smallest noise to clear his throat. His elbow nudges me as he rolls. Does he realise he's woken me? Then he is up, peeling the covers back and slipping from bed. I know he gets up to watch sport, to bet. I know he doesn't have any training sessions to take tomorrow, yet still I feel something is off. Now the door opens almost silently, just the subtlest moan of a hinge that sends a current down my spine. *What are you doing, Cain?*

The door closes, just as slowly and not all of the way. Soft feet on the carpet outside. Then down the stairs.

I wait, rigor mortis still. Minutes pass. I'm not going to sleep, not until I know what he is doing. I could always go check on him, walk through the house like I was getting a glass of water. But clomping my way downstairs would give him ample warning. Stealth is key. Slowly, I sit up and reach for my phone. It lights up the room when I touch it. I listen to the house for a few heartbeats, then turn and lower my feet to the carpet. I move gently, navigating by the dim glow of the phone screen. Through the door, sucking my stomach in so I don't touch it. Then to the stairs and down on the balls of my feet. The air is cool, and I can hear the distant whir of his computer. He's in his study. I creep towards the door, holding my breath. I'm suspended between flight and fight, compelled forward by a *need* to know, to understand what my husband is doing. It's probably nothing, I'm sure it's nothing. But how can I trust him after finding out he had been to that WeStay on Hillview Terrace? And why come to bed at all if he was just going to use his phone and get back up? I grip the handle and turn it so slowly that it doesn't make a sound. Pressing inward, I feel weak as though all of my energy has been sapped by the cool door handle.

Cain is there, standing hunched before the computer in his pyjama pants, peering close to the right monitor, blocking it with the bulk of his bare back. On the left monitor I can see he has his emails open. Whatever is on that other screen has his full attention.

I move a little closer now. Stepping carefully, watching him. His right hand comes to his mouth, covers it and he leans closer still. I keep moving. Sidestepping to open up a view of the screen beyond his shoulder.

He's watching a video. He's clicking through . . . footage. Of me. I freeze. He's watching me. He has the footage. I can't breathe. This is the moment I've feared most. But then I realise it's not the footage from the night with Daniel in Auckland, but the night at the lake house. I'm cuffed to the fire. Daniel is there on the couch. It's . . . It's *the video*. Could it be? My husband is on Peephole. What if he planted the camera? The room seems to twist around me and a small gasp escapes. It's so tiny but he hears. His head jerks around, his eyes find mine. I jump back but he's on me before I have a chance to run. Something Rata says comes to me. *If it's not feeling right, or you're worried things are going south, get out and call me.* His hand reaches for my throat, gripping the front of my gown. I'm trapped. He's got a crazed look, his eyes all white.

'What the hell are you doing?' he yells.

The room seems to vibrate. My vision blurs. Panic courses through my veins and my phone slips out of my hand and crashes to the floor. My knee rises instinctively, it catches him and his grip loosens enough for me to tear away. *Get out.*

'Lina,' he calls after me. But I'm already running, out the door of the study. I sense him behind me, but I don't look back. I throw the door closed, hear him tearing it open again. I rush down the stairs to the front door. If I make it out I can get away, I know I'm faster than him with his bad knee and I can run further. There's no thinking, no room to stop or consider what I saw. I pull, turn and twist through the door then I'm out in the dark of night, my head swimming. I sprint, the cool air claws at the inside of my throat. My feet carry me away from the house. I don't stop until I get to the corner, searching in the cones of light thrown from the streetlamps. *My phone is back in the study.* I could knock on doors until someone answers. No one has that video. It's not online. The police can't find it, can't access the servers that host it. But *he* has it.

I hear a car in the distance and turn to see headlights. Turning back to the house, I can't see Cain anywhere. The car slows as I step out into the road and hurl my arms around in the air. It's a taxi. I look back again – I see Cain pass beneath a streetlight and his form is thrown into full colour. He's coming now, chasing me.

'Stop, please!' The taxi slows. Pulls over just past me. I run to it but the back door is locked. The window drops a crack.

'Hi,' the driver says. 'Where are you heading?' then a pause as his eyes take me in – my pale sleeping shorts and top, torn at the front from Cain's grip. 'Is something wrong?'

'I need the police. Let me in quick.'

'What's happened?'

'We don't have time. Just open the door.'

The lock rises, I rip the door open, drop inside. Then I see him. Cain hobbling closer three house lengths from the corner. His angry eyes fix on me. Despite his grey pants he looks like an animal.

'Go,' I scream. The tyres give a little squeal as the Prius accelerates. I look back and see Cain watching me, his hands on his hips.

Investigation notes for Task Force Riding Hood

Transcript nine of eleven from Deepchan message boards, in which agents attempt to gain access to the service Peephole:

Anon4qJjy4rE: it doesn't exist otherwise I would be on it by now

Anon6AsRk9k1:   it does. I am not going to risk my money and my access. Just trust me it's there online. Dozens of streams.

Anon4qJjy4rE: send one screenshot. Unless you're full of shit.

Anon6AsRk9k1:   here's all I will tell you. It costs a lot to join. It's better/more real than any porn, or video leak site you've been on. If you're a voyeur there is no better or safer service. The streams are from dozens of different countries and nobody knows they're being watched. You will not find anything else like it.

Anon4qJjy4rE: don't hold out on me. You've known me for months. give me the referral.

Anon6AsRk9k1:   you don't understand. You can't tell anyone, you can't screenshot. Everyone's streams have a unique overlay, leak a single frame and you get banned and lose your deposit.

Anon4qJjy4rE:	I'm not going to tell anyone shit.
Anon6AsRk9k1:	I can't do it.
Anon4qJjy4rE:	refer me, I will pay your next year subscription.
Anon6AsRk9k1:	Bullshit.
Anon4qJjy4rE:	I'll send any crypto you want right now to prove it. I've got money.
Anon6AsRk9k1:	You're a fucking fed aren't you?
Anon4qJjy4rE:	Yep. And a voyeur and I'm sick of the same shit porn and the same hard candy. Of course I'm not a fucking cop. JUST LET ME IN. come on dude.
Anon6AsRk9k1:	Let me think on it for a day. They don't mess around. You break a rule, we both lose out.
Anon4qJjy4rE:	If it's as good as you say, if it's really worth it, I'll be on my best behaviour.
Anon6AsRk9k1:	don't make me regret it man. I'll refer you as thanks for the shit you've sent me in the past, but please don't make me regret it. They take it all pretty seriously.

TWENTY-SEVEN

I WAS SO wired when I arrived that I barely noticed where I was. I'd taken the taxi driver's card – he'd eventually left me here when I'd promised I would pay him double the fare when I got my bank card. Now, as dawn breaks, the forecourt of the real Auckland police station reveals itself to me outside. It's different to the place Rata took me last time. This one is all glass, modern yet imbued with authority.

Waiting areas are never designed for comfort. Police waiting rooms are cattle stations. The cold plastic chair does its utmost to cut off circulation below the knee and when I stand to stretch, I get pins and needles. My nerves are frayed as it is, but sitting here for half the night has only made it worse. I think about the baby, stress is bad for both of us. I make myself breathe slowly and try to relax. I imagine her or him growing, expanding.

The doors open. I see Cain and a cool blade of guilt runs down my spine. I've never felt like this looking at him before; the shame, the sense that I barely know my husband. My eyes avoid his and settle somewhere near his waist, where his hands are cuffed. Then they fall to his feet, he's wearing neat sneakers, then up over his pants, his button-up shirt. But no higher. I can't look at his face. He's the biggest person in the room but he seems diminished. His head turns to me as he passes, and I freeze. I'm not angry or stressed anymore. I feel . . . sadness.

'Lina, this is a mistake,' he says. 'You don't understa –'

Then I meet his eyes and see they're pleading but before he can get another word out, he's pulled through a door by the beefy arresting officer. I almost rise to stop them, to tell them to let him go but then I remember what he was watching. How could he access it? What does it mean? He's my husband, and I still love him, I just don't understand why he was watching that footage. In place of the panic that rose so suddenly in the study there is something else: doubt. I'm not even sure what really happened. Was he actually going to hurt me? *He would never hurt me, would he?*

A second officer follows him in and I continue doing what I have done for the past few hours: thinking about my husband, him visiting that house on Hillview Terrace, him volunteering to go to the lake house so often without me, and now watching the footage from that night. All while I wait for Rata. The taxi had dropped me here at around 2 am, and it's now almost six.

•

Next time the doors gasp open, it's Rata coming through. He gives me a curt nod and approaches the front desk. He speaks briefly with someone out of my view.

'Lina, let's go,' he says. I rise and pass through the door he holds open for me.

This time round, the conversation is much more direct, just a timeline, the facts of what happened last night. What I discovered on Cain's computer. Did I want to press charges for assault? *Of course not.* But he grabbed you? It says here by the throat. *No, not technically by the throat but that seemed to be what he was reaching for.*

No, it didn't feel like assault, not now in the light of day. *Everything happened too quickly. I don't even really know what happened.*

There's no subterfuge, I'm barely cognisant.

'I can understand your loyalty, you've been married to the man for a long time. You probably feel like you should know everything about a person after seven years.'

I just shrug. 'I guess so,' I say. 'I just want answers. I don't know why he was looking at that video or how he got access to it, I wish I knew but I don't have anything else to tell you.'

He squeezes his lips together and gives a small nod.

'Some men need control. In the military all they have are rules. As odd as the rules are they will stick to them. I started out in the army in my early twenties. Willie Apiata was my hero. But they're not all heroes. I'm sure you know.'

'Why are you telling me this?'

'I'm thinking aloud I guess.' He runs his tongue over his top lip. 'It's possible that your husband installed the cameras in the lake house. I'm not saying he did, I'm just saying it's possible. He has the footage and he visited that house. He might have done it for the money, he might have justified it to himself as a victimless crime. But why were *you* at that house that night, Lina?'

'Someone had stayed there as well as our place. That's the truth. I just wanted to check it out.'

'So why didn't you visit all the other places that profile had booked? There was another place in Auckland, one in Whitianga. That profile booked eight places in New Zealand in total, but so far we have only found evidence of cameras in two properties, yours and the one you booked at Hillview Terrace. So why choose that place?'

'I'm not going to beat my head against the wall trying to convince you. I've answered your questions. I want to go home.'

The room is silent for a moment. Then he drums the table. 'Do you have somewhere to stay for now?'

'I can stay at home,' I say. 'I'm fine to be home.'

He rises, opens the door. 'I'll arrange a car for you. If and when your husband is released, you will be notified.'

'I've really got to get going,' I say. 'I have work.'

'You're working today? After last night?'

I just shrug. I feel compelled to go in. I don't want to wander around the house all day thinking through everything that has happened, and it's too late to find someone to cover my shift.

'I'll get a ride for you now. A couple of my guys are picking up Cain's computer. He's volunteered access to assist in the investigation.'

•

It's a silent trip to my front door, and I notice a second police car following us.

I don't have my keys, but Cain has left the door unlocked.

'Help yourself to whatever,' I say to the two officers. I quickly shower and find my clothes for work. The officers spend most of the time in Cain's study, carting his computer out to their vehicles. I have two missed calls on my phone from an unknown number this morning. I don't bother calling back. Probably journalists.

The cops go through Cain's drawers, take zip drives, old CD-ROMs, hard drives. They clean it out, then they're gone. They're efficient. There's five minutes to spare when I walk out the front door.

It doesn't make sense, nothing makes sense, I think on my way to the station. I see Daniel again, those green eyes staring down at me on the ground. Why would Cain have the footage? How did he get it? Is it possible my husband set the cameras up to spy on

the guests then Daniel turned up and derailed his plans? Or . . .
what if they knew each other somehow?

In the end I arrive a touch early to the station. I park and put
my seat back in the car, waiting for my shift. I close my eyes for
a second. Next thing I know someone is tapping on the window.
It's Judy, one of the old heads who I've worked with a few times.

'Lina?' she says.

'Oh sorry. I just dozed off.'

'Are you okay?'

'Yeah,' I say, scratching at my eyes. 'I'm just waiting for my
shift. What time is it?'

She looks confused for a moment. 'You're not rostered on today,
darling.'

'Sorry?'

'You're not rostered on. It's Erica and August taking over now
for us. You're off today.'

'Oh,' I say, blinking. 'It's Thursday, right?'

'It is, but you're definitely not on. I checked the roster when I
saw your car.'

I swallow. 'Oh, my mistake. I must have misread it.'

'No worries. Go get some rest.' She taps the roof of the car with
her fingers and starts out towards her own vehicle.

I can't muster the energy to drive home straight away. I tip my
seat back again and stay like that for a period. I could sleep right
here with the radio soothing my mind, and for a moment too long
I stay in that position because when I open my eyes, the car is full
of mid-afternoon sun. I check the time to find it's almost three
o'clock. It's been hours. Pressing my fingers to my eyelids, I let
out a long yawn before reaching for the keys and starting the car.

The gate opens and I head off.

At home something has changed. I'm grieving for my old life,
for the man I've loved all these years who might not be who I think

he is. Rata's words, *you should know everything about a person after seven years*, are trapped like flies in the web of my mind. He's right and I'm angry. Angry at Cain. What has he done?

I do something productive to take my mind off things. I print out the next fortnight's schedule and pin it to the fridge with a magnet. Now I'll see it every day.

Dragging my anger and my empty stomach up the stairs to the bedroom, I collapse beneath the covers once more and protectively wrap my arms around my belly. My last thought is about the baby, what this means for it. My connection to it has already grown so strong; the instinct to protect it fuelled me last night.

I don't need my sleep mask, or tea, or rain sounds, I just tumble into the dark hole of slumber once more.

•

The phone call from Rata comes at around midnight. I'm in bed, the same bed I've shared with Cain for so many years. This house is only a rental but like the lake house it's charged with memories. I reach for the phone, see the time and want to hurl it at the window but I know it must be about Cain. I bring it to my ear.

'Hello.'

'Lina, it's Detective Rata, sorry to call you at this hour.' He doesn't sound sorry. He sounds rushed and frustrated.

'What's going on?'

'Cain has been cooperative in assisting the search through his personal computer files, and web use. We have no evidence to suggest your husband has engaged in any criminal activity outside of his use of proxy servers to access international gambling websites – something for which he will be cautioned and not charged.'

'But what about the video? Where did it come from?'

'The footage you discovered your husband watching was sent by an anonymous email address from an encrypted server.'

A wave of relief rushes through me, but immediately the shame and guilt empties me. I put him through hell today. 'So what does this mean?'

'It means we're releasing him. I can't share any other details about this investigation.'

Something dawns on me. My sim card was in that phone that night, so if it wasn't Cain, then someone else has been in our house and taken it. Daniel? Or the second man? 'But he went to that house on Hillview Terrace,' I say. 'He went there before me, he might have removed the cameras. You said –'

'I said to be careful,' he says, his frustration rising. 'We had good cause for suspicion. I can't comment on his motivations for going to that house.'

'Right, so he's free to go?'

'Look, it's not necessarily protocol, but given the late hour we can keep him here overnight without charging him, give you time to gather your thoughts or find somewhere else to stay if you're concern –'

'No,' I say, cutting him off. Rata has asked Cain his questions, now I suppose Cain will have some questions for me. He's innocent. I overreacted. All the emotions of the past week bubbled over and sent me into a tailspin of panic. How could I do this to him? 'I want him home now.'

'Sure,' he says. 'We will have him back there shortly.'

•

I pace about the lounge, my feet wearing a neat figure eight into the carpet as my mind runs over the facts and possibilities. Daniel got into the lake house, he threatened to kill Cain and me. He went upstairs and beat Cain. I got free and when he emerged from one of the rooms at the end of the hall, I shot him. Then Cain visited the property Daniel took me to, where other cameras were installed. Someone anonymously sent him video footage of Daniel in the lake house. At some point, my sim card was taken from the bottom of my wardrobe.

I should feel relief because intellectually I'm beginning to see this was all a misunderstanding. Cain has done nothing wrong. In fact, he's been mostly patient with me throughout. I've done wrong, not him. There's an aching knot of guilt in my stomach. *Guilt.* There's only one question unanswered and it's the one I'm most afraid to ask: did he go to that house because he knows what happened with me and Daniel? Was there another photo left in our letterbox?

After some time I hear the key scratch into the lock at the front door. I ball up my courage, and stride over to meet him as the door swings open.

TWENTY-EIGHT

ANGER. NO, NOT anger. Resentment? Defeat? Whatever it is in his eyes it drains me. 'Well, that was an interesting day,' he says.

'Cain,' I begin but the rest of the words don't come at first, I have to push them out. 'I'm so, *so* sorry.'

He raises a hand, seems to wince as if my apology is spit that's hit him right in the eye.

The hand goes to his forehead, slides down, straightening out his face. *Say something, Cain.* The tension presses against me, thick as water. *Brain, pharynx, larynx, lymph nodes, lungs, heart, spleen, liver . . .* if I get through every organ in the body before he speaks, I might collapse. *Gall bladder, stomach, kidneys.*

'Thought I was conditioned to deal with interrogations but after today I . . .' a pause, a deep exhale. 'I'm done. I'm spent. It's taken so long to try to build a normal life and I feel like it's just slipping through my fingers.'

'No,' I say. 'Cain, please.'

'I just want to go to sleep and forget about everything.'

I move to let him through. He leads me into the kitchen.

'That's it for the betting,' he continues, ignoring me. 'Just when

I was starting to do well. And I don't want police digging into my past, or journalists.'

'What do you mean?'

He turns, leans against the island. 'I mean the Skelton stuff, Lina. I mean me snapping at customers at Axel's gym. We need to be on the front foot. We need to show a united front, which is hard when you don't trust me. When you run away from me to the police in the middle of the night. How are we going to raise a child together when this is what you think of me?'

Under the hanging kitchen lights his eyes are dark, his laughter lines are deepened by the shadows. He's right.

'You have to see it from my perspective too, Cain. I've been on edge since the home invasion. I panicked.'

'Yeah,' he says. 'I see it from your perspective but it doesn't change anything. I was making good money and now I can't. I'm not the cleverest, my body is damaged, I don't have great business sense obviously. I just wanted to take care of you, and the baby. I want to do good for this family.'

The ache inside intensifies. *What have I done to him?* 'I'm so sorry, I didn't realise using betting agencies outside of New Zealand was illegal. I just didn't think when I saw that video.'

'They've given me an official warning.'

He pulls a glass out of the cupboard and fills it from the tap. Takes a slow, thoughtful sip.

'It might be time to swallow my pride and get a boring job with a steady pay until the baby comes.' He pauses, takes another mouthful of water. His sad eyes stare down at the benchtop.

A fresh ache below my sternum. He's too proud, too principled. Those rules of his: *A man must look after his family, his wife. Don't take the dole if you can stand on your own two feet. There is nothing worse than hurting a woman or a child.* Yet I feared him. I feared for my life. I'm thinking of something to say, some hope to offer but before I can open my mouth, he's speaking again.

'What I don't get, Lina, is why you ran away. Why you went to the police. You could have asked me about that video and I would have explained it. Did you think I could actually hurt you?'

I shake my head, hot tears come. 'I don't know, Cain. I was overwhelmed. The people that had access to that video are perverts and –'

'Did you actually believe I had something to do with recording the video? That's where your mind went?'

'I panicked. I thought . . .'

'You thought it was me. You thought I was a creep, despite knowing me for seven years, and swearing to always love and trust me. You thought I could do something like that?' Now his eyes come back up to me with a sour look. I hold my elbows, sniff as tears come.

'You grabbed me.'

'That's my instincts, Lina. You gave me a fright. Then I wanted to calm you down but you were already sprinting.' He finishes the glass of water and sets it down. 'They asked me what porn sites I visit, they wanted to know everything about what I do online. They asked if I'd ever watched child pornography. It was mortifying.'

'I got scared.' I use the heel of my palm to smear the tears from my cheeks.

'Why did you book that house on WeStay?'

I become still, an insect trapped.

'What hou –'

He shakes his head, resigned, and I feel a deep aching sadness. I can see it already by the way his shoulders drop.

'Your work email was on my phone from that night at the restaurant,' he says. 'I saw you'd booked a WeStay. Are you seeing someone, is that it?'

'No, no one,' I begin. How can I explain it? 'It's not that, Cain. Don't ever think that, I only want you.'

That is how he knows. Everything seems to loosen with the relief. *He doesn't know about Daniel and me.*

He scratches the back of his neck and squeezes his eyes closed. When he starts speaking again he keeps them screwed shut. 'The truth, Lina.'

If only it were that easy. There's no *truth* for him. I can't put him through more hell.

'I was working, so I didn't get there until later.' I pause, thinking, and he decides to fill the silence.

'You booked the WeStay. That's all it takes to cut loose my imagination. I could see you with someone from your runners' group or from work. Maybe Scotty.'

'Scotty?' I say in disbelief. Never in a million years would I be interested in Scotty. Cain knows that, surely. 'No, Cain. Not him.'

His expression changes.

'Not *anyone*,' I continue. 'I booked that place because I realised that the last guests that stayed at Tarawera had also stayed there.'

'You thought you'd just check it out?' he asks.

'That's right, the police can confirm it. They found me there at six in the morning. They were monitoring it for that same reason. I knew if I told you, you would just think I was being paranoid. You don't believe that there was a second man.'

Cain exhales slowly. 'I *still* don't believe there was a second man,' he says. For a heartbeat I think he might cry. 'If you were seeing someone else, I would never live with it.'

A dark implication in his words.

'I'm sorry,' I say, coming around the kitchen bench to him. 'I'm sorry for ever doubting you and for not telling you what I was doing.'

'I get it,' he says. His voice has shrunk. 'It looked bad.'

I hug him now and, reluctantly, I feel his arms come around me.

'Now only one question remains, who sent the video?' I say. Someone else is out there, watching, waiting. Terrorising us.

TWENTY-NINE

NOT ALL ALARMS are loud screaming things. Sometimes it's the quietest alarms that shake you the most. This morning it's the familiar chirp of my phone. Call it intuition, I know instantly that something is wrong. I had a similar premonition when I received the message about Grandpa. I was a medical student, hungover with a boy from my class in bed next to me. It was a Sunday morning and the moth-eaten curtains in his flat did little to keep the sun out. There was a text from Wiremu, *Hi Lina, call me when you can.* I'd gotten up and made it to the privacy of the bathroom before I'd begun to cry. I called Wiremu, already knowing. Grandpa's heart was bad by that stage, but I kept telling myself he would find a way to keep going. The moment Wiremu began to apologise I broke down. I remember thanking him at the end of the call, something that seems absurd now. Then telling him I'd be okay and hanging up. The boy found me balled on the cold tiles, his flatmate was waiting to have a shower. He offered to drive me home.

It was a gut punch that left me winded for years. After that, every time I got drunk with other students my mind wandered to Grandpa, dying alone in the lake house. So I gave up medical school. I didn't want to be a doctor, I didn't have it in me.

This time when I wake and see I have a text message from Claire, I get that same feeling, an uncomfortable fluttering in my stomach.

Watching you both on the morning show, it looks terrifying. I hope you are doing okay. Please get in touch if you need us.

Watching you both. Watching us do what? Cain, as usual, is already awake. I can hear him down in the kitchen. I roll out of bed, scratch the sleep from my eyes as I descend the stairs.

'Cain, I think we are on the tele.'

'What?'

I rush towards the lounge room, reach for the TV remote and turn it on. It's the first thing we see on the screen. That same video Cain was watching.

'And here she is, Lina Phillips as the assailant known to be Daniel Moore leaves the room going back up the stairs in the corner of the shot to her husband who is bound. Mrs Phillips contorts her body, as you can see in the imagery on your screen.' Cain approaches, stands beside me. *'She manages to lift the fireplace enough, which according to the manufacturer's website weighs seventy-five kilograms, quite some feat. If we could just zoom in a little. There, see there is an inch gap for her to slide the other handcuff underneath. It's incredible really, to have this vision into the night that shocked the nation, and sent a wave around the globe. I'll remind viewers this is exclusive footage, not even my producers know the exact source of the images you are seeing right now other than an email address.'*

Cain clears his throat. 'How the fuck did this get to the media?'

A new voice adds to the conversation now. *'It's remarkable the strength Lina Phillips shows here. Given the earlier footage of her helping her highly inebriated husband inside and up the stairs, it's clear that only one person was going to save her and that was herself.'*

The screen dies. I turn to Cain, he's still holding the remote tight in his fist.

'What?'

'I don't want to hear it. It's a beat-up. You're the hero, we know that.'

'Cain –'

'It's true. I'm glad, of course I am. But these people have half the story. I *wasn't* drunk, I was drugged. And how did they get the footage?'

'Probably the same way you did,' I say. 'Someone might have sent it to them anonymously.'

'Or the police leaked it. I bet that's what happened.'

•

We cook together. According to my schedule, I've not got work for four days so this is a good chance for us to reset, but I know he'll be stewing on that comment from the talking head. The way the footage makes us look. He'll be assessing it, internalising it. His mistrust of the police, his anger at the media. He's wanted to give an interview since it happened, for the payday and to clear our names. He wanted to be the hero not the drunk husband. It should have been him that saved the day.

'At least this should confirm there was just one person there that night,' he says. 'You acted in self-defence. The police can stop trying to build some conspiracy now. Case closed, it's all there on TV.'

I don't need to remind him again that someone sent the footage, someone has it. Case *not* closed. And they may have the other footage from the Hillview Terrace property too.

•

Later in the day, while the police are dropping back his computer, Cain is tapping away at his phone. I walk past him, slowing to peer over his shoulder. He's punching out a reply in the comments section of a news article.

'What are you typing?'

'Nothing. Just these people starting rumours. Bullshit about us.'

'Show me?'

The reason for his irritation is clear when he raises his phone to me. *WeStay Horror House: Hidden cameras in every room, but who installed them?* It's the *Daily Mirror*, a UK paper.

I take out my own phone and google our names. Someone has written an opinion piece on the dangers of the 'gig economy' for *The Age* newspaper in Australia, using us and our experience as an example. *The New York Times* has run an investigative piece linking the home invasion and the cameras with the Colorado murder and a home invasion in Berlin.

I click on the trashiest article I can find, from *The Sun* in the UK. I wade through the scum that sinks to the bottom of the article, the comments section. I see what Cain means. They've found out he served in the military, that he was scheduled to give evidence into the unlawful killings in Afghanistan when Skelton died; they know I'm a paramedic. Some think the entire thing was staged, some calling it a 'false flag'. A conspiracy theorist ironically believes it was all faked to help the 'NWO' enhance surveillance powers on the internet. Another comment reads: *Who would install cameras inside a WeStay anyway? Maybe this guy that turned up with a shotgun had stayed there, found the cameras THAT THE OWNERS INSTALLED and discovered what these perverts were doing. I'm not saying what he did was right, violence is never the answer, but it smells fishy if you ask me and there is DEFINITELY more to this story. If they did install the cameras to spy on their guests they're sick and they deserve to go to jail themselves.*

I close the browser. 'It'll pass,' I say to him, unsure of how long that will actually take.

'Someone is feeding them,' he says. 'And the only good that could have come from the footage is it should have settled the discussion about a second man. But instead it's just sparked a whole bunch of new conspiracy theories.'

I grab his hand now and place it on my belly. 'Just remember we've got this to look forward to. Soon, when the baby comes, we can start looking at moving. We can leave all this drama behind and go off grid for a while. Just the three of us.'

'You still want to move to that house, after everything?'

Maybe not. Who knows what emotions will well up when we go back there. 'Let's wait and see.'

Cain goes outside to his punching bag. I can hear him all afternoon beating it to within an inch of its life.

•

That night when Cain goes to get groceries, I find Scotty's number in my phone and step into Cain's study. I've still not heard from him and, after all these years, I feel oddly insecure about how our working relationship abruptly ended. I despise the feeling that someone dislikes me so much; I should ignore it and move on but I can't.

'Lina,' he says. 'This is a surprise.'

'Hi Scotty,' I say, keeping my voice light. 'I'm just calling because my last couple of shifts were with someone new and I wanted to ask why.'

'Because I asked to be moved,' he says, his voice uncharacteristically flat. The room seems to heat five degrees.

'Oh,' I say. 'I figured that might be the case, but it seems odd all these years working together. You know I had to ask about the drugs, Scotty.'

'It was time for a change, wasn't feeling the chemistry anymore.'

Chemistry is an odd choice of word. A spike of anger. 'I wonder what would happen if I contacted the ambulance service and mentioned my suspicions? I could have taken that approach, but

I chose to speak with you directly. You know I can still mention it to them.'

A long pause, I can hear that deep nasally breath. Finally he speaks. 'I wouldn't do that if I were you.'

'Yeah, and why is that?'

'I saw you on the news, Lina. You had a rough time down there at the lake, didn't you? Shot that poor kid right in the guts.'

I freeze, my mouth is open and no sound comes out. My mind jags on something. *Scotty.* He's been close to me. He could access my emails. He knows so much about me and knew I had listed the lake house on WeStay. And there was something he said, *you are not so squeaky clean.* What could he have meant by that?

He speaks again. 'What if I told you that things could get a lot worse for you? What then?'

'What are you saying, Scotty?'

'Be careful, Lina. I know you've got secrets.'

The line cuts out. Some time passes before I move the phone from my ear. *It's him.* I scan the edge of our property as if he's out there watching me from our tiny backyard, or the street.

The moment Cain gets in, I run to him. 'It's Scotty,' I say. 'It has to be. He threatened me. He said things are going to get worse.'

'Slow down,' he says, dumping the bags of groceries on the bench. 'What do you mean?'

'I had a feeling, an intuition, so I dialled his number.'

'You think he somehow orchestrated all this? He's the second man?'

'It's possible, right? I'm going to call Rata.'

'Alright, maybe get them to check him out. I'm not convinced but what's the worst that could happen?'

'I'll call now.'

Rata answers after two rings. 'Lina.'

'Hi,' I say. 'I think I know who might be involved in all of this.'

'Who?'

'Scotty Pearson, a colleague. I don't know why but I have this feeling and he threatened me. Can you check him out?' *What if he knows about me and Daniel? What if he contacts Cain in retaliation?*

'Scotty Pearson? Address? Date of birth?'

'He works for the ambulance service. Early forties.'

'That'll be enough. I'll take a look.'

•

We barely leave the house for the next two days – deliveries for lunch, phone calls with friends rather than meeting at cafes. I've had a few missed calls from a random number but I don't want to talk to journalists or police about what happened. Cain does burpees and chin-ups out in the yard, and spends hours working over the boxing bag, coming back inside with blood trickling between his knuckles despite the training gloves he wears. He postponed the PT sessions he had scheduled in. I take my prenatal vitamins and read in the sun slanting in through the windows in the lounge room. At times I have to read the same page four times before any information enters my brain. When I'm not thinking about everything that happened, I'm imagining this baby inside me swelling, then eventually out in the world; a child growing up. Even now at this early stage, I can barely find the words to describe the love I feel for her or him.

We've not heard from Rata about Scotty, and I'm not holding my breath. I would take the next couple of days off work if it was possible but there's only so much leave I can take, and we still need the money despite Cain's windfall.

When my next shift comes around, I drive to the station with the radio turned up, trying to mentally prepare. I've been feeling more fatigued of late, which I know isn't uncommon with pregnancy but I was hoping to be one of those mums who gets through without the vomiting, the nausea, the anaemia – the sorts of complaints that make birth, or rather the time *after* birth, such a relief. I guess then it's sore nipples, less sleep and no sex for a while. We will manage. Especially with a perfect little baby to dote over.

When I pull up, the gate is already wide open. I find a car park. I notice other cars there, not just the usual working-class fare I normally see at changeover but a silver BMW. I climb out of the car and start towards the entrance of the station. It's cooler today. The station has codes for the gate and the door entrance. The only cameras are at the entrance of the building overlooking the car park. Even the drug lock-up and safe have their own codes. But today when I punch in my individual door code, those four familiar numbers I've used for all these years, the door does not buzz unlocked. The keypad beeps twice.

I try again. The door won't open. I see someone coming from inside to let me in. But they're not in an ambulance officer's uniform, they're in a suit. What would a suit be doing here at 6.30 am?

His face – clean shaven, mid-forties with sunken pores – doesn't change as he approaches the door.

'Come in,' he says, after pressing it open.

'Thanks.' I go to stride past him, towards the lockers and kitchen.

'This way please, Lina.'

'Sorry?'

'My name is James O'Brien, we emailed you last night. I wasn't expecting you until nine.'

'Nine?' I say. 'My shift starts at seven.'

He looks unperturbed, rolling his tongue beneath his bottom lip. 'You didn't read the email we sent you? We also tried to phone you a number of times over the last week but we couldn't get through.'

That's because I've been ignoring calls from unknown numbers.

'I've been getting loads of calls and emails every day. What is this about?' I say.

'Why don't you come on through to the meeting room?'

I hesitate.

'I'll explain in a moment,' he says, 'come on now.'

I follow him into the training room, there's a laptop on the table and a second man there.

'Rob,' he says. 'I'll need you to phone Jessica from HR into the meeting.'

Jessica from HR. This isn't good.

'I'm sorry, will this take long? I've got to start in fifteen minutes.'

Something unspoken passes between them. James has his phone to his ear then he speaks. 'Hi Jess, so sorry to bother you this early in the morning, I've not woken you, have I? . . . Good. Well we have Lina Phillips here at the station now. She didn't see our emails or listen to the voice messages evidently, and so she has arrived for her shift. Are you okay to do this remotely?'

Do what? What the hell is happening? He nods. 'Okay, I'm putting you on speaker.'

Rob speaks quietly to me. 'I'm your union rep, Lina. I emailed you but when I didn't hear back I had a feeling you might turn up for your shift. We're going to get you through this, just follow my lead and don't answer any questions you don't want to.'

I open the mail app on my phone, see dozens of messages in my inbox. I find the one from the ambulance service. *Disciplinary meeting.* I don't open it because they're speaking again.

'Alright, Jessica is with us now.'

'You didn't check the roster?' James asks.

'I printed it out. I didn't realise it would change.'

'Hi, Lina,' the woman on the phone says. 'I'm the representative from human resources for this meeting and can answer any questions you might have.'

'Sure,' I say, more blunt than I'd like. 'First I want to know what exactly is this about?'

'Well,' James begins. 'Recently we received a complaint from a fellow ambulance officer.'

'A complaint?'

'Concerning your behaviour on the job, notably a suggestion that you might have been under the influence of pain medication or some other mind-altering substance.'

'Me?' I say, my skin suddenly hot. 'Wait, was this from Scotty?'

Jessica speaks, her too-bubbly voice coming down the line. 'We can't identify the complainant.'

'God, you can't be serious?'

'We take these complaints seriously and, given the nature of the complaint, we've expedited things until we can complete our investigations. Part of the complaint concerns a call in which you failed at first to correctly diagnose an abdominal aortic aneurysm.'

'*That* was Scotty.'

'I understand you were the lead on the call.'

'I took over for him!'

'When you arrived at the hospital your colleague was driving.'

'This is bullshit.'

'It is, there's no proof that you were using on the job, Lina,' Rob adds.

'No,' James says. 'But four nights ago, two hundred ampoules of fentanyl were removed from the medical lock-up. You were spotted loitering in the car park, despite the fact you weren't rostered on.'

I search my mind, tracing back to the day. That was just after Cain was arrested. I was exhausted from the night before. 'I had a nap. I got my dates mixed up.' I pause. 'Look, I've had a lot on my mind.'

Rob seems to double-take at this. Why is it so often the people we have to rely on are the most comically inept?

'This doesn't prove she did anything, this doesn't prove she took the fentanyl.'

'No,' James says. 'But at some stage over the course of the evening her passcode was used to enter the building and the safe.'

I'm shaking my head, tears starting. 'Test me,' I say. 'Test me for fentanyl.'

'That's not going to help with our investigations, Lina.'

'It's him. It's Scotty. I called him out and he's setting me up. He was groggy, he messed up the call. He's seen me punch my code in a thousand times.'

'If that were the case, why didn't you file a complaint about him like you're supposed to?'

'Because I'm an idiot. Because I thought maybe he was developing an addiction and it would cost him his job. I was trying to help him.'

The irony hits me – I wish there were cameras here like at the WeStays. I wish they had surveillance on the drug room 24/7.

'Eight months ago, we discovered over one hundred ampoules of fentanyl had been taken from another station. That's an ongoing investigation but we can't take any further risks.'

'Call the police,' I say. 'Search my property.'

Jessica speaks now. 'A thorough investigation will be conducted. For now, Lina, the best course of action is for you to be placed on leave. This will be paid leave and, given everything else in your life, it might be a good opportunity for you to reflect.'

'Reflect?' I say but she's still speaking, powering through.

'We've also organised for you to speak with a drug rehabilitation counsellor. The ambulance service is fully invested in your psychological welfare through this time.'

They're covering themselves if I become depressed and their investigation confirms I had nothing to do with this, as it certainly will. I want to scream, or cry. I want to sink through the chair to the floor and sleep for a week.

'Can I go home?' I say.

Rob and James look at each other. 'We'll need to check your locker before you go, and would ask that you wait until police officers arrive.'

'Police?' Rob says, there's heat in the look he gives James.

'It's a lot of drugs to disappear, Rob. This isn't just someone having painkillers before their shift.'

'You don't have to wait,' Rob says to me. 'You can go home right now.'

'I've got nothing to hide.'

'Good,' James says. 'Perhaps we can start with your locker.'

When I open it, I'm barely surprised to see the two glass ampoules sitting there, empty, on top of my things. Anyone can see they've simply been pushed through the grate on the door but James takes the moment to smack his lips.

'Well, that's not a good look, is it?'

'Yeah, if I was taking fentanyl before my shift I'd just leave the evidence sitting there like that. This isn't fair.'

James clears his throat.

I can see it rolling out before me. Administrative leave, therapy, a big red 'A' emblazoned on my chest. They might find somewhere to hide me in an admin role or training, watching me closely for the rest of my career. Or maybe the suspicion and *evidence* will be enough to sack me. Two hundred ampoules. This could put me in serious legal trouble. *This is just a speed bump*, I tell myself. *This will be fine.* But I know it won't.

Scotty has come for my career. What will he come for next?

DANIEL MOORE: 'A SINGLE BLOKE, HAPPY-GO-LUCKY, A BIT OF A DUNCE BUT WITH A GOOD HEART,' BEST FRIEND SAYS.

The man at the centre of a crime that has shocked the country was 'your average guy – a bit of a joker, got in a bit of trouble at school but nothing like what he did to those people,' his best friend says.

Andrew Mohi – who knew Moore for nineteen years – accused the media of representing his former best friend in a way that was 'biased, and straight-up wrong'. He says Moore made a mistake and probably had his reasons that no one will ever know but he wasn't 'some criminal mastermind'.

Mohi, who viewed the footage of the invasion that was recently released, added, 'I wouldn't have believed he did it if I hadn't seen it with my own eyes.' The footage is from two of the cameras in the home. One showing Moore terrorising a woman. The next shows Moore walking down a hallway in the dark with his mask off moments before he died.

The criticism is in stark contrast to the comments made by Wellington academic Sloan Drake who bemoans what she calls 'the good bloke defence', a reaction she says the media and public have to 'mostly white domestic abusers and general criminals who do horrific things'. Drake joins a chorus of voices who have expressed a need to protect and support victims.

US TV personality Terrence O'Dwyer addressed the crime in his late-night talk show. 'I don't know this man, I know nothing about him other than the fact he installed cameras in a WeStay and drugged, captured and threatened the owners of that WeStay at gunpoint. I don't give a damn what his high school teacher thinks of him, or the fact he had a Batman poster on his wall. He's a sadist and a murderer, that's it.'

'No one is denying what he has done, ' Mohi said. 'But the focus should be on why he did it. What drove him to that. He had been tied up with one or two bad people, he'd done a bit of drugs, another thing everyone seems obsessed with, but no one can answer why he did it. And no one can explain why there were something like ten cameras in that house and we've only seen footage from two. He wouldn't come up with this all on his own.'

This is one piece of the puzzle police are hoping might help to paint a fuller picture of the evening. The rumours of a second assailant have not abated, despite the release of the video which seems to suggest Moore acted alone. Many theories have emerged on social media, and the police have been reluctant to rule out a second offender.

Another piece that might help understand the motivations of Moore is his missing phone. Police divers have trawled Lake Tarawera near the scene of the crime, along with the banks, and inside and outside of the house but as of yet the phone has not been recovered. The coroner has also confirmed that Moore was on drugs at the time of the offending.

THIRTY

MANY PEOPLE DREAM of paid time off, filling their days reading, or watching endless Netflix, pursuing silly childhood dreams of becoming a writer or a dancer. For others, like me, it's exactly what the seventh circle of hell looks like. It's not the nerves about the pending outcome of the investigation, it's the absence of a distraction. The boredom breeds thoughts, and everything I think about brings a fresh cut of anxiety, each deeper than the last.

Many paramedics use drugs, some become addicted. In the medical profession only chemists have greater access to opiates than us. I will be supported with *my addiction*, they say. The implication being my defence will be addiction, which means a treatment plan and an eventual return to work in a limited capacity with less access to medications. Any real career progression will be permanently shelved. The plan was to be a stay-at-home mum down at the lake house yet this mark against my name still hurts and Cain's income just isn't enough. I don't want to be seen in this way, like my mother, unable to control herself.

At home I go over the conversation with Cain in my head in anticipation.

He's sweaty when he walks in the door – he had clients today, more than usual. The cynical part of me suspects that, given our new status as the survivors of the infamous WeStay attack, strangers are much more inclined to book in one-on-one time. The photos of him in the paper, taken from his military days, probably added to the appeal. He told me he's got a wealthy new client who has him booked for three sessions a week, a friend of Axel's.

'Hey,' he says. 'You're home.'

'I am,' I respond, forcing a smile. 'I had a meeting this morning, I'm going to be on paid leave.'

He puts his backpack down, and when he straightens, his brow is dropped in scepticism. 'They just gave you leave because of what happened? Just like that?'

I'm sick of lying to him, but he doesn't need the added stress right now. 'Yeah,' I say.

'For how long?'

'Four weeks to begin with,' I say, guessing at a realistic time frame, although I really have no idea.

'That's kind of them. It'll be nice to have you around the house. You can help me schedule all my new bookings,' he says. 'I still think we need to give an interview, Lina. It's easy money and it'll put so many of these rumours to bed. Plus I'll likely see an even bigger spike in new clients. Might even bump my prices up.'

'No,' I say, thinking about being interviewed by a journalist. What they might uncover. I've never been a great liar, and who knows what might happen if they use body language experts and all the rest. I know it's an opportunity for Cain to clear up the misinformation, particularly about him being drunk that night.

'Think about it,' he says, pinching the front of his gym shirt and pulling it away from his chest. 'I'd better have a shower.'

•

Days pass in a state of ennui waiting for something to happen. I've not heard from Rata, but we've been following developments online. Every media update makes me sick with dread. What if someone has the video of Daniel and me from that night in Auckland? Maybe Scotty is sitting on it, planning to blackmail me, or release it to the world.

Tonight on *Sunday Night* they have the first guests who stayed at the lake house on the show, Cherry and Dan. They look different to their photos, he has put on a little weight and she is wearing much more make-up than in her social media photos.

'And have the police confirmed whether or not you two were filmed as well?'

'No,' she says in her Canadian accent, turning to her husband as if to confirm her answer. I think about their dog Donald.

'But it's possible?'

The woman pantomimes shivering, and the husband drags his lips to one side, shakes his head. He speaks now: 'I guess it is possible. Someone might have footage of us, in the shower, or on the toilet.'

'It's a scary thought.'

The interviewer nods; an open, interested expression on her face. 'And Cain and Lina Phillips, did you have any dealings with them?'

'This is unfair,' I say to Cain now. 'The show didn't contact us.'

'It doesn't matter,' he snaps, his eyes fixed on the screen.

The man turns to his wife. 'They just let us know how to check in and sent us a nice welcome message. Oh –' he pauses now, turning to his wife, a half smile plays at his lips. 'Remember the LinkedIn thing?'

My heart drops. I see and hear it all in some hyper-slow reality where every millisecond drags for a minute.

'That's right,' the woman intones. When she speaks again there's more energy in her voice. 'We had an odd thing happen on LinkedIn.'

'And what was that?'

'Well, Lina had visited both of our LinkedIn profiles. You can see who has viewed them and she came up.'

'She viewed them,' the presenter says, annunciating *viewed* with a cock of her head. 'That must have creeped you out a little?'

The skin at the base of my throat becomes tight.

'Yeah, it did creep us out a bit,' the woman says. 'Makes you wonder what else they looked up of ours. We had lots of really positive reviews from previous stays so they shouldn't need to snoop into our personal lives.'

'Looking back on it now, that probably should have been a bit of a warning.' The man laughs.

I want to scream at the TV. *You are not the victims.* 'This passes as journalism? She doesn't even point out that nothing happened to these people, their involvement is incidental.'

Cain turns to me, hisses, 'Shhh.'

'More after the break,' the interviewer says.

Ads come on and Cain mutes the TV. 'I agree with you. It's gutter journalism to make a story out of nothing. The sooner they figure out who has the footage, the better. We just need to hunker down until that happens or wait for everyone to just –' he flings his hand, 'get over it and bugger off. It's probably just sickos in another country trying to keep the story going.' He goes to the kitchen and makes a protein shake. His bicep tenses as he rocks the shaker in his hand. 'We could squash this, we could clear our names and show them all we are normal people.'

'They know the truth,' I say, frustrated. 'They've all seen the footage of me chained up, you in a stupor. That man coming in. He looks straight at the camera, you can see him looking up at it, he knew it was there. He installed them. Anyone who can't see that needs their eyes checked.'

'I know, I fully understand that, but most people, *regular* people, probably don't. We can get a PR person to help us,' Cain says.

We've missed part of the interview, Cain unmutes the TV and their voices come back.

'And you have other news?'

The couple, grinning now, share a look. 'We got engaged last week in Queenstown which made it better.'

The woman holds her ring out.

The presenter gushes, squinting so her crow's feet fan out, but her forehead is rigor mortis. 'I'm pleased to hear things took a turn for the better later in your trip.'

I blurt. 'They didn't even know anything about the cameras when they stayed! They gave us a good review.'

'So has this whole experience changed your opinion about New Zealand?'

'Well,' the woman begins. 'You think it's this nice, friendly place where nothing bad happens. But then bad things do happen here. There are bad people everywhere, even in the most beautiful places. But we would come back.'

'Definitely,' the man adds.

'I'm glad to hear.'

The show switches to the next story

'Now that should piss off a bunch of Kiwis.' Cain scoffs. 'Tap into that jingoism, make them think this will hurt our global image or cost tourism dollars. We've got to fight back, Lina. Set the record straight.'

He turns away from the TV, and ambles from the room.

I can hear my phone chime upstairs. I assume it's a concerned friend wanting to check in. Watching the program about us, discreetly mining gossip. After Skelton's death the NZSAS were all painted as brutes by the media – a boys' club killing indiscriminately in Afghanistan. So why does Cain trust them now?

I reach the top of the stairs and go to my phone. I see the number on the screen and recognise it instantly. I've not seen it in weeks. Not since I received those long-deleted text messages. It's Daniel's number. My heart is racing as I open the message. It takes a moment to load. A photo. It's of us. The still from that night in Auckland. My face pressed to his. A second message comes. Just nine words. Bile is rushing up my throat. This can't be happening. I read the words once more.

This is a warning: forget about the second man.

Peephole transmission

Given the recent scrutiny from authorities, members will no longer be able to access archival footage. In the unlikely event police breach our servers, this measure will help to protect the planters involved. Past footage will be stored offline for the foreseeable future. We apologise for any inconvenience caused.

Enjoy the show.

THIRTY-ONE

RATA ANSWERS AFTER a few rings.

'Hi, it's Lina Phillips.'

'Yes, Lina. How can I help?'

I'm breathing too quickly. I shouldn't have called, this is exactly what the message warned me against. *Forget about the second man.* I have everything I wanted out of the situation, a baby and our financial problems are manageable. I need to just forget about it.

'I've been thinking,' I begin. 'The second man . . .' I can't think of how to put it so I just say the words. 'I made a mistake, I know there wasn't another person there that night. It was just Daniel Moore.'

'Right and you just decided out of the blue –'

'I remember everything much more clearly now.'

'Sure. I wasn't part of that original investigation but there doesn't seem to be evidence either way of a second man.'

'Exactly,' I say, with relief. 'Has there been any other progress?'

I hear him draw a deep breath, as if preparing a long speech, but all he says is, 'I don't have any major updates at this stage I'm afraid. Just theories, lots of theories which are useless until we have something concrete.' Another pause. In the near silence I feel like I can hear him thinking, considering what he is about to say. 'We only ever catch the tip of the iceberg with this sort of thing. Peephole and cybercrime in general. You've got to get lucky because of how decentralised it is, and the lengths people go to conceal their ID when they're breaking the law online.'

'But who would use this Peephole?'

'I only have theories, nothing concrete. I'd guess the users are mostly your garden variety voyeurs, but also others.' He inhales. 'I spent three years on a task force in New Zealand, working with teams in other countries to monitor suspected paedophiles. We had a few arrests, every so often a ring was busted, that was the high-profile stuff. It won't work like that in this case here.'

'Why?' I ask, my heart still racing. I see the picture again in my mind. I must delete it the moment I hang up the phone.

'We would never get enough resources to be effective. No one sees this as a threat anymore. As far as anyone is concerned the case at Tarawera is closed, it's *interesting* but there's zero risk of the criminal reoffending.'

'Especially given he acted alone,' I say now, reinforcing the idea.

'Possibly. The police combed the property. We know it was Daniel there that night. But was he the one who installed the cameras? It's very likely but we can't be certain. Someone has access to the footage and has shared it. How Daniel's phone disappeared without a trace is a mystery to me.'

It doesn't make sense. The phone pinged towers suggesting Daniel was travelling to the house, then it disappeared. Until today.

He continues talking. 'I assume the phone is probably in the lake, or dropped somewhere in the bush.'

'And Scotty? You checked in with him?'

'I knocked on his door myself. Hardly the most accommodating man.'

'No,' I say. 'He was fine for years but he's been different lately.'

'He was with his partner and her kids at home the night you

were attacked. I checked his search history via his ISP, and interestingly we found the term Peephole.'

I frown. Could he have sent the message?

'There were other phrases and lots of news sites about the home invasion. It's clumsy and, if he was involved, I doubt he would be simply searching these things on Google. This has been all over the media and lots of people are probably searching similar things online just for news, but I'll keep an eye on him.'

•

'Who were you talking to?' Cain says, entering the room after the call has ended.

'It was Rata, the detective. He checked in on Scotty.'

'Right,' Cain says, frowning. 'And?'

'There's nothing too incriminating but they're monitoring him.' I exhale. Still holding my phone tight, thinking about the message. 'I was also thinking, maybe we should do the interview. Take the money and run.'

He smiles now. 'You want to do it?'

'We'll need to book a PR person first, to talk us through it, but I think you're right about setting the record straight.' An appearance on national television would be the perfect platform to make it clear there was only one man: Daniel Moore.

'Good idea,' he says. 'I'll call Axel. He has a PR contact. We'll be swimming in money by the time the baby arrives.'

I hear him rushing downstairs to his phone. I unlock my own phone. Read that message once more before responding.

Okay. Done. Please stop this now. I'll forget all about the second man. Just don't share the photo. I'm begging you.

A moment passes. I squeeze everything inside hoping this is the end of it.

Good girl.

THIRTY-TWO

I HAVE MUCH more foundation on than I would ever otherwise wear. They just kept smearing it on, the make-up artist chatting as she went. Even Cain has a little powder on, despite his protestations.

'It's because of the lights, no one will be able to tell at home,' she'd said to him in the seat. 'All men on TV have to wear just a little.'

Cain sat there with a slight grimace, judging himself in the mirror.

My hair is a fire hazard, but I'm aware of what bright lights and a camera can do to your complexion and hair so I trust them. I trust I won't look like this woman I see in the mirror by the time I reach the screens in living rooms around the country. *Think about the money.* It's twenty thousand dollars just to sit there and talk for an hour. They've already started advertising it. Think about the fact this will clear your name, Cain's name. It will remove any doubt about the cameras. Cain is right, this is for the best. Think about that text message. *This is a warning: forget about the second man.* Someone is still out there and they want to disappear.

The PR consultant Axel referred us to had organised the interview. The terms, she assured us, were fair and although we would never get 'copy approval' she said she had a good working relationship with the producer and had her word that they would show us in a favourable light.

'Lisa will be gentle on you. Trust me, this will be a breeze.'

She told us this despite the reputation of the host, the formidable Lisa Stoke. I'm reminded of the fierce interview she did a few years ago with Bill Bennett, the Australian Rugby player who famously tore his microphone off and stormed from the interview when he disagreed with her line of questioning. Her status in the New Zealand media landscape is legendary. She's broken politicians, turned international best-selling authors like Oliver McDuffy into bumbling fools, and grilled half-a-dozen prime ministers in her thirty-year career but, as we've been told over and again, if you're honest with her, if she senses you are telling the truth, she won't push any harder. She only wants the truth. Which is bad news for me, because I can't give her the truth.

The producer primes us with a series of questions, marking them all on a clipboard to be passed on to the interviewer. The questions are all softball, things we'd already covered with the PR woman. Then a bearded man comes over with mics. 'Alright, guys, just going to need you to feed this down your top. He hands me a receiver, and I lower it down my blouse, the microphone staying in his hand close to my face so I can smell the cigarette smoke on his knuckles. He clips the tiny microphone in near my mouth and I hook the receiver on to the waist of my jeans. He checks our levels, radioing the producer, 'Check these levels for me, Bev.' Then to us, 'Alright, tell me about your day.'

'Me?'

'Yes, you.'

'Okay,' I say. 'Well, I had a smoothie this morning for breakfast then we went for a wal –'

'Stop there,' he says, then into the mic, 'All good? Great.'

'Now you, what did you do today?'

'Same as her really. A quiet day, went for a walk and when we got home we –'

'Excellent, sounding perfect,' he says. Then he's gone. The room is too hot.

'I get the feeling he didn't give a shit about our mornings,' Cain says, and I give a laugh that breaks up the small clots of tension inside me.

Soon the producer comes back through to the green room, grinding her palms together as she approaches.

'Alright, Lisa is ready for you now. It's going to be fine, just relax and pretend no one else is in the room. Alright? Follow me.'

She leads us down a short corridor and through a soundproof door into a dark studio. *Keep breathing.* In through the nose, out through the mouth.

Lisa is smaller than I was expecting. On TV she seems to have this immense stature, as if her power and control in this domain translates to physical size. It's in the way she smiles, a slight tweaking of her lips, her eyes fixed on the fresh meat before her.

'Pleasure to meet you both,' she says, offering her hand. The cameras are already rolling, I know this part of the show. It will show us greeting her as the intro music plays, before anyone can hear our mics, before the coverage cuts and dives right into the interview.

'Hi,' I say, taking her hand.

'Please, have a seat.'

We sit in the two seats opposite her. Stiff backed, not nearly as soft and comfortable as the chairs in the green room. Cain naturally sits erect, core active and head high. His shirt is still crisp but it stretches around his shoulders and chest. Impossibly, he's both focused and relaxed. It gives me some confidence knowing he's by my side.

'Thank you both so much for agreeing to come on the show to speak with me, I'm sure it's been a rocky couple of weeks for you.'

There was no warning that the interview had started but when she pauses and raises those neatly manicured eyebrows, I realise this is the first question.

My racing mind searches for a way to describe what we have been through but defers to the cliché. 'It's been a rollercoaster.' Did I mumble? *Annunciate, Lina.* The lights are a little too bright, too hot. My heart is already thrashing in my chest.

'Yeah, we've been through a lot,' Cain adds, 'but we're just glad to make it out the other side relatively unscathed.' He is much more eloquent. High pressure makes a diamond of him and coal of me.

'You say *relatively* but of course it's impossible not to look at you and see that scar healing above your left eye.' She turns her head slightly to encourage Cain to show where a knock had split open his brow. He does exactly what she wants, showing it, touching it with his forefinger.

'I'm a big boy,' he says with a smile. 'It'll heal just fine. But it was a very scary night for us.'

'What was it like, Lina, that night? Knowing Cain was incapacitated? Tell us what went through your head.'

'I swallow, count to four before I answer. 'It was terrifying. I was certain at times I was going to die and I thought Cain was already dead.' I can feel tears starting, but I sniff them back. 'Cain has always been there, he's my rock and I knew I needed to do everything in my power to help him, to help us.'

'You must have felt pure relief when you discovered Cain was okay?'

I find myself nodding. 'Relief, yes. And just an overwhelming sense of love. But it didn't last very long.'

'Oh?'

Don't mention the fear of a second man, I tell myself. 'I knew for certain that there was only one intruder in the house that night, but until the police arrived I still felt like he had one last trick to torment us with. I wanted to get away from him as quickly as possible and away from the cameras,' I say. 'Then when the police arrived and the paramedics said Cain was going to be okay, that was when I let myself feel relieved.'

She turns back to Cain. 'And you've been through . . .' she pauses, skews her head searching for the right word, '. . . *trauma* before, haven't you?'

Cain nods before answering. The nest of snakes in my stomach quivers, threatening to wake.

'Yeah, I mean Afghanistan was scary for different reasons, but nothing prepared me for the helplessness and the . . .' he's thinking now for the word.

'Impotence?' she says. He stares at her, I feel the intensity of it, radiating more heat than the lights. Of course she means ineffective but it's enough to throw him for a moment.

'Ah yeah, I suppose that's one way of putting it,' he says, his composure coming back. 'In my time with the military, I felt I had agency, I felt like my fate was in my hands and I was never taken prisoner. I never feared dying, not even when I was hurt. I always had faith in those people around me and my own abilities. I'd not really thought I was going to die until I woke in that house with my hands bound. And the scariest part is I couldn't do anything to help Lina. All I've ever wanted was to be a good husband, to start a family and keep my loved ones safe. I failed.' He exhales, his eyes finding his palms in his lap.

'Lina *saved* you.'

He looks up now, puffs out his cheeks with the hint of a smile. 'That's right. She did. She's a hero.'

I reach over and take Cain's hand, giving it a small squeeze. It's the lines he'd spoken with the PR consultant but when he delivers them, I feel warmth blooming in my chest.

'She is a hero. Now, Cain, you've also spent a little time recently with the police. Photos emerged of officers removing what appeared to be computer equipment.'

I feel his hand in mine, the dampness is from my own hands. He's calm and still. He squeezes, and he might as well be whispering in my ear, *I've got this, don't worry.*

'That's right, Lisa. As we own the property that the cameras were in, I thought it right to volunteer my computer and hard drives to eliminate myself as a suspect in the ongoing investigation into the cameras.'

I squeeze his hand again, it's the perfect answer, just how we'd practised.

'But, of course,' Lisa continues, 'the rumour mill was sent into overdrive when a taxi driver came forward saying Lina stopped his car, that she was terrified and you were seen running after her down the street.'

He gives a small laugh, it comes across as genuine if a little dismissive. 'I think we've quashed this rumour too but we all know how people love to talk.'

'People do love to talk, so what would you say about those who sight the coroner's report into Daniel Moore's injuries? Some have pointed out that there were no bruises on his knuckles, despite your report to the police that he punched you. That's how you sustained the injuries, is it not?'

He tucks his free hand in under his elbow, as if hiding his own knuckles which bear scratches and bruises from the boxing bag. 'I thought he did, but maybe he used his elbows, or knees, or the gun. I was drugged so everything is foggy. I just remember getting hit. It's unsurprising though, Lisa. We've heard all sorts of bizarre rumours and conspiracy theories. From a plot by the government to install surveillance in *all* homes, to theories about the military spying on civilians with me working as some undercover agent.'

That crooked smile, it reaches his eyes. He's doing so well. 'I'd like to think I was Jason Bourne, but I'm just an ordinary guy caught up in this mess.'

'Right. But people have good reason to produce their own answers when so many questions still remain.'

'Here's the fact at the heart of the issue – that man, Daniel Moore, showed Lina the footage on the phone, as you can see in the video that was released this week. We know he knew about the cameras, so it follows that he likely installed them. Everything else is frankly rumour.'

Again he hits it out of the park.

'So you're saying it didn't happen, you didn't chase her down the road? The taxi driver lied?'

'I'm saying this is a combination of different rumours and possibly mistaken identity. There was a morning we snuck away early to the police station so we wouldn't be spotted by the media outside our house. Maybe that's where this rumour came from but I've been cleared of any wrongdoing. I *volunteered* myself and my home to a search to help the police.'

I've never thought of him as a good liar, but we had rehearsed these answers so much maybe he believes it.

'The police have released a statement clearing you of any suspicion but some viewers at home would perhaps say that you only handed over your hardware because you knew there was nothing on it. What would you say to them?'

We never prepared for this *question.* 'Honestly, Lisa, I would tell them to get a life. Get off reddit, or Twitter or wherever else conspiracy theorists loiter, and they might gain some perspective.' He's getting frustrated.

'Strong words,' she says.

A small shake of the head. 'Well, you know, I've had a gutful of it. Imagine if this happened to you? Imagine being beaten half to death, being traumatised and taunted in your own home then you come out the other side of it and have to deal with the crazies online that want to turn this into some fantasy, or some sort of political issue. We see it online everywhere, grist for the journalists' mill, the different takes from talking heads.' He pauses now, brings his voice down a notch. 'I'm just looking forward to the next big story. Something else to focus on because we're not the story. The cameras are the story, the footage is the story. *Daniel Moore* is the story. Not us.'

'Yes, but you can see why *this* story attracts particular interest from the public? In fact the international media has been following it closely with CNN, the BBC, Fox News, Al Jazeera all running follow-up stories this week alone.'

'With all due respect, Lisa, *you* are the media. They're only responding to your interview last week with the guests who stayed at our home. You made headlines.' He gives a small laugh. 'You paid us to come here now to keep the story going. If people want the truth of the matter it's already out there.' He shrugs. He's gone off script now.

'It's of public interest, Cain. People want to know they are safe when they stay in other people's properties. That's the role of a journalist, to seek out the truth and present it to the public.'

'That's a fair point to make but keep in mind this is one WeStay.'

'Two,' Lisa says. I see Cain's surprise, his dark eyebrows rising. 'Two?'

'Police have now confirmed cameras were once installed in a second property in New Zealand. A WeStay in Auckland.'

He nods, realising now it's the Hillview property. He knows I was right. 'Well, maybe there is something to fear then. I don't have any answer for that.'

'And you, Lina. I hate to bring this up, but it's something that I'd be loath to overlook, given the way stress and trauma can affect addiction.' The snakes all squirm inside, sliding up toward my throat. I try not to react. If I speak now, could I stop it? 'But do you have any comment to make about the fact you were recently stood down from your work with the ambulance service?' There it is. The gut punch. Cain's head turns sharply. All the oxygen leaves the room. It's obvious to anyone this is news to him. Turning my head, I see the question in his eyes, *Is it true?*

'No,' I say. 'I don't have anything to say about that.' I'm shaking my head.

'Nothing? Because your mother had her own issues with alcoholism, didn't she?'

A flush creeps up my neck. 'No, it's got nothing to do with what happened to us at Tarawera. It's an ongoing issue. So . . .' I shrug. 'Can we move on please?'

She's leering; a moment, a dozen heartbeats. *Brain, pharynx, larynx, lymph nodes, lungs, heart, spleen . . .*

'You don't want to say anything about it.'

'I'm not going to make any further comment. This is an ongoing issue with my employer, one which is based on a misunderstanding.'

'We'll move on then, shall we? What makes you think Daniel Moore targeted you?'

Cain goes to speak but she raises her hand. 'This question is for you, Lina.'

I look around, see the man behind the camera, his eye closed, the woman with headphones holding the boom mic over us, the producer nearby. I see them all staring at me and I turn back to Lisa. *Does she know? Is the photo out there?*

'I believe what the police believe.'

'Which is?'

'He chose us at random. He had a fake WeStay profile, our house was available and in a remote destination. He set the cameras up, watched and waited until he felt it was the right moment. The cameras were streaming to others online but I believe, I *know*, that Daniel acted alone.' I think about the image. The message on the back. This is what he wants – me to kill the rumour about a second man.

'Daniel?' she says.

'Sorry?'

'You called him Daniel. It's just most people are using his full name.'

Again, I look around. I see the scepticism on the producer's face. I know I've made a mistake.

'Sorry, I wasn't really thinking.' My shrug is quick, and suspicious. Cain's posture changes. Still rigid, only now he raises a hand to his chin and scratches gently at his jawline.

'Can we maybe end it there?' he says.

'Just one or two more questions,' Lisa says, smiling. 'Because I'm led to believe you both have some much more exciting news.'

The baby stuff is coming up now. The PR agent insisted we talk about it, connect with viewers, end on a high.

'That's right,' I say, my hand coming to my navel. 'We're very excited because early next year we are having our first baby.'

'How wonderful.'

Peephole
Live Cam Premium
Stream: 045A
Viewers: 056

He rolls his chair through the front door and places the keys on the coffee table along with his wallet and phone. The bag sitting across his lap he drops in the bedroom as seen on camera 2 – 44 viewers. He moves closer to the mirror and assesses himself, combing his fingers through his groomed beard, before running a hand back over his dark crew cut. He finds a pack of cigarettes in his bag and rolls his chair out to the balcony, grabbing his phone off the table on the way. He can be seen on camera 1, through the glass, lighting a cigarette and taking a drag while he looks down at the phone in his hand.

THIRTY-THREE

THE CAR RIDE home is tense, there are no words, no sound other than the voices on the radio and the hum of the tyres. When we are parked in the driveway, we sit as if bracing to step out into a storm, wide-eyed, waiting for the other to do something. Finally he speaks. 'Why didn't you tell me what happened at work?'

I shake my head, still reeling. Filled to the brim with an anxious energy that, if I opened my mouth, would bubble out like toxic gas. The radio is quietly playing a song now and when it finishes the news starts. It's dark outside the windows, I find my gaze lingering on the front of our house. He asks again. I turn to him, my head already shaking. 'I don't know, Cain. I couldn't tell you. Not with everything else.'

. . . the psychologist was apprehended at the train station in Melbourne . . .

I tune out the news story.

'And you called him Daniel? It just seems odd, Lina.'

'I froze up. Forgot his last name.' It's a lame excuse but it seems to do the trick because now he says, 'Oh well. Twenty grand, and we did what we went there to do. Nothing we can do about it now. I actually feel kind of relieved. Like we can move on at last.'

Inside, Cain goes to the bedroom to call Axel.

I climb the stairs to listen in.

'You're probably right,' he's saying, his voice quiet. 'It just seemed like an ambush at times. The same thing happened with the Skelton stuff. They just seemed to know.'

A pause.

'No,' he says. 'She barely touched upon it and didn't mention Skelton, we've got nothing to worry about.'

Another pause as he listens.

I press the door open, and he turns to me. The unmistakeable look of guilt etched in his eyes. He's still listening to Axel.

'Hey, I'll have to call you back,' he says into the phone.

'You've got nothing to worry about?' I say.

'Sorry?'

'You said, "We've got nothing to worry about." What did you mean by that?'

'Oh nothing just . . .' He pauses, swallows.

I feel heat in my chest. 'I need to be able to trust you, Cain. This isn't helping.'

'That's rich, Lina. I just learnt from a reporter that you've been stood down from work.'

'You know I've never touched drugs, Cain.'

The tiny muscle at his jaw bulges; he tilts his head back. 'I don't like to talk about what happened to us in Afghanistan, Lina. I don't like who I was, who we were, what we did. It changes you.'

They trained us to kill but they can't untrain us, I think of those words in the leaked letter Skelton wrote his mother.

'I know but that's not good enough right now, Cain. Trust me, please.'

'The psychologist –'

'I don't care what the psychologist said. Tell me what that phone call was about.'

He closes his eyes hard, like a man battling a migraine. 'Skelton killed that family, but he did it to protect me.'

'Protect you from what?'

His eyes are still squeezed closed. 'It was an accident. We were so highly strung, so paranoid after the attack. When we got to that village, we were looking for any threat. I rushed a house and it looked like a man was reaching for a gun but he wasn't. I had already pulled the trigger.'

The nightmares. It's the first thing that comes to me. What if they're not from the blast that almost killed him but from this? 'You killed him?'

He opens his eyes now, his nostrils flare. He gives the smallest nod. 'It changes you,' he says. The sadness in his eyes. He's talking about me now. *I should have been the one to save you.* He didn't want me to live with the weight of a death on my mind. The guilt that comes on so suddenly, so fresh and raw like it happened yesterday. He lives with it too.

'You were at war,' I say. 'You can't blame yourself for the rest of your life, or live in fear of it coming out.'

'It wasn't the first unlawful killing or the last. Loads of blokes killed civvies. But this one was investigated.'

'It won't come out now, Cain. And if it did you could always just explain.'

'Don't be naïve, Lina. Axel was going to testify with me, that it was all Skelton. Instead of us both going down, Axel and I decided it would just be Trent. Then Trent took his life.'

The nightmares, the guilt. He's got a secret that could ruin his life and so he gambles and drinks, he has nightmares and snaps at people at the gym.

'It's not your fault, Cain. You can't carry all that around alone.'

'It comes and goes, the guilt, the grief, but I manage it. It's mostly the fear that the secret will get out, that my world, *our* world, will come crashing down. I want to control it but I can't. And now the stakes are much higher, with the baby coming.'

It's like he's plucked the thoughts right out of my head.

THIRTY-FOUR

DAYS LATER, CAIN watches the interview when it airs but I can't bring myself to sit through it. I know it will only confirm all my anxieties, that everything I said and did in that studio would be manipulated, the drama scaled up. I go for a run instead.

When I get back, Cain wears an unreadable expression. 'They'd edited out what I said about the media, I should have guessed. Except a couple of snippets to make me seem a touch unhinged.'

'What about me?'

He smiles. 'You did really well, you came across as a saint standing by her slightly deranged, deeply damaged man. It was perfect.'

'Really?'

'Yeah, I think we did good in the end. We can put this whole thing behind us, and the money has landed,' he says. *I hope you're right, Cain.* He takes me in his arms, my sweaty top presses against his. 'Cold out there?'

'It's fine,' I say. 'I was distracted.'

'I bet.'

'I can't stop thinking about the house.' All the years with Grandpa and Grandma, summers in the sweltering heat, the first time Grandpa took me across to Hot Water Beach, when I wore his too-large life jacket and he didn't wear one at all. The tiny outboard motor strapped to the back of the dinghy whined the entire trip.

'It might be time to start thinking about putting it on the market,' I continue. 'It's worth a lot and I just don't know if this dream of starting a family there will be the same now. We could sell and buy somewhere else.'

He lifts his chin, rests it on the top of my head. 'Well, it's your decision, Quin. I'll do whatever you want.'

'Thank you,' I say, squeezing him back. 'We're starting a family, Cain. No point holding on to the past.'

Cain nods. 'Whatever you think is best.'

I swallow. It still doesn't feel right, it's a sort of betrayal but what choice do I have?

He releases me. Reaches for the bottle of beer on the benchtop.

'What's on for tomorrow?' I ask him.

'I'm fully booked,' he says, taking a swig as he walks to the lounge, settles back on the couch. 'Can you believe it? Wouldn't have imagined a couple of months ago I would have a waiting list.'

'I think we should probably get down to Tarawera soon, check in on the place. Pack up.'

'Axel and Claire were pretty keen to see it,' Cain says. 'They've never been. Who knows, we might be able to convince them to buy it.' He laughs.

'Do you think you could stay there again?'

'I think so,' he says. 'I mean, yeah. But could you?'

I nod. 'Yeah, I might be a little scared but I think I can manage. I'll text Claire, see if they're busy.'

•

I think about those posts from the last guests. The ones they took in the house. Cain said there was almost no power usage for their stay. They're easy enough to track down again on Facebook, and sure enough the photos are still there but there's been no new posts since that night. No doubt Rata and his team have viewed them, but it's only now I realise that you can't see their faces. The photo of the man in bed simply shows dark hair on a pillow but whoever it is, they're facing away. And in the photo in the mirror, the flash blocks the face so you only see blonde hair. And finally that photo before the fire, the glasses clinking together – again, there's no faces, no evidence of who they are. I pause, staring at it, then zoom in.

'Cain,' I say. 'Look at this.'

'What is it?' he says coming closer.

On one of the glasses, you can see the windows reflected. It's just a silhouette.

'This is from the last guests, the account that had booked both the properties with cameras.'

'I can't see a face,' he says. 'It's just a shape.'

'*A*,' I say. 'Singular.'

'Sorry?'

'The photo is staged to make it look like two people are holding glasses but look, you can tell one of the glasses is resting on the table and in the reflection someone is holding the other glass. It's just one person.'

'People stage photos all the time,' he says. 'But why go to the trouble when someone else could just hold the glass?'

'Exactly,' I say. *So if there was only one person staging the photos, then maybe there isn't a second man. So who the hell has Daniel's phone? Who sent the photo of us in the house in Auckland, and released the footage from Tarawera?*

'There was only one man,' he says. 'I knew it all along.'

The threat that accompanied the photograph of Daniel and me was clear, so I know I must leave this theory behind. 'There was only one,' I say. 'There was always only one. Daniel Moore.'

THIRTY-FIVE

WE'RE IN CAIN'S car. Me and Claire in the back, Cain driving with Axel beside him up front. Taking that familiar route out of Auckland. We stop in at the Bombay Hills BP and Cain fills us up.

'Snacks for the road?' he asks.

'I'm fine,' I say. He saunters into the service station to pay, his right leg stiff.

'Despite everything I'm actually looking forward to seeing the place,' Claire says.

'Well it might be your last chance. We're putting it on the market.'

'You are?' Axel says, with a note of sadness. 'It was your grandparents' place, right?'

'Yeah,' I say. 'We'll find something else.'

'I'm glad you'll be in Auckland for a little longer,' he says. 'But I'm really sorry, Lina. I know it was a special place for you.'

'Better go out in style,' Claire adds, turning to me across the back seat. 'Have one last good weekend down there. Weather is supposed to be nice.'

'Gets up to twenty-four on Saturday,' I say.

Cain is coming back now. He climbs in, tosses a Snickers bar on Axel's lap. 'You beauty,' he says, tearing it open.

'I know your only vice,' Cain says, before starting the car and setting off again.

It's a nice easy drive down, and the boys are talking about training together for selection. Reminiscing. Although Axel's never outranked Cain, he's always seemed to carry an authority over him. I'm watching them, grinning as they recall a time when they were eight days into the gruelling SAS selection process. Most had already dropped out. Crossing the Waiouru desert in the centre of the North Island, their food intake had been restricted every day and they were on a pack march carrying one twenty-kilogram jerry can of water each and one extra to be passed between the group throughout. They were at the outer limits of what humans are capable of, physically and psychologically.

'It was thirty degrees, remember?' Cain says now.

'I can't remember much, just thinking I was going to die. We were about fourteen hours into a twenty-hour march. My legs were jelly and no one had said anything for about two hours.' He's already got laughter in his voice, they both do. 'And out of nowhere someone decides to loudly –'

'Very loudly,' Cain adds. 'Like a grenade.'

'– pass gas.' Axel is struggling to speak, through the bubbling laughter.

'My brain wasn't even functioning,' Cain adds. 'It barely registered. Then in the debrief someone said –'

'It was Trent who said it,' Axel says, they're both telling the story now, speaking at the same time.

'*Right, fess up, who farted back there, you almost killed me.*'

They're roaring in the front seat. I smile and Claire flicks her eyes up. *Boys will be boys.* They're talking about Trent Skelton. I think again about what Cain had told me. Cain killed someone. It shocked me, but it shouldn't have been surprising. The man was a farmer. This detail alone is lodged in my brain. I'd read the notes in the news. It's so much worse given that the man was innocent. Now I know Trent Skelton didn't kill the entire family. Cain killed the father and Trent killed the daughter and mother.

'I just can't believe we've not been down here,' Axel says. 'Can't wait. Might get a swim in today.'

'It'll be cold.'

'I like it cold,' he says. 'Remember Wanaka?'

'*That* was cold,' Cain says. Another boys' trip, Cain's stag do. The stories start again.

For the rest of the trip down, Cain and Axel are talking about the new gym Axel is opening. Cain has been trying to convince me to go in on it with him using some of the proceeds we'll get from the house.

'Military training for office workers,' Axel says. 'Who would have thought?'

Not me. It didn't work for Cain, not until our fifteen minutes of fame defibrillated Commando Fitness.

'No phones for the weekend,' Axel says.

I notice Claire roll her eyes again. 'He's trying to detox. Don't drag us down with you.'

'I like it,' Cain says. 'See if we can last until midnight.' He tosses his phone in the glove box.

'Good man.'

•

'Wow,' Claire says, when we pull in. 'It's beautiful, Lina. You actually grew up here?'

'Mostly, yeah. My grandpa built it. It's got a few quirks, but I love it.'

'Deck could do with some work,' Axel says, teasing Cain who built it.

'Cheeky prick.'

There's no police tape, no sign of what happened that night. I can see the freshly painted patch where the weatherboards have been repaired from the shotgun holes in the side of the upstairs bedroom. The new window looks much tidier than the rest, but the paint on the new boards is just a touch off the others. It hasn't faded like the rest to the sand colour it will end up.

My palms are damp. Until recently, the lake house hadn't seen much action: the squatter sleeping in the empty house for those months before moving on to another home, and that day Mum came to take me away. She could barely walk, let alone drive. I always tell myself it was an accident, it was the booze. The official cause of death was accidental drowning, but she was unconscious before the car hit the water. There were no brake marks. I could have hugged her, that day before she left, I could have told her I loved her, whether I believed it or not. I could have told her she couldn't take me away but she could still visit.

'Lina,' Cain says now, his arms loaded up with bags. 'Coming inside?'

I turn from the house, smile. 'Yeah.'

•

The boys cart the food and bags into the living room, Axel insisting Claire and I don't do any lifting. So I go ahead and open the place up. It seems just the same as always inside, as though nothing happened, yet I feel anxious, fearful of going into rooms alone. The fireplace is there, right where I was cuffed. The blood has been cleaned from the carpet, the floors. When they come in, Axel drops his bag near the door. 'Sorry,' he says, rushing past me to the bathroom. 'I'm busting.'

'It's just down the hall.'

He turns back. 'Thanks,' he says.

I look around the room, memories of my childhood overlaid with memories of that night. A sickening double composition. I don't know if I can make it upstairs, face the spot where it happened.

'Where are they sleeping?' Cain says, holding Claire's bag.

'Do you mind sleeping upstairs?' I say.

'I'm happy with that,' Claire says. 'Wherever you want to put us.'

I lead Claire upstairs, pausing at the top. I look down and swallow. There's no sign of what happened that night, not even here, yet my breath catches in my throat. 'In here?' she asks, stepping past me.

'Yeah,' I say. Cain comes up, drops the bags in the room for her and heads back downstairs.

I breath out and step into the room. 'Wow,' Claire says. 'Pretty view. So isolated.'

I hear the boys walking through the house. They emerge outside on the lawn below us.

'Look at them,' Claire says. 'Axel tries to be macho but they're just a couple of little boys when you get them together.'

'I was just thinking the same.'

Cain pushes the swing he hung, it twists on its rope. Can I really sell this place? I watch as Cain points to something across the lake, then Axel throws his head back in laughter, his hand cupping Cain's shoulder.

'It must be scary being here again?' she asks, turning her eyes away from the boys to me.

'Not scary, just off. I don't know, it's nice to have you guys with us though.'

•

Claire helps me prepare dinner and we eat at the table, fresh snapper, salad and asparagus. Cain and Axel are already a few beers deep. Claire brought non-alcoholic wine but it tastes like someone mixed apple juice with dishwater. We drink it anyway.

'So,' Axel says, resting on his forearm over the table with a spear of asparagus hanging limp on his fork. 'What's the story with the cameras? Any updates?'

'They're hopeless,' Cain says. 'Lina's been chatting with a cop, they reckon they've almost got access to the website that hosts the videos.'

'The streams,' I correct him.

'Sorry, the live streams. The cops have been trying to get access but it's not easy apparently.'

'Right,' Axel says, thoughtfully. 'Who is the cop?'

'You know any?' Cain says.

'Yeah, I've got a few contacts.'

'Rata,' I say. 'Detective Rata.'

'Doesn't ring a bell. I hope they bust them anyway.'

Cain drains the last of his beer. 'Another one?'

'Yep,' Axel says. Cain goes to the fridge. Claire sips her fake wine. Makes a zombie face at me.

'It's not so bad,' I say, forcing a mouthful down.

'So what's the plan for after dinner?'

I look to Cain, he's already speaking. 'Could take the dinghy over to Hot Water Beach, should be quiet this time of year,' he says, pausing and taking a slow thoughtful sip of his beer. It's a natural hot spring plugged into a seam of native bush, running to the sand. 'Although we would need to fix the boat. Might be best if we do it tomorrow.'

'And they've not found the guy's phone?' Axel says, still fixated on that night.

'No,' I say. 'They can't figure out where it is.'

It takes effort to keep the conversation going with Claire while the boys sink deeper into their session. I'm tired and fading fast. She makes the most of our chat but I'm only staying up so I don't have to go to bed alone. There's still fear, and the high-pitched hum of anxiety. Cain will climb in eventually, with that dampness of drink. Years ago, when we had first met, he was more courteous about it – taking a shower after an evening at the pub, brushing his teeth and delicately slipping in beneath the covers.

When I eventually get to bed, I can't sleep. From the downstairs room, I can hear the music clearly through the walls. They've put on Metallica. Any pretence of sophistication those two have sober is stripped away when they get a few drinks in them. They're back in their late teens, a couple of wannabe soldiers drinking themselves into oblivion and listening to heavy metal. Fortunately, I brought down melatonin, after half an hour of lying there I find myself reaching for it. It doesn't take long to feel the lulling effect, soon I'm dozing off. I hear more music. It's a song I recognise. My grandfather used to play the Rolling Stones a lot when I was a child. The plucky intro of the sitar. Then that marching percussive thump of the tom drums. What is this song? It comes to me in the first line of lyrics. 'Paint it, Black.'

BREAKING: POLICE CONFIRM DANIEL MOORE ACTED ALONE

A spokesperson for the task force investigating the alleged installation of cameras in WeStay properties has confirmed they now believe Daniel Moore acted alone.

The news comes days after *The Herald* broke the story that a second property located in Mount Eden also contained evidence of cameras.

The cameras were removed prior to their discovery. No footage or camera equipment has been recovered but guests who stayed at the property have been notified.

A WeStay profile that is believed to be linked with Daniel Moore had previously booked both the Lake Tarawera property and the Mount Eden property.

Police indicated that they're not looking at any other suspects at this stage, and that the method of installation and equipment along with other factors indicate Moore was responsible for both.

Police also acknowledged that there is no evidence that Moore had an accomplice the night of the home invasion. Their attention will instead turn to tracking down the footage and pursuing those who have viewed and shared the material online.

More details to follow.

THIRTY-SIX

IT'S LATE, OR very early. A peel of moonlight passes beneath the curtains and Cain's breath tells me the whisky came out after I went to bed. I don't know what woke me but I'm awake now. I close my eyes again.

The rest of the night passes in gasps of restless sleep. I find myself inexplicably crying for my grandparents at times, for the house and my past. If we sell, where will we end up? When morning eventually arrives, I wonder if I can stay another night here at all.

Light fills the house. Cain goes straight to the fridge, pulling out a slab of bacon and the carton of eggs. Axel is on his phone on the couch.

'What's the plan for today?' I ask.

'I was hoping to get the boat out on the water,' Cain says. 'If we can get it going.'

'I'll have a look at it now,' Axel says, glancing up from his phone.

'Good idea. Lina, can you show him where it is?'

I unlock the back door and take him out to the tiny boatshed.

'So this guy was inside the entire time?' Axel asks.

I meet his eyes. 'Yeah, I think so,' I say. I reach for the padlock and push the key in but it doesn't turn.

'Careful,' he says, taking the padlock now from my hand. 'Last thing we want is the key breaking in it.' He tries it himself, but still it won't turn. 'Give me a moment.' He strides back to the house and returns with a can of lubricant. He sprays it inside the padlock, tries the key again. It doesn't open. 'You sure this is the key?'

I peer at it closely. 'Maybe not.'

He pulls it out, holds it up to the sunlight, looks at it closely. 'They always look the same, don't they?' he says, with a grin. 'You got any others I could try?'

I try to remember the last time we opened this shed. It's been three or four years at least. 'In the basement there's a shoebox of junk where we keep old keys. Could be in there. I'll run and grab them.'

'No, you stay,' he says. 'I'll go have a look. The basement you said?'

'Yeah. Under the workbench.'

When he returns he paws through the shoebox of bits and pieces, pulling out a charger for a mobile phone they stopped making in the nineties, old drill bits, a UK plug adaptor.

'A few keys at the bottom,' he says.

Claire is coming towards us.

'Come on, Axel,' she says. 'We need to pick up bread and coffees. Cain's already got the bacon on and the hash browns in the oven. Decaf latte?' she says to me.

'Yeah,' I say. 'Sure. I'll have found the key by the time you get back, Axel. It's got to be somewhere.'

'Otherwise we could bolt cut it open,' he says.

Claire turns back to me with a smile. 'Cain said he desperately needs your help to make your famous scrambled eggs.'

'Hope he hasn't talked them up too much,' I say.

They go to our car and climb inside. Axel starts the engine and they back out.

I pull more junk out of the box, finding keys at the bottom. I'll try them one at a time. I see a key attached to a key ring with a tiny buoy. It looks new, too new to be in this box. I hold it up, noticing something odd. It's not one key but two. A key for a modern lock and a key that looks old but is polished and new, long and thin with a blade at the end shaped like a U. *Where have I seen this key?* I freeze. *They always look the same, don't they?* Axel had said but I know this one is the same as another one I've held. My eyes go to the house, the kitchen window. I see him there. Cain, staring out the window at me. His eyes are wide. Why would this key be here? I drop the keys. Why would we have the same key as the Hillview Terrace house? There's only one reason. Time stops. Everything trembles. My body aches with a new fear. Now I know for certain: *It's him. Cain installed the cameras. Cain cut the keys. Cain knows.*

THIRTY-SEVEN

I'M STILL STANDING there. Wide-eyed and rooted to the spot when the back door opens.

He's out on the deck now moving through the sunlight. The hulking form of him in his singlet, with all those tattoos and scars. My hand goes to my navel, rests there. The bump. I can't outrun him anymore. He knows, he *must* know that the baby may not be his after all.

'Come on inside, darling. I need your help.'

'It was you,' I say, my voice trembling with fear. 'You installed the cameras. You know.'

'Shh,' he says, stepping closer. 'We don't need to do this, Lina.'

A rush of heat to my face, my breathing is growing faster and faster. 'How?' I take one step back towards the lake. 'How did you do it?'

'We get to make up our history. We decide what happens. What *happened*. We can just forget you found those keys, Lina.' He steps closer. 'Nothing has to change.'

No, it can't be him. He can't know what I did. My breathing is fast and heavy, my hand comes to my brow. 'How did you do it, Cain?'

He wets his lips, looks past me over the lake. 'It really wasn't so difficult to become him,' he says. 'Contact lenses. A mask ordered online from a military replica store. And a black-market shotgun. Finding your sim card made things much easier. I got into the dating account and organised a meet-up with him.'

'You lured him here? So he was innocent? You're telling me that I killed an innocent man?' The familiar creep of guilt rises like bile; this can't be happening.

'It was supposed to be me. I was supposed to do it. Killing changes you and you pulling the trigger was the last thing I wanted.'

I remember Cain's shock that night when he realised I had killed Daniel. We had gone off script; I was never supposed to escape from the fireplace, and I wouldn't have if someone hadn't made that comment and helped me. Cain was supposed to save me.

'The hard part was setting up the cameras, capturing the footage in a way that exonerated us of wrongdoing. It had to show that we acted out of self-defence. So it showed me stumbling to the bedroom, but it didn't show me taking the ladder and sneaking back out through the laundry while you were in the shower. It didn't show me meeting him at the road with a shotgun and forcing him up that same ladder and into the bedroom.' He clears his throat. 'I stripped him and told him if I heard him or if he moved, I would kill him. And he was good, silent as a mouse. I locked him in that great big chest, then later the cameras showed *Daniel* dragging a body in a sheet to the spare room. But they didn't show me forcing clothes back on him, pushing him out into the hallway. The hole in the wall and the smashed window let the rain in, filling up the chest, rinsing the floor and washing away any evidence that went against what the cameras showed. It was easy enough to open up the old gash above my eye on the door knob. Everything went to plan, except I was the one who was supposed to escape, rush out with my hands still bound and push him down the stairs. The camera would show me desperate to save you.'

My head feels light, filled with helium. My body is trembling. He did all this to get rid of Daniel. The viewers. Maybe this was his way of punishing me too. 'But you didn't save me.'

'The princess saved herself,' he says, a wry smile. 'But you wouldn't accept that he acted alone. You needed to keep pushing and probing. You didn't trust me.'

I was right about seeing someone else – there was Daniel, and the second person I thought I saw was Cain. Just a glimpse of him behind Daniel. I can feel hot tears pricking my eyes. 'I killed him. He was innocent.'

'You have to believe he was evil, Lina. You have to accept the version of events you've believed all along. We have a choice, you and I. You can ignore those keys you found. You can go back to how things were. We can both forget each other's secrets. I installed the cameras for us, for the money. I never watched anything, I'm not a pervert. I was training Rick Reynolds, complaining about money and he put me on to Peephole. He told me there was good money to be made, easy money. I could take all the earnings, all he wanted was local streams in his time zone. It was foolproof.' His voice is rising now. 'The money was laundered through international betting agencies.' He chuckles to himself now. 'It was Rick who alerted me to what you were up to. I asked for the video clips and he sent them. It wasn't easy to watch, Lina, but I still loved you. The funny thing is, I did what I did for you, for us. And I worked out that you did what you did for us too. That's why I still love you, Lina. In spite of everything. Some would say we deserve each other.'

My molars are numb from clenching my jaw. How could he have done this, plan that whole terrible nightmare in this house? He put me through hell. He chained me up and taunted me, just to make me hate Daniel, or the person I thought was Daniel. Just for the viewers and the money.

'We've both got secrets, Lina. We're bound to them, and to each other. There's no untangling this mess. I'm prepared to forget, I can move on. You just need to decide if you can too.'

I can hear the crack of gravel, of a car on the driveway. He looks in that direction.

'They're here,' I say, more to myself than him.

'Come on,' he says. 'Axel and Claire have heard all about your scrambled eggs. Be a shame to let them down.'

I hesitate for a moment. *We both have secrets.* I follow him in, keeping my distance and feeling an ache in my chest. The pain of knowing. I could call Rata, I could tell him it was Cain and put him onto Rick Reynolds. But what would that mean for me? The world would find out what *I* did too. This baby would one day know as well. Slowly but surely, I come to a decision.

THIRTY-EIGHT

'FIND THE PLACE alright?' Cain asks Claire with a smile as if nothing has changed.

'Yeah, easy enough.'

He takes the long black out of Claire's hand and brings the decaf latte to me at the stove. 'For you, Quin,' he says, offering it. I continue stirring the eggs, and he sets it down beside me. He takes a sip of his coffee. 'Need this after Axel made me down that last double of Glenmorangie at midnight.' He's so *normal* now.

Axel laughs. 'Had to really twist your arm, did I?'

At the table, we sit and everyone begins reaching for grilled tomatoes, scooping scrambled eggs or spearing the crispy bacon with their forks. Everyone but me. Does no one else feel the thickness in the air, or see the heat in my cheeks? The energy in the house has shifted, like the moments after a strong earthquake, but one only I felt.

'Not hungry?' Cain says.

I realise he's talking to me. My eyes, fixed on the empty plate before me, rise now to his face. 'No,' I say.

'Morning sickness?' Claire asks.

I turn to her. *Do you know?* No. They couldn't know. Cain wouldn't risk it. 'Yeah, possibly.'

'Well, everyone else dig in,' Cain says. I force a mouthful of my decaf latte down.

'Sometimes,' Cain begins, 'I wonder what we would all be doing now if it didn't happen. You know? If that bastard didn't do what he did to us.' He's looking at me. 'I can forgive him and what happened, I can pretend it never happened knowing that he's dead.'

No one speaks, so he continues.

'I guess that makes me emotionally primitive. Forgiveness in death. Maybe . . . I'm just a caveman.' He laughs. Axel gives a snort.

I am a fucking caveman. Those words Daniel said; no, not Daniel. *Cain.* He can forgive what happened because Daniel is dead, a dead man can't replace him. Something else he said comes to mind now. *I could never raise someone else's kid, knowing the real parents were out there in the world.* Did I force his hand? I imagine him now, heading to the hospital that night with Daniel's phone on him. Flushing the coloured contact lenses down the toilet. Believing he had committed the perfect crime. Impervious to interrogation, built to survive the toughest environments and prepared to go further than his enemy. I see that tattoo on his chest again. *Who Dares Wins.*

'No need to dwell on it now, though. This weekend is about giving the house a proper farewell,' Claire says.

'Let's get that boat in the water after breakfast,' Axel says, changing the subject.

'Good idea. We'll get the bolt cutters out,' Cain says. 'You can be the skipper.'

'Bloody oath I will be.'

I'm still looking at Cain, catching his eye for just a heartbeat. Then he looks back to his food. I put my coffee down and wait for breakfast to be over. A flush of guilt rushes over my skin. I think about that gurgling sound; Daniel Moore bleeding out almost directly above where we now sit and his only crime was pursuing the wrong woman.

'Why don't you lie down after breakfast, Quin?' Cain says. 'You don't look so well.'

'I've got magnesium oil,' Claire says. 'I'll grab it for you, it's supposed to help with the nausea.'

'I'll be fine,' I say, swallowing hard. 'I am fine. It's just being back here in this house; the light of day gives that night context.'

'You did the right thing,' Cain says. 'You saved me. And you saved yourself.'

Claire helps me pack up the dishes and Axel and Cain go out to the boatshed. Is he going to continue life as usual, carry on like nothing has changed? I know the ball is in my court and I know what I need to do.

'Back in a sec,' I say to Claire, hanging the tea towel over the handle of the oven.

I take my phone out. It's got one bar of reception and I dial the number for Rata. I hold it hard against my face as it rings and rings. He doesn't answer so I leave a message.

The boat engine chugs now, it turns over but doesn't start. Cain must have found the key. Again, someone pulls the starter and this time it roars into life and I step closer to the window looking over at the two men on the lawn. I've loved Cain so much, from that first moment. Lots of others from his unit became involved with drugs or crime, to chase that thrill, or to make money. Cain wanted to make it work for us, he was desperate to earn a good living and look after me, but he took it too far. My phone rings, it's Rata. I see Cain rushing across the back lawn towards the house. The door opens.

'Come on, ladies, let's go for a spin,' he shouts into the house.

I look down at the phone in my hand.

THIRTY-NINE

'YOU WANT A lift?' Cain says to Claire, turning and presenting his back to her beside the edge of the lake.

'Alright.' She climbs up. He sloshes out through the water to knee height and backs her up to the boat where Axel has it idling. Cain sloshes back through the water for me. There's tension as I climb up onto his back, feel the muscles pressing against me through his t-shirt. *I know you*, I think. *I've loved you all these years*. He ferries me out. The words are there, but I can't say them. I won't. I've made my decision, and nothing can change it now.

I climb over the side of the boat and then Cain lifts himself in. We take up seats opposite each other, on the sides of the boat. Claire faces forward in behind Axel, watching her husband.

'Ready?' Axel calls but before anyone can answer he throws the throttle forward. In a heartbeat we're flying. The water rushes by. The engine dials up to the timbre of a buzz saw and lake water drifts over the front and sides of the boat in sprays.

Suddenly we are in the middle of the lake, the house just a pale square in among the green.

Cain is watching me, completely neutral, a laser focus.

Axel slows it down a little now, turning around and yelling something out with a grin, but the words are stolen by the wind. We keep moving until we are so far from the house that I can barely see it behind us.

Would he hurt me? It's one of those odd principles he lives by. He would never hurt a woman. But he has killed men. *They trained us to kill but they can't untrain us.* He'd never accept the dole. He'll always protect me. I tell myself it's true, even now after everything.

Claire stands, puts one arm around Axel's waist, bracing against him as the boat rocks. Halfway towards Hot Water Beach, my eyes move back to my husband's. A moment of eye contact. We both know each other's secrets. He looks down and I follow his gaze. He's holding those two keys, now without the buoy key ring, and a phone. I know it's Daniel's phone. It has the dating app, the messages, the evidence that he was lured to our house. His arm moves out over the side. And now I see a question in his eyes. I nod. *Do it.*

The phone and the keys fall and are swallowed by the lake where it froths and boils at the boat's edge. They're gone in the growing tail of foam in our wake. Just the slightest lift at the corner of his mouth as if to say, *it's done, the past is behind us.* Cain was using the photos and the phone to force me to forget about the second man, to stick with the narrative, to do the interview and clear our names, but now they're gone. Twisting and turning through the murky depths.

I breathe in, breathe out, give just the smallest nod once more. Our indiscretions confined to a point in time, a place that soon we will never see again. Our secrets plummeting to the deepest part of this lake that has given me so much, but taken even more.

Peephole
Live Cam Premium
Stream: 021A
Viewers: 006

This stream is a favourite with the viewers. It's one of the longest running
streams on the platform and, unlike many of the others, it's rarely new
people staying in the home. It's almost always the same couple, the
muscle-bound man and the tattooed woman with the short black hair.
They're there so much of the time, with that little brown dog. After so
many months, viewers feel like they know them, viewers can *inhabit*
them. *They can see the woman's stomach growing with her pregnancy.*
Today someone else is in the house. He's in a black balaclava and comes
through the front door. He punches in the code to the alarm and carries
a stepladder and a small toolkit with him. He goes directly to the corner
of the living room and climbs up the stepladder to the camera. It's quick,
methodical work. Viewers drop away as one by one he removes all of
the streams. In the living room, the bedrooms, the bathrooms. They all
drop out and it's almost like the cameras were never there. It's like *he*
was never there.

SECOND ARREST MADE IN WESTAY HIDDEN CAMERAS CASE

Police have arrested a man and raided his Grey Lynn home, seizing computers, hard drives and other hardware in dramatic scenes. The arrest is believed to be in relation to the Tarawera home invasion and an online network of voyeurs who produce and share covert footage within holiday rentals from websites such as WeStay.

The suspect has been granted interim name suppression, but it is understood that he has a 'significant profile' and is refusing to cooperate with investigators.

It is alleged the individual has engaged the illegal service Peephole, which investigators learned about earlier this year.

The raid came after NZSAS personnel received a tip-off.

'Obviously it's a major concern for the public, and it's an important part of our tourism industry that travellers can feel safe, particularly with the places they choose to stay. We're confident that we are on top of the situation and will be in contact with all those who may have been affected,' lead investigator Ed Rata explained. 'Anyone caught distributing, recording or viewing this material will be prosecuted to the full extent of the law.'

Given the anonymity of the video-sharing platform now known as Peephole, it's unlikely there will be further arrests.

EPILOGUE

Fourteen Months Later

SHE'S A PERFECT little girl. Esther Rose Phillips. I had to give her my grandma's name because she came out with Grandma's eyes, and Cain wanted his mother's name as her middle name. It was a fair compromise in the end. They say you fall deeper in love with your husband when you have your first child, when you see the unfiltered joy, the silliness, the cooing soppy man this tiny infant makes them become – and it's true. My big macho husband is putty in her hands, the doting father who can see no wrong in his child. You will never see a little girl who loves her father more and a father who would do so much for a child. We are the parents neither of us had growing up and I couldn't be prouder of my family.

I watch him now from the kitchen window, the new hammock swinging beneath the blooming pohutukawa. The red haze of the flowers. The hot ceramic sky, mirrored in the lake. The saddle of the mountain with its deep, rich greens and those two out there lazing in the mid-afternoon heat. Cain bends to the shape of the hammock's net, looking out at the water with Esther nestled in against his chest.

Sometimes I have thoughts about Daniel, and the odd nightmare. Collateral damage, that's what Cain would say if we ever talked about it. But we don't talk about it. We will never talk about it. I try my best not to think about it and I find it works: I think about it less and less with each day. Some shrapnel the body must press out, some stays in there sealed in scar tissue.

I'm somehow a hero, but Daniel's friends and family still want answers, even now. Where did he get the gun, why did he do it, why was there so much ketamine in his body as detailed in the coroner's report? There's more evidence still out there, on that video that has continued to circulate. Of course, the terror in my eyes was real. Daniel stepping into the hall was real. But I've watched it a few times and now I can see moments when 'Daniel' exhibits signs of weakness in his right leg. Anyone who points any of this out is labelled a conspiracy theorist, something I'm grateful for.

•

Scotty's new partner reported him when he almost sideswiped a cyclist, and he tested positive for fentanyl. It's justice, but I didn't need to take my job back. Without the high Auckland rent we can survive just fine. My paid leave carried through until my due date and then I had maternity leave. Cain's new gym in Rotorua is providing more than enough income for us now.

Cain carries Esther along the lake's edge. Her pigtails bounce and her lilac cotton dress presses against his side as he points out the ducks floating by.

'That's the mummy and those are the babies,' he says.

She turns to me as I stride across the lawn with her sunhat in my hand.

'She'll get burnt,' I say. I see that grin, the two white nibs beginning to punch through her bottom gums, and those eyes and I feel the stirring inside. The feeling only a mother knows. These are my people, this is my family and my home.

It feels good to build something new, build it from scratch. We start again and leave old bones in the ground, never to surface again. We move on. Silent but knowing. That's the key, I think now, to a long and happy marriage. That's the grease that keeps family life turning smoothly. Our secrets are as quiet and as deep as Esther's beautiful green eyes.

ACKNOWLEDGEMENTS

I'M BEGINNING TO realise that the author does *not* decide how long a story will take to write. If you're lucky and pay close attention, if you stick with a story long enough, it might one day reveal itself to you. *The Last Guests* took about eighteen months longer than I anticipated to complete. I worked harder and spent more time with it than any other project I've commenced but I never lost faith in the premise of the story, and the incredible people I've managed to surround myself with never lost faith in me.

The first thanks, as always, goes to my incredible literary agent Pippa Masson. I have no idea what I would be doing if you hadn't always shown faith in me and my work but I'm certain I wouldn't be up to book number four. Thank you also to the other agents helping to get my work out into the hands of publishers and creators in other territories, including Gordon Brown, Dan Lazar, Kate Cooper-Adams and Jerry Kalajian.

Thanks to my publisher Rebecca Saunders and my editor Emma Rafferty along with the rest of the team at Hachette who have all helped to whip this book into shape and get it out into the world. Thanks also to Mel Winder, Tania Mackenzie-Cooke and the Hachette Aotearoa team. Thanks to the many others who have had eyes on this story at various stages, including Deonie Fiford, Ali Lavau, Lyn Yeowart, Tiffany Plummer and my number-one-fan/ mother-in-law, Jackie Tracy.

Robert Watkins, Brigid Mullane, Tessa Connelly and Lydia Tasker have each played significant roles in helping to establish my career for which I will always be grateful.

Thanks to Lily Cooper and the team at Hodder Books for finding me a readership in the UK. Thanks also to Helen O'Hare and everyone at Mulholland for getting my work out in the US.

This book took a lot of research and my odd method/writing habits saw me develop a mild gambling habit, get more fit than I would ever care to be again and led me to shave my head (again). I also spent time around the stunning Rotorua Lakes area and made a number of trips to New Zealand as research before COVID-19 stopped further travel plans. Right before the lockdowns and the chaos that was 2020, I completed a fellowship at the Michael King Writers Centre in Takapuna. I cannot overstate the importance of this unbroken writing time in such a historic house for the completion of this novel.

Along with researching the setting, I sought to understand the life of a paramedic. I spent countless hours on the phone with Kierin Oppatt, quizzing him on both the most pedestrian aspects of his job along with the most interesting. Kierin, in the extremely unlikely event you've made it this far into the book, thank you for everything.

I spoke with former members of the New Zealand SAS and Army Corp who served in Afghanistan to gain a greater understanding of life both before and after deployment in 'the unit' and how such an environment affects one's psychological landscape. Many thanks to Barrie Rice and Carol Kitsen. Thanks to Nathan Blackwell who also helped with police procedural matters.

To understand the inner workings of the 'dark web' criminal networks, I relied heavily on the insight of James Waters to add plausibility to the story. Thanks, Jimmy, for showing me how Peephole might function in the real world and explaining why it's almost inevitable an equivalent service does or will exist.

And to the usual suspects: the Tracys, the Pomares. Thanks for everything.

Finally, thank you, Paige, for your belief and patience.

J.P. Pomare is an award-winning writer whose work has been widely published. His debut novel, *Call Me Evie*, was critically acclaimed and won the Ngaio Marsh Award for Best First Novel. Pomare's novels *In the Clearing* and *The Last Guests* were critically acclaimed bestsellers, while his novel *Tell Me Lies* was a #1 Audible bestseller and was shortlisted for the Ngaio Marsh Award for Best Novel and the Ned Kelly Award for Best Crime Fiction.

He was born in New Zealand and resides in Melbourne with his wife and daughter.

www.jppomare.com/

 jppomare

 jppomare

 JPPomare